ALSO BY JOHN G SMITH

Barn door to balance sheet

Derbyshire born

Quantitative Wheezing

Poems about

JOHN G SMITH
EUGENE

Matador
9 Priory Business Park,
Wistow Road, Kibworth Beauchamp,
Leicestershire. LE8 0RX
Tel: 0116 279 2299
Email: books@troubador.co.uk
Web: www.troubador.co.uk/matador
Twitter: @matadorbooks

ISBN 978 1785893 384

British Library Cataloguing in Publication Data.
A catalogue record for this book is available from the British Library.

Printed and bound in the UK by TJ International, Padstow, Cornwall
Typeset in 11pt Aldine401 BT by Troubador Publishing Ltd, Leicester, UK

Matador is an imprint of Troubador Publishing Ltd

This book is dedicated to my late and much
lamented son Christopher

The author gratefully acknowledges the moral and technical support
unstintingly and unselfishly given to him in the preparation of Eugene
by:-

His wife, Julia
Angus Macrae
John Watson & Don Miller for the poem

It was long ago. It was far away.
But it has always been here. It has always been now.

PROLOGUE

For a Fen Tiger to be pounced upon in a land stalked by a Chinese dragon would require a leap of 9,000 miles and an even greater leap of the imagination. Yet it has happened.

It was January 1942 and George Whitby was reading the long letter from a lost sister four years his junior. It was written in an affectionate tone as if he was the sweetheart rather than his namesake George, whom she had married three years before, at the tender and virginal age of twenty-one. They always started with "My dearest brother over the seas" and ended with "xxx". She already had a daughter and was seven months pregnant with her next child. There might be no electricity on that farm in the valley but sparks had come from somewhere, he was thinking, and he was thinking about his young wife whom he had left behind and he was thinking about the baby she was holding on that railway station in Lincolnshire, as through watery eyes he watched the platform disappear in ever-darkening steam and smoke.

The Territorial Army was fair enough: thousands of others would be first. They would take the front lines. Yet as the Cambridgeshires (or the Fen Tigers) boarded ship, the secondary role was obscure, at least to him it was. It was not obscure now. This sweat bath called Adam Park, with its taut tough grass, encircling Banyan trees and four-square colonial houses standing universally proud, white and forbidding, was where the 1ˢᵗ Battalion was going to hold its position, stand this foreign ground against the Japanese 41ˢᵗ regiment. The bush telegraph seeped into the tents telling of 25,000 Japanese men swarming over the Strait of Johore, surprising 80,000 of our boys, all facing south – the wrong way. But Fen Tigers never retreat and George's head shattered like a coconut hit by a wooden mallet as the single Japanese bullet hit the centre of his temple. The order to surrender this Singapore post came just ten minutes later. Ten minutes in wartime can be an eternity.

★

What surprised Eugene was that the main gate off Wood Lane, normally closed and padlocked, was wide open. Although the sun had gone down there was enough light to follow the red-shale drive down through the first field and around the sharp left-hand bend that he knew bordered the duck pond. Rising up the final two hundred yards or so to the farmhouse, they could just make out that the main yard gate was closed, but James did not have to stop the van because Mr Bell was already swinging it open by pulling on the thick rope, waving them through and directing the van behind the crew yard.

Willy got out first and by the time Eugene had scrambled from his hidey-hole, his two brothers were talking in whispers to Mr Bell. He could hear nothing of what was said but noticed James point him out and saw the farmer nod. He followed the three men through the main cow house to a small brick building at the back that had no proper door, just an opening wide enough to lead in one animal. And an animal was in there. He could make her out by the light of an oil lamp hanging on the back wall which was casting shadows that flickered over the cow's haunches. These shadows were heightened by the draught from the three men entering. He could see that they had walked into a narrow passageway and now stood together facing the cow. Now in profile, the distinction between Eugene's older brothers was stark. James, the younger of the two, was tall and bean-pole thin and in place of the long thin nose which characterised most of the Whitby male clan, his was shorter and more bulbous. So distinctive was James that a family joke had it that Mam must have played away on the night he was conceived; of course that was just a joke. Willy was different in build and facial appearance. Although only in his early thirties, the thick overcoat failed to conceal the start of a Whitby belly, exaggerated by his short stumpy profile.

Eugene knew enough of this game by now to recognise a large, and he supposed, old and milked-out British Friesian. The black and white rump was all he needed to identity her. He walked round the side, through the open doorway and squeezed into the narrow alleyway so as to be next to Mr Bell. His hands trembled and he sensed his pulse racing. This was his first trip: he knew what was about to happen. Mr Bell signalled to him to stand beside Willy. He then put his fingers to his lips and motioned him to remain perfectly still.

The cow would be accustomed to Mr Bell, and probably others, coming into the passageway. She would be fed twice a day by forking hay over the three-foot or so wall into her standing area so she was accepting the handful from Willy with the resigned solemnity common to all milk beast. James had the cattle killer pointed with its bell end on the upper forehead and Eugene could see clearly the word "Top" pointing upwards between the cow's horns. The Friesian chewed nonchalantly. Jolted by the cold tingling of his toes Eugene was thinking about what brother James had told him as they worked together in the making-up room yesterday. How in the old days his granddad had to use his strongest man to wield the huge poll-hammer to hit the head of the 1,000 lb bull in just the right spot. 'If tha misses the spot, tha's left with a raging bull seeing thee as its target.' He said that nowadays we use the captive bolt humane killer, a stunner with its loaded blank cartridge. It takes little strength to hit the firing pin; getting the position of the bell-end on the sweet spot is much more important than the blow. 'Think of a line tha's drawn from left eye to right ear and right eye to left ear. Where lines cross, that's thee sweet spot. The blank cartridge explodes and that explosion drives the killing rod straight into the animal's brain. It's a stunner Eugene, a stunner. Tha just needs thee knife to finish job off.' James explained that a Greener Humane Killer was a standard tool for horse dealers and vets and, as they still had a few animals of their own down Common Road field, why shouldn't he carry a Greener, nothing unusal in that.

James drew the mallet from down at his side and struck the free end of the rod, hard. There was a muffled thud and the cow dropped to its haunches. Willy leaped over the low wall, drew a sharp knife and cut deep into the neck from top right to bottom left in a single slashing movement. Blood poured from the wide gash straight onto the shed floor. It poured and poured. Eugene felt himself shaking but he didn't know why. The big Friesian's head lay to one side, still solemn and eyes still open.

James cut the engine to a mere tick-over and turned off even the tiny side lights as the van rolled silently from the brow of Harper Lane and down towards the village. Eugene was thinking that of course they would be descending because only last week they had learned at school that their village name of Huthwaite came from Old English with a spattering of Norse. It meant a clearing on a knoll. He also knew why everything out there was pitch black. Blackout regulations had been imposed on 1st September last year even before the declaration of war. These required that all windows and doors should be covered at night with suitable material such as heavy curtains, cardboard or paint, to prevent the escape of any glimmer of light that might aid enemy aircraft. The Government ensured that the necessary materials were available. External lights such as street lights were switched off, or dimmed and shielded to deflect light downward. Essential lights such as traffic lights and vehicle headlights were fitted with slotted covers to deflect their beams downwards to the ground.

The occasional chink of moonlight in an otherwise dark cloudy night was all James had to help him keep to the road. Eugene crouched low between his brothers, wedged behind the gear stick and in front of the van partition. A partition that separated a front-quarter of the cow hidden in the secret compartment under Willy's passenger seat while the rest of the animal was secreted under the false floor of the load space behind them.

As they came into the village James pressed gently on the brakes and the van eased to a stop. The stillness heightened the tension that had been in the van's stale air since its doors had been slammed shut back at Bell's farm. Eugene heard his two brothers grumbling about how the blackout was disrupting everyone's life. How low morale was affecting the butchery trade with even the most loyal of their customers deciding not to venture out after dark for what before the war had been just a few extra bits of meat. But then Willy was saying that for runs like this, it was a blessing 'least seen, least known'.

The three waited. They had their story prepared, should anybody leaving the Peacock pub walk – or more likely, stagger – past. The turning-out hour would benefit them too.

A drunken rabble is ideal for drowning out any noise from a passing butcher's van. In any case, they had been to Arthur Bell's to fetch the rabbits for fattening up in the yard. The rabbits were real enough; anyone could take a look in the back and find seven hutches, each holding five young rabbits. James had just whispered that they were getting better at timing this run when, sooner than expected, a pin-prick of light glowed, down below, faint but visible, and moving in a vertical figure of eight. He released the hand brake and the van started its slow descent, now in total darkness, ever closer to the moving light.

The Big House stood in the most prominent position facing the Market Square. From the front view, there was no hint of the butchery trade that underscored the success of the large family in residence. But from the side road leading off the Market Square, there could be no mistake. The retail shop with its imposing gold lettered sign told everyone from doctor to school teacher and from coal miner to builder's labourer. This was where to come for the finest meat for miles around "Whitby and Sons – Master Butchers". The high wooden gates to the right of the shop led to an inner yard accessible only to the family. It was within this large space that the real business took place. The cutting-up room, the making-up room, the blood bath, the knife safe, the sausage stuffer, the vice-clamp mincer and other machinery were all housed in this private place.

Eugene was first to spot his dad and poked his brother James in the ribs. The light was gone as James swung the van through the high wooden gates into the yard. The relief was palpable. Willy was first to light his fag, taking a deep drag and leaning back on the side of the van. He was smiling to himself. He felt good and better still for having heard the solitary click that told the adventurers that their dad had pulled the wooden gates together and dropped the iron latch into place. Each player knew his silent part. James stayed at the wheel to steer whilst Willy and young Eugene pushed the van into the garage. James got out, walked round to the passenger side and hauled out the seat. Meanwhile, Willy lifted up the compartment floor but as he was pulling the board out it slipped from his sweaty hand and clattered onto the yard. The three stood there, mesmerised by the bullet-ricocheting sound. A mistake. The first bad mistake of the night. But nothing happened; no response. The air was still and all was quiet.

What seemed like an eternity passed until Willy tugged James's sleeve motioning him towards the open van door. Together they pulled out the front quarter and Eugene came across the yard to help by putting his arms below the fifteen stone mass of warm animal. The three moved slowly over to the making up room. They heaved the front quarter onto the cutting-up bench and returned to the garage. Dad had already taken out the rabbits and removed the false floor so the two elder sons could get at the second front quarter and, again with Eugene's help, they carried it to the making-up room. Willy closed the door, bolted it and stubbed out his fag with a heavy boot. The rest was easy. James would separate the two rear quarters but leave them in the van with the doors and windows wide open. The airflow would allow that thirty stone of back-end animal to set overnight.

Eugene ran into the Big House. He had to get to bed and should have been there hours ago but he was a man now, big brother James had told him as much, and the sooner he learnt the business the better. He stopped in the outhouse to take off the heavy leather boots which, like all his stuff, was a hand-down from one of his elder brothers – Harold he thought. And it was Harold his dad was shouting at. They were in the main sitting-room but the door was ajar and Eugene could hear quite clearly what was going on. How dare Harold pour scorn on, criticise at every turn and downright bully young Eugene. He might be five years younger than Harold but he would be the man Harold could never be. He was bright. When did Harold ever get 18 out of 20 spellings right at school? Had Harold ever worked out the joint prices per weight for hanging in the shop? More than that, young Eugene was a worker and he was brave. Had Harold volunteered to help his brothers in a night run? If Harold caused trouble again over Eugene then Harold would feel the steel tip of his dad's boot on his arse.

Eugene found himself shaking; he hated these now common family rows. His fingers twitched as he struggled with the thick square leather laces that stubbornly resisted being pulled through the eight holes on either side of each boot. But the boots would not come off until they were undone and the stiff boot tongue pulled out. Eventually he did it and then peeled off the thick woollen socks, hand knitted by his mam, who stood there small and quiet against the thick wooden door frame, watching him with an air of resigned calmness. She held a glass of milk poured from a jug in the pantry, where she had been listening for the creak of the heavy gates and the unmistakable rumble of the van tyres on the cobbled yard. They were back. Her boys were safe. Dad had pulled off another run. The risk worried her and that worry was etched on her face. She put her left hand on the shoulder of her youngest son and led him across the outhouse floor, into the kitchen, and through to the big room. In the dim light she pointed to the door at the far end leading to the stairs. Eugene took the glass of milk, nodded to his mam and walked towards the door. Not a word had been spoken.

The steep staircase took a still excited young Eugene from a man's secret world to his own private space. As the youngest he had the smallest room in the attic. The room had a solitary window overlooking the Peacock Inn next door. Even after this special night, he could not resist, as he never could, looking down into the back yard of the pub and waiting for shadowy figures to emerge and make their way home. Eugene took off his trench coat, hung it on the peg behind the door, removed the thick jersey and folded it neatly on the chair which he could just make out in the faint moonlight. Because he did not want to draw the blackout curtain, he could not risk pulling the cord to switch on his single electric light bulb, even though it was shielded heavily by a thick orange mantle.

The day electricity came to the Big House was a red-letter day. It was only last August, on the first day of the school holidays, that the van arrived and the tall thin man in a brown smock came in with wires bundled over his shoulder. Mam had been so excited, bustling from bedroom to bedroom, agreeing with Mr Electric just where each ceiling light could be located and where the dangling cords should go. He watched hypnotically all day as the man used his ladder to connect his wiring to the new pole planted right outside the big gate on the causeway and began drilling under the eaves above the back outhouse. He followed Mr Electric's every move as he drilled the hole, fished the wire through and fixed the cords and knobs. By five o'clock it was done and they all stood by for the big switch on. Mam fetched Willy and James from the making-up room with Harold loping behind. Sister Eve ran up the stairs still with a butter knife in her right hand and Molly had changed from her factory uniform. Eugene could tell that Mr Electric was used to an audience. These first business people to get the new light were special and that made him special. He was bringing in a new, clean and brighter era to people who wanted to believe that, somehow, this war could be won.

But now the new electric wasn't so special anymore and anyway there were still the foul smelling gas lights downstairs and in the yard, shed and shop. This was a total blackout night but he knew the room like the back of his hand. A hand that even at the age of thirteen was large and calloused from work in the shop and the big shed. He undid his thick leather belt, unbuttoned his black woollen trousers and placed them carefully over the back of the chair. Care was important here because, along with the checked flannelette shirt, all his clothes were for school tomorrow. He climbed into the high standing bed still wearing vest, long underpants and under-socks. He shivered. The room was cold and the water bottle, that had earlier warmed his bed, had long since lost its heat. The night run had taken much longer than they had expected. He lay back and stared at the clouds as they floated past the window. He could not sleep.

Eugene was puzzled about the meat supply; whether it was the whole ham as boiled by Mam this morning on the big stove and carried by James to the table for carving, or as fillings for the two big pork pies already at the centre of the table. He had in his bedroom the rationing list that they had all written out at school (just one year and one term left – he was mentally ticking off the months). He had checked things the family sold against a table printed last week in the Daily Express. He was sure that from last January, only between one shilling and two shillings worth of meat and between four and eight ounces of bacon was allowed per person. His mam was right. He had learned the business. He had been on the run to Bell's farm last February and two more since. He knew where the extra meat came from. The puzzle was how it helped, given this rationing system. Was an inspector about to peer over the wall from the market square and add up the shillings worth multiplied by the nine of them at the table? He knew that his dad, Mr Bell and all of them were taking a risk, that he must not talk outside the family, and that they were "of means", since his pals often told him so. He remembered brother Harold revealing the secret tin of money (over £300) which Dad had taken to Evertons before returning with the beautiful black gleaming ten horsepower Ford HRR 118. As Harold had pointedly said, "the only car for miles around". He was with his dad when it was filled up with National Benzole at 1s/4p per gallon. True, he got his driving licence two years ago, but would Dad ever let him have a drive?

Brother Harold should not have told him about the savings. Nor should he have taken young Eugene aside in the back yard that morning, his birthday morning of all mornings, to announce in his high-pitched snivelling tone of voice that it was obvious – now Winston Churchill is Prime Minister – that the war will not be short. Someone on the BBC thought there would be five more years of blood. 'In five years you will be as old as I am now but, unlike me, you will get your call-up papers and that will stop you eating up our profits. Bad luck Eugene.' Harold was a troublemaker. Eugene had known that since he was, as Dad said, 'knee-high to a grass-hopper.' They all knew. Eugene was being called to the big table to sit on the right of his dad. He beamed his biggest smile and looked happy to be a teenager. Yet, even now, he was making a vow. A vow to find out how their means came about and to read more about the war. Could Harold be right?

It wasn't a very posh scrapbook. It did not need to be because it was Eugene's private thing. It was his idea and he decided what to paste in it; a job for Sundays when things were quiet, and in the privacy of his bedroom he could cut and paste the articles he had collected over the past week. He could make his notes from what he had heard at school from teachers but mostly from his pals and he wrote down what he could remember of the BBC news bulletins. Calling it a book was a bit grand. Actually it was a collection of sheets cut from the thick wrapping paper used in the shop and which Eve had stitched together for him down the left-hand edge. Being next youngest to him in a large brood, Eugene was close to his elder sister and she shared his secret of the growing scrapbook, though not its contents. She knew he kept it in the bottom drawer of his chest of drawers, rolled up and hidden under his vests and pants. She did not peep at what he pasted in. It was their secret.

As well as the latest books, Percy Blackmore always had yesterday's Daily Mirror. On two consecutive days came the milk scandal stories. Two farmers in different parts of the country had appeared in court for selling milk to which water had been added. Both were prosecuted and for Frederick Smithers the fine was £15 with £3/3s costs. No sum was reported for farmer Cruthers.

A story in the Daily Express concerned The Paradise Café on London Road, Brighton. An employee of the local Food Control Officer kept watch over the number of customers entering over a six-day period. This record had been used to estimate that the defendant (the café owner) was entitled to 850 points whereas, based on the number of meals he claimed to have served, the Food Office had issued him with 2,150 points. The magistrate fined Oliver Wright £5 with a 10 guineas cost. Another report concerned a well-known London butcher who, it seems, required a tip of two shillings and sixpence (a considerable sum as the magistrate pointed out) for supplying his customers with under the counter meat. He did an excellent trade. A witness said she stood in a queue outside the shop with her half-crown in hand and overheard a small boy standing in front with his mother say, 'Mummy, why do you have to pay extra when you buy meat from this shop?' The magistrate wondered how we are going to bring up our children to be honest after the war with this sort of behaviour. She also speculated that more butchery branches would certainly be opened by the said butcher, once peace arrived and on the back of his pecuniary greed.

The eyes of a rapidly growing-up Eugene were opening. By the spring of 1941 he was pasting in his scrapbook a published announcement by the chairman of the North Midland Region Food Price Investigation Committee, Sir Douglas McCraith that cans of soup sold by manufacturers at 6s/6d a dozen were reaching the public at 14s/6d a dozen having passed through the hands of six middlemen, one of whom had bought the goods twice. Other abuses included the canning of dried beans, prunes and peas for sale at a large profit and the peddling of worthless substitutes for once common but now rare foods. Favourite amongst these scams was milk substitute consisting of just flour, salt and baking powder.

At least, he thought to himself, his family supply of the odd Friesian cow or two produced real meat. And perhaps getting a bit extra on the side was the same with the litters from the two Big White sows kept on the land Dad rented down Common Road. Once weaned the last ten piglets had been split into two fives: one group staying with the sow but the other five shifted to the pigsty in the second field. He remembered helping lift the squealing little ones into the cart and as Dad had mentioned to James, just in time before the Ministry man called. Putting things to one side might also explain why they had two identical hen sheds, one in each field. When he washed and crated the eggs each Friday night, one lot went into the shop while the rest stayed in the Big House. He never quite knew why.

The underlying cause of all the shenanigans and profiteering was well-known. As Mr Mottley, the headmaster at Common School, had told his class, rationing plus demand, plus imbalance of ability to pay, plus greed, inevitably leads to a black market. There was no better subject to study, dealing as it did with a bit of history, food sources, food types, arithmetic, market supply and demand, ("economics boys and girls – economics") and most important of the lot, human nature. 'Give me a need and I'll show you a supply'. Eugene was finding Mr Mottley's market lessons fascinating and soon realised that the increasingly dour war news about the supply of food was having a greater effect on him than on any of his classroom pals. And he now knew why.

The Whitby family was no different to any other when it came to tuning into the BBC radio's nine o'clock evening news bulletin. According to Mr Mottley, the nine o'clock news, one of ten news bulletins now broadcast during the day, was listened to by sixteen million devotees and this was half of the entire adult population. Brothers James and Willy would return from the Peacock to be with the rest of them, huddled round the Murphy wireless in the big living room and, as Dad said, the BBC pulled no punches when reporting the war news.

By the time Eugene was in his last year at school, the reports of German success using battleships and submarines to hunt down and sink our merchant ships were both normal and devastating. By now everyone knew the amount of food coming into the country was declining and the nightly dread of our men perishing at sea was heartfelt. If the family could do anything to help, then that had to be a good thing. Eugene agreed with his dad and brothers. Rationing had been introduced only months after the war started. It suddenly dawned on everyone Eugene knew that butter and sugar could no longer be bought in any quantity they wanted and could afford. Even more important was the rationing of bacon. The bacon they could supply as a business was restricted each week to the allowance, multiplied by the butchery customers registered with Whitbys and approved by the local Ministry of Food Inspector.

Eugene was not stupid. He knew his dad soon realised that before rationing they sold much more bacon from their shop in the yard than the total allowance for bacon he was given. He also knew that his dad often spoke to Mr Bell at the cattle market on Saturday mornings. Plus, as brother James said, 'coal miners 'ave plenty money in pocket.' Bacon was small fry but then along with milk and canned fruit, tea, jam, biscuits, fish, cheese and goodness knows what else, came meat. His Dad had the land down the Common together with a few pigs and sheep and he had the butchers shop which faced the road from the yard but the real business was buying from the slaughterhouse and making up the joints and sausages and pies to sell from the shop and off the vans. Mr Mottley devoted one whole lesson to the news item about the debate in the House of Commons. Labour MP Joseph Clynes had called the black market 'treason of the very worse kind' and others called for long terms of penal servitude and even use of the cat-o'-nine-tails.

ONE

The old man was half sitting, half lying, on the diagonal in the corner of a two-seater settee. It did not look very comfortable; it wasn't very comfortable, but with his left leg stretched out on the settee, the right leg braced on the floor and his back pressed against the cushion, it took pressure off. Being alone like this for hours on end and being lonely (he learnt years ago that they were not the same thing), together with the pain up his backside, took over his mind. He knew it did. Yet, staring out of the plate glass window to the super-modern conservatory and the nothingness beyond, what else was left? His sergeant wouldn't have stood for it, 'Eugy – get off your arse, shake yoursen man.'

She was so beautiful. Her face was sort of round like a mantel clock that had been gently flattened at each side and when he first saw it, he instinctively knew that the time was right, that she was leading him through it, that she was talking to him with those sparkling eyes. She must be Burmese and she was entering him.

The ache in his groin came gently, peacefully and with low intensity like the drip, drip, drip of water from one teak tree leaf to another as the first rain of a gathering tropical storm descended. He was thinking that the ache seemed to grow and become deeper as two new things happened; the inside of a sort of tent came creeping into focus and she was holding his

1

hand and talking excitedly in short staccato sound bites. This was his world of no idea. No idea where he was, how he got here, what was wrong with him, who she was, or, what she was saying. But, as the long sticky days passed, so this ache stayed for longer and longer, leaving less and less space to work out the where, why and who of the smiling eyes and soothing hands.

It was a bang on the door that brought him back to the present. The thing was, he could not just leap off the settee, walk with military urgency out of the room and down the hall, unlock the outside door and fling it open. He wished to bloody hell he could. What he did do was curse under his breath – 'qui kaung, qui kaung' – push his old body from the settee onto his right leg and wince as the obstruction up his backside made itself felt. He could walk, he would get there if that damn left hip didn't give way and why do they have to be so impatient? Bang, bang, bang went the door and poor old Eugene, tottering and leaning to the left, made his slow progress as if the only purpose of this lonely day was to stop the flowers being taken back to the depot. The flowers for Dorothy's grave.

*

The now worldly but chastened Eugene met his Dorothy in March 1950 by pure chance. Well not quite. Sister Eve had just about dragged him to the Drill Hall up Main Street on that bitter cold and windy Saturday night. In the big bedroom upstairs, having pushed some of the beds to the wall, he had tried to follow her steps to the lindy hop and the mambo. Then, late one afternoon as they held hands and she swung her flowing dress to the imaginary rhythm, he had he thought, mastered a few of these steps.

But that was then and now was now and he was tired after a full day on the van with brother James delivering the meat orders and collecting the money. And he still had no modern clothes to wear. It could only be his demob suit hanging behind the door of the little bedroom overlooking the Peacock. Although still smart, it was hardly a Scully embroidered red retro western shirt, sported (apparently) by the lad sister Eve had fancied at the dance last Saturday, or the micro suede zip-out bomber jacket of his mate. Then again, his demob double-breasted dark blue suit with matching waistcoat was a marker. It told those locals where he had been. More importantly, what he had been through. Anyway if he was going, that is what it would have to be. No way was he wasting his dad's wages on this modern fad stuff.

It was a set-up. No sooner had they hung up their coats than sister Eve dashed to the far end of the hall and was now bounding back over the wooden floor, dragging behind her a seemingly reluctant young girl, 'my best friend Dorothy from the factory.' He looked at the flush-faced Dorothy. Her face was not round like a mantel clock and flattened at the sides: she was not Chit. The ache was back but in the pit of his stomach. He sat down on one of the bench seats lining the Drill Hall, lit a fag and made small talk with sister Eve and this Dorothy. About the factory work, about the butchery work but he wasn't here. He was on the jetty at Collyer Quay and he was crying.

★

By dint of family tradition, Eugene was not allowed to help with preparations for his own birthday party so he carried, with regal importance, the old canvas deckchair to the shade of the laburnum tree in the Peacock's border, there to start the very latest book borrowed from his pal Percy Blackmore. Percy's dad always got an early copy of a book just out, but how was a mystery, it was a puzzle. He was finding it hard to get into Graham Greene's The Power and the Glory.

'If this table wasn't groaning under the weight of all this stuff, it could 'ave bin sold in the shop and off the vans yesterday.'

"Stop your moaning Harold" said Mam, 'this is Eugene's 13th birthday and we're doing him proud, he has learned the business and is now a fine helper – isn't that right, Dad?'

The table had been put together from planks and trestles carried out to the front lawn from the making-up room by Willy and James earlier in the day just after a light shower had passed over. This Sunday had reverted to the weather pattern of the last ten days, warm and sunny, so the grass and borders were looking at their May-time best. It was a family gathering intended to ward-off the gloom and worry of the latest war news and they were all there. Dad at one end, guarding the carving knife and fork and Mam at the other, doting over the birthday cake made with bits and pieces salvaged over the past week by Molly and Eve, the two girls still left at home. Although it would not occur to Eugene until years later, it was his favourite Eve who, of the two girls, held all the cards in the *looks department*. True she was five years younger than Molly but there was more to it than that. Customers had been heard to say that she could have been the original Eve; pretty, dainty and demure. Not that Molly was ugly, far from it, but she was more thick-set than Eve and shared with some of her brothers a rather stern countenance. Young men tended to take merely a passing interest in Molly. Effortlessly, Eve drew them like moths to a flame.

The thirteen white candles were surrounded by Eve's pink piped icing and Molly's crepe-paper border. All was set now that Mary had arrived. She had walked up the fields from the farm in the valley. Farmer George, her husband of thirteen months had gone back to fetch the cows for milking and Eugene had overheard his mam telling Molly that Mary was two months pregnant. Six left the roost, one gone to war, six still in the Big House of butchers. Thirteen to reckon with on Eugene's thirteenth birthday. Mam was good at numbers. She needed to be.

★

Eugene was in the kitchen when the telegram came. Simple in language and matter-of-fact in tone "George Whitby missing in the invasion of Singapore, feared dead, deepest sympathy extended". Mam was staring at the wall with the picture of the Monarch of the Glen stag. Her face held no expression; tears rolled down her small beautiful cheeks. One of her thirteen had gone. Gone, in a place she had never even heard of and for a reason she could not understand. Butchery to butchery. For the first of what was to be many times, Eugene's world turned black. How could a fit man only 28 years old die? It made no sense.

TWO

I t wasn't a tent. What had made him think it was? It was a small one-roomed house. Her house it must be. Lying on the low single bed he studied the ceiling or rather the inside of the roof. The room was rectangular and each of the two long walls supported a pitched roof. It looked as if the frame and the inner slats were hardwood, teak he supposed, but the watertight covering was thatch made from some sort of broad-leafed grass or maybe palm leaves. Anyway, it certainly worked. Inside was perfectly dry and last night's storm had been some storm. He was thinking that the whole building was not so very different from the smaller making-up room in the yard back home, except the walls were plaited sections of bamboo that had somehow been flattened out; not the solid cold bricks of the butchery.

For the first time he looked at the floor and where the concrete would have been were bamboo planks. The bed had a bamboo frame too but it did not have the iron springs and hard mattress of home. He lay on something very soft and light and was covered, he now realised, with a single sheet made of silk-like material. He had leant against Chit's shoulder when they entered through the veranda which like the whole little house was on stilts.

As if the most natural thing in the world, Chit had lain next to him since the first night. She was small and warm and naked. Back in the Big House he had been smothered and mothered by females, all older than him. He had been washed, clothed, fed and protected by his elder sisters. He knew their shape and he knew their ways and Eve and Molly had been his playmates and then his best buddies. But he had not known a girl. Not one who seeped gradually into his consciousness. Not one who bathed his feet in warm water and held a cool cloth to his forehead and who took his aching head in her hands and looked lovingly at him with those sparkling eyes. Not one who pressed her soft tender body against him nor one whose breasts and nipples were hard against his chest. Not one who started the ache that grew and grew. For the first time in weeks he felt himself smiling. 'Little Eugene' they had called him – they should see him now.

Teaching each other. As Eugene felt his strength returning, that is what he realised they were doing. She could say his name in two short sharp syllables '"U" and "Gene" and he could name the meal she prepared each day as "Moh-Hinga". He could make her "Ming–alar", she could make him "Oh God". Eugene went to paradise and he wondered where Chit went. Wherever she went emotionally, she always came back to him physically in the evening after her workday was over. There never had been, and there never would be again, anything like this.

As he lay on her bed during those long daytime hours awaiting her return Eugene reprised in his mind and then slowly comprehended the successive stages of their lovemaking. From the very first contact, she had taken the lead and perhaps there could have been no other way. He was very ill and very weak. Those paperbacks passed around among the lads in which boy meets girl and they tear off each other's clothes in mad passionate lust could never have been their way. For one thing he wasn't physically capable and for another she had nursed him and her absolute and unselfish care had turned seamlessly to love.

And love it was. Like young children from completely different backgrounds who do not speak the same language, but still play happily together by adopting unspoken rules and leading each other on through action alone. So it was with Chit and Eugene. Slowly and carefully over nights lying in that small single size bed they explored each other. Vigour, confidence and awareness of her body oozed from him in unison with the flushed face, sighs, hardened erect nipples and opened legs. She would sit astride him and slowly descend, drawing his erectness into her small delicate self. After six or seven nights of experimentation, his mind recalled the piston rods of his dad's ten horsepower Ford as his semen spurted in like the explosive petrol ignition deep inside that fine young engine. Eugene and Chit were on their road to ecstasy. Permanently bonded together.

★

Brother Harold had been right, damn it. Eugene had just returned from the Friday van round with James and as he walked across the yard saw Mam standing in the doorway holding a longish brown envelope. There were tears rolling down her small and beautiful pink cheeks. The memory of that same official-looking envelope arriving just three years earlier was still as vivid as it was painful. Her son George had been called to his death in some far off place. Was this now a summons for her last born and favourite, Eugene, to journey to the same fate?

Eugene was mystified. True, he was past his eighteenth birthday, yet it had been weeks since the 8th May street party celebrating VE Day. Surely the war was over? Men had started to drift back and were already walking into the yard asking for work. How could he be asked to leave his dad and brothers only for some other man to take his place? But it was there all right, staring him in the face, "Auxiliary Air Force – Notice of Calling Out". He was the right age, fit and able and not in a reserved occupation, unlike (he was thinking) the miners with their money and the farmers with their cows and pigs. All those he had got to know so well over the past five years had done nicely for themselves. It was just not fair. He was, even at this final hour, being called up: to where exactly?

Once the shock of his calling up had subsided and all those in the Big House had had their say with brother Harold, 'bluddy well knowin'' all along that 'little un wud get his papers', they all gathered in the big sitting room to listen to the nine-o'clock news and then pore over the pile of forms that came with the Calling Out notice. James had now left home but there still remained the butchery clan, Mam, Dad, Willy, Molly and Eve as well as Eugene. Harold had gone over to the Peacock, as Dad had anticipated, 'to tell all and sundry that little Eugene was a goner.' It was well known from the news bulletins and from the headlines in the Daily Express that whilst the conflict in Europe was over, the war in the Far East raged on. The Japanese had still not been driven out of the Malay peninsula. Britain still needed its young men and what is more, needed them in those far away tropical lands in which one of their kith and kin had already perished. Now the odds seemed stacked heavily in favour of a second Whitby sweating it out in Singapore – and maybe further inland.

★

What changes a mind-set? Just like the staid aunt who, when repeatedly invited to go for a walk after tea, would brush it aside with, "I see no point in aimlessly wandering about". That is until the day a friend, who was grieving deeply, wanted a companion to walk with for a few miles on the cliff path south of Scarborough towards Filey Brigg. She went out of sympathy; out of pity really. But it turned out to be a lovely warm springtime day, the wild flowers hung tenaciously to the cliff edge, the new-born lambs were finding their feet in the rolling cliff-side meadows and kittiwakes were swirling from the cliff face far below. That aunt now lives above those cliffs and walks that path every day. What was aimless, no longer is. Or the dog hater who got lumbered with a spaniel when his father died suddenly and is now the proud owner of a best-of-breed. Or the atheist who got half-blinded by a light. So Eugene started to think about the call from the RAF, after all, it could have been from the army. Everybody knew that the boys in blue were a cut above and would he be trained to fly? Did he really want to spend his life butchering and what is more always being the junior butcher with carping Harold somehow, God knows how, to deal with? The real killing war was over and if he got to see the world, how good might that be?

At the training camp just outside Preston, Eugene was chosen to be a cook. Some warped mind must have interpreted his butchery skills as akin to actually preparing food. Quite a laugh really, but then, those preparing meals are not in the front line. So, taking everything into account, he would be in the RAF rather than the Army. There must be a strong likelihood of going overseas and not being stuck in barracks somewhere in Britain. When he got to wherever they were sending him, surely he would be in some cushy kitchen and not out there searching for the enemy. Could it be that Eugene was a lucky boy?

There were sixteen men billeted in Training Hut "G" and Eugene had made a special pal of Billy who was from Kendal and who, before his papers, had been working in a factory making pencils. They had spent many evenings over the past eight weeks talking of home and their jobs and family and trying to imagine what lay ahead. Billy could now memorise the various cuts of beef and Eugene knew what a Groover machine was and heard much about graphite and clay. But this evening was different. Warrant Officer Bates strode into the hut at eight o'clock on the dot to give his briefing. They were to be up with the lark tomorrow and march in full kit to Preston railway station for a day's travel. Two special troop coaches had been reserved on the 6.05 am to London Euston. They would then travel by Metropolitan Underground to Paddington Station in order to catch the early afternoon train to Exeter. A change of trains would then take them to Plymouth and, "to get the stiffness out of your legs", there would be a four-mile tramp to Devonport Dockyard. If all went to plan, they would be on board the ship by nightfall and bunkered down ready for sailing on tomorrow's early morning tide. Billy looked at Eugene through the smoke-filled haze of their hut. No words were needed, their expressions said, *Christ Almighty, this is it.* The luck that Eugene had first reflected upon started to lose some gloss with Bates' final piece of information. The ship was short of crew. The whole company would be required to work their passage and he meant the whole company consisting of one hundred men, six sergeants, two warrant officers and two commissioned officers. One hundred and ten in all would be trainee sailors.

Bates gave every man an information folder which was to

be added to as each section of their orders came through. To pass the time on the journey to Devonport, they were to swot up on HMS Devonshire.

It was during the long hours of the following day, as the trains moved the company southwards that Eugene started to comprehend what military service entailed. Whilst this war had been raging, his family had been supplying the black market with meat and with no regard for the rules intended to save food for a besieged Britain. A second jolt was the dawning realisation that this ship he and his pals were destined to work on, had a history far removed from that covered by the lessons back at school. Perhaps he was after all lucky to be thrust head-first into the real world. Perhaps.

It was interesting to learn that HMS Devonshire had been built at Devonport where she was now docked and had been active pretty much ever since her launch in 1927. During her early years in the Mediterranean there had been a tragic accident when a gun misfired and seventeen men were killed. Later she had been in Chinese waters before returning to the Balearic Islands where she became famous as the ship on which the surrender of Minorca to the Falangist forces was signed. In another notable incident, she evacuated the Norwegian Royal Family two months after Germany invaded Norway in 1940. But Eugene was reading about the service in the Indian Ocean in 1943 and how Devonshire had covered ANZAC troop convoys between Suez and Australia. If the rumour amongst his pals was correct, then the morning tide was about to take this County-class cruiser Down Under – once again. Devon to Australia; so where were they to be dropped off?

Eugene and Billy were bunkered together. They tossed a coin for who could have the upper berth and Eugene had won. In ignorance they had assumed upper as better but that was to disregard the huge iron pipe that passed no more than eighteen inches above Eugene's head. A pipe that they had been told by Junior Ship's Officer Clarke (another "Nobby" a nickname which made Eugene feel a little more at home since there had been a Nobby in his class at school and yet another one on his meat round) led either to or from – or anyway had something to do with – one of the ship's four Parsons geared turbines. While the ship had been at sea for the past three days, the pipe – now christened that bloody thing – issued a low rumbling sound which occasionally changed pitch. This engineering intrusion into their sleeping quarters on top of the, at times, alarming roll of the whole vessel made sound sleep in these early days afloat nigh impossible.

The big map on the wall upstairs had a magnet arrow that was moved by one of the regular crew to indicate the ship's progress. That was how on the second night at sea they knew of their passage through the Bay of Biscay. Disturbed by the ship's movement up and down and side to side together with the drone of the engines and the rumbling of the pipework, sleep came and went. Eugene's mind was racing. He knew that he was good at figures from his weighing and pricing of the meat in the shop and on the vans. Numbers tumbled out of his fuzzy brain and he sorted them into a semblance of order as given by Officer Clarke. When Devonshire was fully loaded she displaced 13,315 tons. She was 633 feet long, 66 feet wide at the beam and with a draft of 21 feet. Eugene imagined this cruiser parked in the market square outside the Big House back home. He mentally strode out 210 of his widest paces. "Flippin' 'eck", it filled the entire market square. He was not sure how fast a knot was, but a top speed of 32 knots sounded a lot, as did a range without refuelling of over 9,000 nautical miles. So from Devonport they might reach goodness knows where. And another thing – how do they cram over 780 men on board? Eugene finally drifted off to sleep.

Whilst on board, he would not be cooking. HMS Devonshire might not have had a full regular crew but that did not apply to the kitchen hands. That had been made clear at the outset. He and Billy were assigned cleaning duties and these duties were not limited to below decks. One or both of them would need a head for heights. The Duty Officer had pointed out the three funnels, the 24 gun placements and the single Supermarine Walrus aircraft and catapult. 'All need a scrub down at some stage – will let you know.'

The arrow on the big map was pointing to mid-way between Sicily and Cyprus when things started to get interesting. There had been no announcement from the upper deck but the junior officers were ripe with rumour. They were no longer alone. Back in May the Mediterranean basin had finally been cleared of German and Italian military shipping including U-boats. However, just to ensure safe passage, HMS Devonshire had joined six other warships to escort up to twenty-five assorted merchantmen towards the Suez Canal en route for the Far East. Using his binoculars Billy could spot at different times of the day freighters, cargo ships and at least one tanker. And then one afternoon he spotted something else, one ship in the flotilla was on fire way off to starboard. Three days later, the rumour mill was grinding again; the freighter had hit a mine and an ex-Italian navy boat, recently commandeered and turned over to our fleet, had come to the rescue. A few months earlier this vessel had been an enemy. On this day it was a friend in need. Eugene was beginning to appreciate how the pages of history turn.

It was now generally felt by the crew that Devonshire, having returned to home port after her second assignment serving with the Home Fleet off Norway, was now detailed to return troops from the Far East to Australia. As Eugene re-studied the big wall map he was, for the first time, convinced that what his mam had dreaded was about to happen. His war service would be carried out somewhere near the graveyard of brother George; the Japanese killing grounds.

THREE

To be at rest in the Princess Dock in Bombay was a complete surprise. It had become clear to Eugene and Billy for days that the more northerly route taken by their ship through the Arabian Sea was unlikely to mean they would pass South of Ceylon and enter the Bay of Bengal for a passage to the Far East. Not only that, but also the lads below deck had picked up a rumour that the company might be called upon to help quell reported unrest in the Royal Indian Navy. As they mustered on deck for the briefing there was palpable unease in the air. Air which, though it was still early morning, was already hot, humid and acrid, or as Billy put it "strewth Eugy, what a pong".

As Group Captain Bennett made clear, they were not about to take on the Royal Indian Navy. After disembarking (Devonshire was indeed going forward to the Far East en route for Australia – "lucky buggers") they were to travel north by train to Thane for three weeks of acclimatisation training and then, air transport permitting, would be flown to Calcutta. If all went well and after a further week in camp, they would take their final train to (Bennett paused for dramatic affect) Rangoon in Burma. There was serious work to do "mopping up Japanese stragglers". The whole company of men, assembled in their ram-rod straight lines on the foredeck, stood in absolute silence, stunned by the news. As one chap said as they went back below to gather their tropical kit, "could have heard a pin drop at a hundred paces".

The next batch of orders to be placed in the, by now, bulging information folder (or from the lips of the lovable sergeant, "study this lot 'til it's penetrated ya thick skull") was headed Recent History and Social Climate in Rangoon. The briefing from Group Captain Bennett on their arrival at the camp in Thane concentrated on the absolute contrast between living in the UK and what they were to experience in and around the Burmese port of Rangoon. Everything they would be given to eat was likely to be based on seafood, maybe some chicken, rice and vegetables but spicy, very spicy because a big influence was Indian curry. It is now the tail-end of the monsoon season and so the air is not only hot but humid, very humid. Expect to sweat like pigs. Sanitation would be basic and toilets are set into the floor, no seats, just squatting down. Otherwise, we will all learn to adapt as we go along but one rule is to be obeyed in all circumstances: 'There will be no fraternising with the local girls, understood?'

It was obvious to Eugene that most of the lads would take the briefing from the boss as sufficient to cope both with the first days of being in Burma and to get by in this Indian place. The batch of written orders could stay nicely in the folder: they might be looked at later. Not so for Eugene. Once off the ship, his brain was whirling. What was it about Burma – why were they really going there? He placed all the papers on his bunk and started to read. A census of 1931 gave the population of Indian Nationals in the whole of Burma as more than one million and of these, about sixty percent had actually been born in India, so they were not even first generation. Only fifteen years ago, anti-Indian hostility culminated in riots in Rangoon when many thousands were killed. It followed that, well before the war started, the Indian population was nervous. Then, on December 23rd 1941, came the first Japanese air raid followed by a second two days later. The civilian population was taken completely by surprise. The lack of any preparation caused chaos in the City of Rangoon. There followed a complete breakdown of law and order and, built upon the civil unrest of 1930 and a spreading rumour that the British were about to abandon Burma, the Indian Nationals began to panic. Immediately, as if by silent psychological instruction, Indians began leaving the city to move northwards, but without them Rangoon could not function since they made up almost the entire working population. Dockworkers were amongst the first to abandon their jobs so that essential supplies were not unloaded and the vessels in the harbour became sitting targets for the Japanese bombers.

One particular news item included in the orders hit Eugene very hard and was to stay with him long after he left this land of turmoil. The keepers of Rangoon Zoo all left their posts. A shooting party was hastily arranged. All animals deemed dangerous were shot. These included tigers, panthers and poisonous snakes. 'Oh God, what a sodding shame.'

We, the British then started to evacuate our officials and staff. Thus, the remaining civilians were pretty much left to their own devices. Bringing the recent history and social climate up to date, the papers state that in the event, and notwithstanding the dual fear of Indians that they would either fall hostage to invading Japanese or would be attacked by the indigenous Burmese inhabitants, well over half of the Indian population decided to stay put. As a result, what one finds in Rangoon in 1945 is a still large but not overwhelming population of ethnic Indians, Burmese now taking a working role but yet a lingering dread of a full-scale assault from a returning Japanese force. It was left to the British to move in to guarantee safety and to purge the land of recalcitrant Japanese.

★

The irony was hard to escape. One hundred young men all drafted into the RAF and not a single one knew anything about, or had any experience of, aircraft. Rather, they had been moved half-way around the world while working as sailors. So on this Thursday morning all was about to change and for the better, or so Eugene and Billy thought as they marched, carrying their full kit, across the already steaming tarmac and towards the twin-propelled DC3. They were fortunate in being part of the first group of 32 to take the flight to Calcutta and up and away into such a gloriously clear blue sky.

It wasn't until they were about an hour-and-a-half into the three-hour flight that things started to happen. Without warning the plane dropped and lurched to the left. Instantly the hubbub of chatter stopped. The plane steadied from its fall as the lads looked at each other in silence. The relief lasted for seconds only. Outside the small windows the blue had turned black and rain lashed the plane. They were on a roller-coaster. The plane dropped again and then like a yo-yo zoomed upwards and kicked to the side. Fear hung in the air like a pall of thick industrial smog. One lad near the front of the plane was catapulted to the roof and his head poured with blood while another sitting next to Billy was being violently sick. Some of the mess hit the seat in front and more was running down his legs below his white tropical shorts. There was a terrible smell. Eugene had grabbed Billy's hand and started to pray using the same words as when kneeling with Mam in St Peter & St Paul's Church down Common Lane. Did he actually pass out? The violent movement just did not stop and there was no announcement from whoever was flying this thing to say that it would. The next thing Eugene knew was that they were descending rapidly, the roar of the twin engines quietened and there was a deep wrenching feeling in his belly; they hit the tarmac of Calcutta with a bang. Bloody hell – why couldn't he have been called up into the Army or, come to that, the Navy for God's sake? Even a butcher can fire a rifle or scrub decks.

During a further week of training in a camp on the outskirts of Calcutta, and as part of a group of ten lads who were ordered to stick together, Eugene and Billy were only allowed one trip into the city. And, they decided later, it had been enough. The write-up in the next set of orders had told them in no-nonsense language exactly what to expect. It had been from Calcutta that the Chindits (the name given to the British Indian Special Force) had launched their operation behind the Japanese lines in Northern Burma. Although the war in Europe was over, it was not over for India. Calcutta was swarming with foreign soldiers: British, American, White Russians and Poles as well as the enormous Indian Army itself. Air sorties were still being flown daily against the Japanese mainland over what was known as the "hump of China". Between 1942 and 1943, three million starving Indians came to die lying on the pavements of their erstwhile homeland. Eugene decided after his day in the city that the order papers gave no more than a sketchy backdrop to reality. To experience the real live city of Calcutta in the year of 1945 was to blow the mind, blow the ear and blow the nostril. A more teeming mass of humanity was impossible to imagine and now the whole company of lads and officers were off to Rangoon. The place from where most of the influx of Indians had started their long journey to death.

"After boat and plane, it has to be train", was the chant they started on the march to Calcutta railway station and the train, when it rolled slowly up to a crowded and heaving platform, was a black monster hauling carriage after carriage of dark red wooden sheds on wheels. As the hissing steaming engine came to rest, Eugene felt the same tingle pass down his spine as when he first caught sight of HMS Devonshire. The flight was forgotten, the stench, the clutter, the clanging of cycle bells and the barking dogs of Calcutta were behind them. If it took a week to travel the one thousand, six hundred and fifty miles to Rangoon, he for one didn't care and he also knew that neither did the rest of the lads. Two carriages in the middle of the train had been reserved and as they stowed their kit in the overhead string racks, it was paradise. Who cares what lies ahead?

If Eugene knew anything for certain about what the future held, it was that reading would be his constant companion. He thought back on what he had learnt and forward to what he still needed to find out. Barely able to settle in his seat before attacking the new order sheets, there was an enthusiasm he never realised he had or even thought possible to possess. Back in January of this year (1945), British troops landed by sea on Ramree Island, off the west coast of Burma and this, the third landing by Allied amphibious forces within an eighteen day period, was significant because the island was an important distribution centre for Japanese supplies. The whole military operation had gone like clockwork. Heavy naval guns opened the bombardment at precisely 9.29 am Indian time followed by heavy bombers at 9.30 am dropping one hundred, 1,000lb bombs on gun emplacements. As a result of this successful landing, troops of the 14th Army drove south and on the same day were within eighteen miles of Mandalay and the centre of Burma.

Rangoon itself had fallen to the Japanese in February 1942, not long after Singapore, and had only been relieved once the Japanese General Kimura ordered his men to start evacuating from 22 April 1945. On the 1st May, literally one day before the monsoon broke, a Gurkha parachute battalion dropped on Elephant Point and cleared the remnants of the Japanese forces from the mouth of the Rangoon River. The next day, the 26th Indian Infantry Division landed by ship. Although the looting and lawlessness was to come, Rangoon City was free once again and after three very hard years, Burma was almost wholly purged of the Japanese occupation. What surprised Eugene most about the recent history of the place they were heading for, was just how many countries had sent forces to help the British clear the Peninsular; particularly the armies from India and latterly from China.

The wonders of travel can start to tarnish after two full days and four hours sitting in the same seat with only the occasional respite of a quick walk on the platform each time the train stopped at a station. The train had no corridor but the five berths and central berth were wide enough for reasonable comfort. Although they had now got used to the hole in the floor type of toilet, the lack of privacy, soundproofing and disinfectant did lead to a conscious recognition that they were all in a confined space and on the move.

They had imagined that once off the train, there would be a comfortable camp close to Rangoon station where their stiff joints could loosen up in warm scented showers. But they were soon disillusioned when the duty sergeant lined them up in full kit for a route march. "Only fifteen miles, do you all bloody good after being cramped in the cattle sheds". So, as far as Eugene and Billy could see, they had simply been taken from one hellhole to another, one country to another and if anything it was hotter, more humid and more smelly in Burma that in Eastern India. But at least they were now in the open air and on the move and there would be proper accommodation when they arrived at wherever they were going.

"Knackered" was the only heart-rending, foot-numbing, back-breaking word that Eugene could utter as he slumped to the ground in what Group Captain Bennett was describing to all the company as, "our jungle clearing". It was no more than an open space with a few less trees than where they had tramped during the last six hours. There was no camp or buildings of any kind. The orders this time, the truly astonishing orders, the morale-sapping orders consisted of a set of drawings for each man; "How to construct a rudimentary shelter". Were they really being ordered to build their own accommodation – after the balls-aching journey from Calcutta and this great tramp through the jungle? "Bloody unbelievable".

The idea was for each man to locate two trees about five feet apart. According to the drawings, a thin branch should be cut and tied about four feet above the ground, horizontally linking the two chosen trees. Just short of each end of the horizontal spar two further branches should be secured to form an inverted "v" shape to the ground. Once this basic frame was in place, more spars could be placed across the two ends from top to bottom. The final task was to lay broad leaves over the cross-member spars to form a roof. Importantly, this layering had to start at the bottom and work upwards, so that the rain and condensation would run off the shelter keeping the inside dry. The instructions recognised that some people would make a better job of building their shelter than others and so it was a good idea to keep an eye on what the more practically minded were doing. Good luck.

Actually, for a pencil-maker and a butcher working as a team, Eugene and Billy were rather proud of their little homes. They even constructed some side pieces by sharpening thick twigs into pegs to anchor bamboo leaves to the ground and again working upwards to the gables. With their groundsheets in place supporting a padded bedroll, life could continue. If only those back home could see them now.

Once the whole group had made some sort of effort to bunker down for the first night, Eugene could not have been the only one to wonder after all this journeying, all the reading of orders and all the acclimatisation training, what the hell they were doing here.

★

The skill of a cook comes into its own when he not only feeds his own flock but understands what the ingredients are needed for and appreciates the necessity of supply. On the third day of settling in, Group Captain Bennett stood on a table he had purloined from somewhere and addressed the whole company. "In a nutshell – no pun intended" he said pointing upwards at the tree nearest to him, "our job, and why you men have come to this land, is to save as many native Burmese as possible from starvation. Many of these local people are now hiding in the jungle. All the able-bodied men were taken, along with many of our captured lads, to work on the death railway – Bangkok to Rangoon. Many perished and those rescued are in a pitiful state. As for the women and children, least said the better. We will fly and drop rice and whatever other supplies we are given into the jungle villages of Southern Burma. We will help the poor buggers to pick up the pieces after three years of sheer horror. That is all".

As a result of a vote taken by the lads in the camp back home, Eugene and Billy had been elevated from being one of the cooks to each being joint main chef. Whilst this had started as a bit of a joke, it arose from the hot-pot dish they had jointly developed and which in turn derived from Eugene's knowledge of beef and lamb cuts and Billy's secret sauce recipes sent by his Lancashire Aunt Maria. The irony of this family supporter did not escape Billy when, along with Eugene, they were called by Warrant Officer Bates to meet their "Aunt Sally – and do not even try to pronounce her real name – you will stand next to her for as long as it takes to learn what goes into and how to prepare this stuff we are all going to eat, got it?"

To the joint main chefs, Aunt Sally's pidgin English was just fascinating and they soon deduced that the soups and main courses were Chynna and the spices were Indee-er . She got the food hot on the charkole, the heavy iron pan with two handles was her wok and the names of the rest of her tools were never quite mastered. But they both knew what these tools were for and stemmed probably from the many years of British domination of Burma. The pestle and mortar was hardly ever out of Aunt Sally's hand. There was a large sieve for separating the white fish from its bones, a bamboo spatula for tossing the chicken in the rice, many colanders for draining (absolutely the same as Mam used back in the Big House at home), the big stone for grinding nuts and pressing ginger and of course all the implements of Eugene's butchery past – cleavers, knives, skewers and ladles.

But the serving and eating of the food was far removed

from home. The lads had to learn how to lie on floor mats, eat off low tables and to understand the need to gorge on the first course. That was because this was also the last course. Aunt Sally got all the dishes for the meal ready as a single task and delivered them to the table at the same time. But the overwhelming difference to anything they had experienced before was the smell of the spices and the broadside assault on their taste buds. After the first few Aunt Sally banquets, all the company agreed that, whilst there were many more visits with the spade to the jungle, it was worth it.

Kitchens are notoriously fraught places: even in the open air, even in exotic climates, even with a dominant head chef and only two joint main chefs, they are fraught places. Although Eugene and Billy were buddies, getting these concoctions together all at the same time could mean wanting the big stone at the same time and needing the large knife to slice the chicken when it was already being used to chop the main vegetable. So, heated discussions took place from time to time but when the hurly-burly was over, there was one thing on which they both agreed. Joint main chefs should not be air crew. They picked up pidgin English and crushed spices. Aircrew dropped rice. Two quite different things. But that was not how Warrant Officer Bates saw it. If there were to be any post-war casualties he wanted no more family grief, "seen too bloody much of that already". However, in the eyes of the younger lads, that did not make selecting air crews fair, far from it.

The first morning of the sorties' selection process was both a surprise and a charade. "Men with a wife and child back home move from wherever you're sitting now to the benches at the back and those you displace move to the front – understand?" The lads looked surprised but shuffled as directed. "Men with just a wife back home do likewise," – more shuffling. "Men with a mother back home, move to the back" – more shuffling. When the dance of the airmen was over and the gabble had subsided, Eugene and Billy found themselves three rows from the front. "Right oh then my merry men, this is where you sit each time we assemble – I pick from the front every time, unless feeling especially bad tempered or if one of you buggers has upset me, in which case I pick from where I fancy – got it?"

It some ways it was a welcome relief to be out of the cooking zone on the chosen days; to be up above the green, mountainous jungle and to allow the vastness of this tropical place to leach into the soul. At least that was how Eugene was beginning to feel. He hadn't been to the High Peak in the county next to his home although he had seen pictures of Kinder Scout and he had read about The Great Trespass that eventually opened up the Pennine Way. Was it as wild and rugged as the land he now saw through the open flap door of this aged DC3? Why hadn't he ventured west and north into Derbyshire? Because he had been too bloody busy butchering cows and making sausages for the shop and vans, that's why. Of course, up here in the skies of Burma there was another blanket of pure happiness that Eugene wrapped around himself. Something he had never, ever, felt before. He was doing good. He, little Eugene, the butt of jokes at school about cows' udders, and having felt the weight of brother Harold's boot in the yard, was now up in the heavens feeding the poor sods far below. Who would have thought it? Not he.

After three months, Eugene calculated that four out of five of the rice-dropping trips were happy ones. The fifth was a bugger and even worse was not knowing in advance when one was in the offing. There were some clues; when the maids could be seen closing the wooden shutters of the huts even though the sky was the usual deep blue and the air was still, there was a storm gathering. How they knew was a mystery but they were always accurate at forecasting bad weather. Then there was the lunatic pilot who though easily identified, could not be avoided. It was a lottery who sat in the pilot seat; he could be a goody but now and again he wasn't. On those trips and even in the absence of electric storms, Eugene was literally terrified and never got used to it. Worse, the lunatic man knew it and played on it. The Dakota's engines could be fired up or cut gently and the plane could be banked steadily and cautiously. On the other hand, Captain Daring the stunt ace, might decide to show the earthling that this workhorse of the sky could do a few tricks and still stay airborne and in one piece – bastard!

Somehow, Aunt Sally had managed to communicate to Warrant Officer Bates that Eugene "he the bestest kuk". That was why he was being seconded to the main British camp in Mandalay and why he was being promoted from AC2 ("Aircraftsman 2nd class or colloquially AC Plonk" as Bates kindly informed him prior to the square–bashing back in Preston – "the lowest of the low my lad"), to AC1. Eugene found himself standing in front of the make-shift bamboo desk of the big boss, Group Captain Bennett, to receive the departure briefing. The boss never got involved in the day-to-day running of things but rumour had it that he was a good chap, experienced, reliable and straight and Eugene was overawed by the big framed and ruddy faced senior officer. But his nervousness soon passed as he received his papers and listened carefully to a potted history. A history of Burma's second city.

"The British conquered Mandalay in 1885 and Burma as a whole was detached from India in the Government of India Act 1935. It thus became a Crown Colony as indeed it is again now but not without two big adventures, both involving the Japanese. In the late 1930's Burmese Nationalists plotted to get the country out of the British Empire and into the Japanese one. This attempt failed but in December 1941 the Japanese decided to take the country by their own direct action; they invaded. Mandalay itself fell on May 2nd 1942 and one huge consequence of Japanese control of Central Burma was that China was cut off from the West.

"The tide turned in February this year (1945) when medium tanks of the 14th Army under General William J. Slim formed a bridgehead on the eastern banks of the Irrawaddy River, about fifty miles north of Mandalay, where the Japanese had been attempting to prevent our ground troops from extending their hold. These tanks were the first to cross the river and, with infantry following, made steady progress. By March, the 14th Army had re-captured Mandalay and as we know from our earlier briefings, Rangoon was restored to our control two months later. So there you have it lad, a potted history of the second city and the privilege this posting gives you to visit up-country. We've picked you out as a bright one and if you fit in well at the Irrawaddy River camp, I personally will see you get your 2-tapes as a Provisional Corporal. Off you go and get your kit ready – good luck – oh, and by the way, Squadron Leader Hanger is also being seconded, they need another senior flyer up there".

As he walked back to his billet, Eugene was floating on air and he found himself listening to the gramophone in the parlour back at the Big House and he was singing along with Peter Dawson "On the road to Mandalay, where the flying fishes play". What are flying fishes anyway?

★

Aunt Sally would have been proud of the kitchen in the Mandalay camp because it was a proper kitchen and it had been created by partitioning off the end bay of the largest rectangular hut. Being under cover, the cooking stoves were made of brick with iron grills and most of the pots and pans were exactly like the ones Eugene's mam used in the Big House. This was as British a kitchen as could be imagined and, Eugene was thinking, a tell-tale sign of this land being a colony for the past sixty years. There was even a huge frying pan where the wok should be. It didn't take long to work out why since being inland, as distinct from on the coast, the cooks had much more meat to prepare than fish which had been readily available in Rangoon. Eugene was in his element; who knew more about chicken and pork than he did? He was in the throes of making a pork-based stew when Hanger swaggered in looking for all the world as if he had been promoted to Air Vice-Marshal. "Eugy, guess what, there's a bloke outside asking to see thee and this is a good 'un, ses he's yur nephew. Cheeky bugger, looks same age as thi sen, should I send 'im packin'? Ses his name's Paul".

It was like one of the romantic films being churned out in Hollywood in which something really surprising happens and is, on first sight far-fetched but, as the story line develops, it morphs into a kind of reality. Billy had been left behind along with their chats over a fag, reading their letters from home and swapping the latest gags. Now in replacement and quite out of the blue, Paul appears. Not that there was any similarity in appearance. The apparent conjuring trick revealed a Paul with the semblance of a long thin Whitby nose and the elongated thin frame of a James; not to mention from the very first sentence he uttered, the broad Notts/Derbys accent that was close to, but not quite as harsh as, that of Hanger or Bates heralding as they did from the more northerly county of Yorkshire. Billy on the other hand was stereotypically of Lakeland blood. Blood that flowed through a big-bodied frame with broad wrists and huge shoulders atop thick thighs and long legs. Eugene's instant thought was that any of the lads in camp who were spoiling for a fight wouldn't think twice about taking on Paul, but Billy – best not.

Years after the event, his elder brother Frank told Eugene what Dad had once said, "The Whitby clan is big enough to deal with this and we have to for the sake of the business. That bloke Albert is going to marry our Alice and sharpish". Exactly one month after Eugene was born, his elder sister Alice gave birth to Paul. Alice was seventeen years old and having mothered many of her younger brothers and sisters, was now a mother herself. What on earth was Paul doing in Mandalay?

After the men had been fed and the plates and dishes all washed up and put back on the racks, Eugene left his beloved kitchen and joined his nephew Paul by the river. Each lit a fag and both felt the same. How they came to be here was unbelievable, just unbelievable. Still only eighteen years old, they were born in neighbouring villages located each side of a county border, one was a butcher and the other an apprentice engineer. But the most amazing thing of all was that one was uncle to the other. As Paul elegantly put it "couldn't bloody well make it up" and now they found themselves in central Burma having arrived by completely different routes. After his training at Catterick Army Camp, Paul had been shipped to Mombasa in East Africa but never got started on anything because of orders to all his company to set out on a different troop ship to Rangoon, having arrived just six weeks earlier. They had been moved up here to help rebuild river bridges blown up by the departing Japanese. The Japs were just sods, all the chaps thought so.

Then there was the question of the monkey. One of Paul's pals had been taking his early morning trip into the jungle with his spade when he spotted a baby snub-nosed monkey sitting amongst the coarse grass in the clearing he was about to dig up. It was all alone, making soft screeching sounds and staring straight ahead with large appealing eyes. Still there an hour later and almost certainly starving, what else could his pal do but pick up the small brownish/black bundle and bring it back to camp? They had built a little cage out of scraps of metal brought back from the bridge and were taking turns to feed Monty a diet of bananas and betel nuts after the seven-o'clock sundown. Monty monkey, now the company mascot, was growing fast and getting noisier by the day – perhaps too noisy. Could that be due to the nuts, because when betels were ground up and rolled in tobacco leaf to smoke, the locals went slightly bonkers? Paul's engineering pals thought that it would be a good idea to move Monty's cage onto the veranda just outside Eugene's kitchen. That way, he would have some human company all day and could be weaned off the betel nuts via the scraps Eugene could feed him from the kitchen. Of course, he must not be found by an officer. And that is how Monty and Eugene got attached and how Monty started his travels.

FOUR

'Could have done it, should have done it. What are you talking about, you half-drunken old bugger? It's taken until well into that third pint to loosen your tongue and get you off your bloody health problems; what should you have done? I come all this way to see you on your birthday and to get you off that settee. You limp along with me half carrying you to this dump and now, at last, when I get a semblance of a proper chat, I have no idea what the hell you are moaning about.'

Old Eugene was only half listening, leaning to the left and staring into his beer and almost talking to himself.

'Should have stayed there, should have stayed with her, should have done what a couple of the chaps had the guts to do – stayed in Mandalay, disappeared into the North and set up home. We would have made a living, we were so very happy, I have never been truly happy since. Chit was so beautiful, three years we'd been together and she saved my life. A futile life spent in England when I should have been back there, what a stupid fool I was, what a lie I have lived ever since.'

'That's pretty deep stuff Eugy; pretty damn sad too – why don't you tell me, before it's too late, what actually happened in the end? You've always clammed up before; make this time different.'

'Can't remember everything now, taken years to blot it out

33

of my mind and it's so long ago but I was standing with Chit on the flat roof of her Aunt's flat, somewhere in the Queenstown District, when two of the Military Police burst in and just manhandled me off. I didn't even have time to say goodbye, all I remember was her squatting on the floor, head in hands and screaming. I was bundled down the stairs, pushed into the back of a military truck and driven off.

'Next thing I remember was being thrust under a canvas awning on the Padang and ordered to stand to attention in front of the desk. There was a huge fan whirling, it was a typical stinking hot Singapore afternoon. I tell you what Billy boy, Bennett was furious, bloody furious. At first he just stared at me, his eyes wide and his big face redder than I had ever seen it. It did not take an Einstein to realise that I was in for the granddaddy of bollockings. After what seemed an eternity with me standing there rigid and he just glaring, I think it began with him asking if I remembered his briefing at the camp in Thane after docking in Bombay – "Do you remember lad, do you remember? No fraternising, I said no fraternising didn't I?" And how the bloody hell did you get her and a sodding monkey all the way down the peninsular to Singapore, without him or any officer knowing? "You should have been in the Secret Service lad." Well, there was a decision to be taken. "Do you want to marry this girl?" Without a second's hesitation, I said yes. He then said that if I did marry this girl, I would be court-marshalled for committing an act that was strictly interdicted. As Bennett used that word, and how well I remember it, he drew his fingers across his throat. And another thing I had better understand was not to expect her parents to approve of a marriage; she would most likely be cast out of her village and, in addition, I might face a civil action back in Burma. My option, my only option, was to get on the boat leaving for home tomorrow and the whole sorry business would be hushed up.'

'Christ Eugy, are you saying you never saw Chit again?'

'Yes.'

'Are you saying you never had any contact with her ever again?'

'Yes.'

'Bloody hell. No wonder you were so cut up when we met again boarding the boat in Singapore Harbour to come back home – we'll have a whisky with the next pint.'

The Ex-Service Men's Club had been on Eldon Street since the 1920's and not much had changed. The two old men were sitting opposite each other at a table in the far corner of the main concert room. It still had its brown-painted woodwork, its worn planked floor and non-too-comfortable chairs. Not that, by this stage, Billy and Eugene were in any mood to notice or mind. Billy plonked the tray of renewed drinks down on the table, leaned back in his chair, looked closely at his life-long friend through watering eyes and let the other man continue pouring his heart out in tune with the drink pouring into that battered and tired frame.

'To give him his due, Group Captain Bennett was a different man when we got back to Portsmouth. He asked me, almost pleaded with me, not to apply for my Demob Papers. He said there was a good career for me in the RAF. He would make me up to Corporal straight away and on £2,12s 6d a week, with most expenses avoided by living in Quarters, I would be far better off than if I returned to butchering. And if I kept my nose clean (with the business of the girl forgotten) there was every chance of a Commission. The RAF needed bright blokes like me to sign on as regulars. He said I should think of that smart new uniform and the overseas postings in peacetime "You'll have the pick of all the pretty lasses, mark my words". But I knew better, didn't I Billy? If I went back to my dad's business and eventually took it over, then one day I would be a millionaire – it would be too late after my RAF days were over to start up in business again. Billy boy, I was a bloody fool.'

★

It was his day off and Eugene was strolling the back streets of Mandalay when he noticed the book shop. He had barely started to browse when he saw it on a dusty shelf at eye level; he could hardly have missed the bright orange cover – The Teaching of Buddha. Opening the cover he read,

Chapter One – The Life Of The Buddha. The Shakya clansmen dwelled along the Rohini River that flows among the southern foothills of the Himalayas. Their King, Shuddhodana Gautama, had settled his capital at Kapilavastu and there had been a great castle built and he ruled wisely, winning the joyful acclaim of his people.

The Queen's name was Maya. She was the daughter of the King's uncle who was also the King of a neighbouring district of the same Shakya clan. For twenty years they had no children. But, one night, dreaming a strange dream, in which she saw a white elephant entering into her womb through the right side of her chest, Queen Maya became pregnant. The King and the people looked forward with joyful anticipation to the birth of a royal child. According to their custom the Queen returned to her parents' home for the birth, and on her way, in the beautiful spring sunshine, she took a rest in Lumbini Garden. All about her were Ashoka blossoms and in delight she reached out her right arm to pluck a branch and as she did so a prince was born. All expressed their heart-felt delight with the glory of the Queen and her princely child; Heaven and Earth rejoiced. This memorable day was the eighth day of April. The joy of the King was extreme and he named the child, Siddhartha, which means, "Every wish fulfilled." In the palace of the King, however, delight was quickly followed by sorrow, for after several days the lovely Queen Maya suddenly died. Her younger sister, Mahaprajapati, became the child's foster mother and brought him up with loving care. A hermit, called Asita, who lived in the mountains not far away, noticed a radiance above the castle and, interpreting it as a good omen, came down to the palace and was shown the child. He predicted: "This Prince, if he remains in the palace, when grown up, will become a great King and subjugate the whole world. But if he forsakes the court life to embrace a religious life, he will become a Buddha, the Saviour of the World."

Eugene bought the book and was still reading from it as he walked back into his kitchen. That same book, now somewhat tattered, sits on a bookshelf above the settee on which an old man spends most of his day thinking of the past. And the past included Monty. Mascot monkey Monty. The lads' mascot that got them back safely and the puzzle was only partly untangled by the Primate Keeper of Singapore Zoo on that sad, sad day when he and Chit handed Monty over. Monty, it turned out, was a Burmese snub-nosed monkey and had a nick-name, the sneezing monkey. That made sense since the lads made fun of him every time it rained. Monty bowed his head in rainfall and if he didn't do so in time, his little snub-nose seemed engineered to catch water and that is when he sneezed.

The zookeeper was not surprised at Monty's survival in captivity because *"Monki he like us he jus want nice company and food – we proud hav im – he very rare – he be star for torrists – many thanks to yu for bringin im."* But how did Monty get to Mandalay? His rare family live in the north-eastern section of Kachin State, the northern most part of Burma. Had he jumped aboard a banana truck heading south? Had he been a pet before being abandoned? Who knows, but he had clung to Eugene for grim death as the lads made their way down that death railway. It was almost as if he knew what had gone on.

Eugene and Paul were now bosom pals and had learned enough about the *system* to ensure their *days-off* coincided so they could explore Mandalay together. A favourite day out was to walk up the 750 ft. high Mandalay Hill for the panoramic view of the city and the Plains of Shan. To the north were ox carts being driven in the fertile lush-green paddy fields and beyond those the old and strange-shaped wooden buildings disappearing into the distant jungle. As they descended the hill on that Friday afternoon, Paul was saying to Eugene that, for him, it was the bright light and the bright colour of everything they saw that made this land so different from the cloudy skies and drab clothes worn back home.

'Eugene, just look at the gold-leaf covering on that pagoda and the burgundy robes of the monks as they walk past us. Another thing: that pale powder smeared in patterns on the faces and arms of the women and children. You haven't seen that back in Huthwaite – eh? Cheap red lipstick and brown dyed legs passing for nylon stockings was about the lot when I left.'

Both lads laughed. Eugene was thinking of the worry etched on his mam's face when the brown envelope arrived. He would write to her tonight. He would describe the wonders of Burma. He would bottle the scents and jungle sounds of this walk to camp by the Irrawaddy River. But the smell of the durian fruit and the ear shattering high pitch of the crickets cannot be bottled and brought back home – silly Eugy.

★

The last thing he remembered was Squadron Leader Hanger reading out the message that had been relayed down the line from Bennett, it was something about intelligence from mainland Japan. Apparently it had been established that the Japanese Field Service Code said that surrender was not possible. The soldiers of the Japanese occupying Army had been told that they would be killed or tortured if they fell into Allied hands and consequently any Japanese still hiding in the jungle would fight to the death or commit suicide. That was why the new order had been issued: under no circumstance must any man, other than on a flying sortie, venture beyond the perimeter of Mandalay City.

Sometimes he could hear voices. People were talking softly but not to him. Sometimes he could make out the shape of people standing at the foot of his bed but it was all blurred and fuzzy. For long periods there was nothingness; blank nothingness. How long had he been like this? One day his eyes pierced the blanket of cloud, albeit with a big effort, and after such a clearer spell the mist returned. Eugene was thinking of what Mr Mottley had said about the grammar in his composition at school *Coping with Rationing* 'Two steps forward Whitby and one step back.' But he was not mistaken this time. There was a tube sticking into his right arm and attached to it a plastic bag hanging from a metal contraption above his head. And, there were two people by the bed and one was definitely Hanger. He was talking softly to a figure in a white coat but in a language something like the pidgin English he and Billy had learnt from Aunt Sally. The white coat was worn by a Burmese nurse and he could see her quite clearly as she bent closer to him and placed a damp cloth on his forehead. The cloth was cool, very cool and he drifted into heaven on a wave of perfumed air.

Eugene was sitting on a low-slung canvas bed propped up by pillows. He was out of his comatose state, everything was clear now and the jungle insects were at their noisiest. It was like the conjurer on the makeshift stage in Calcutta who whipped off the cloth covering the cage and coming from nowhere, absolutely nowhere, was a white rabbit. Except this wasn't a white rabbit, it was Paul.

'Honestly Eugy, you couldn't have made this up if you'd tried. You were brought over here to help feed the starving after the Japs had done their worst and then we're all told to watch our backs in case the little buggers are still hiding in the jungle, and what happens to you? You catch Japanese Encephalitis – and it wasn't even a booby trap they left for you! One good thing is that, apparently, it might have damaged the brain long-term but that won't bother you since you didn't have much of a brain to start with and Christ Eugy, did you have to be so dramatic about it? They told me that Hanger was briefing you lot on the latest Jap thing when, with no warning, you just fell flat on your face. That's why your big conk is still bandaged.

'Thing is Eugy, I've been having a serious talk with Squadron Leader Hanger – he's a good chap you know and a rock-solid Yorkshire bloke to boot. Now that the medic says you will pull through, we think you should take up an offer of being nursed away from here with all its comings and goings. It's a bit risky but as Hanger says, he is the most senior of the RAF blokes here and he can keep it under wraps for a few weeks, long enough to get you back in the kitchen with no questions asked. What do you think?'

'Sorry Paul and I know I'm still dopey but when you say away from here, where do you mean and nursed by whom?'

'When you were in a coma, the medic asked Mandalay

General Hospital on 30th Street if they could spare a local nurse for a few hours a day to be with you here and this young girl, who is called Chit, arrived and basically hasn't left your bedside since. In fact, she seems to have made herself a little hut thing further down the river, bit like your lot had to build outside Rangoon. She's been coming at sunrise each day and feeding you whatever the medic said you could eat and drink as you gradually regained some feelings in your limbs. Did you know that as well as being in a coma, you were also paralysed? She's been washing you, cleaning you up and in fact every bloody thing that needed doing. The medic just left her to it. Tell you another thing Eugy, the medic told me in confidence that without her you would be a goner. Upshot is, Chit has somehow made it known, God knows how 'cos she can't speak a word of English, that she wants you taken to her home in the next village for, we suppose she means, recuperation. Want to go?'

*

Eugene had fallen asleep. Why was sitting up on the settee such a big effort? There was a bottle of Bells whisky on the table and a note from Billy – *Thanks old mate and keep in touch* – the struggle getting to his feet and to the table was due to the pounding in his head, his backside hurt again and the left hip wouldn't move properly. Getting old is a pig he thought, at least the pigs he used to cut up never had that problem – Eugene even managed a smile to himself. Why had he spilled the beans to Billy? Perhaps they had to be torn from his heart before it was too late? Maybe it was just the booze? What they hadn't talked about, and just as well because he couldn't remember much about it himself, was how he got from Mandalay to

Singapore. He hadn't met up with his old pals until they all boarded the boat to come back home.

The effort, with help from his new mates, to conceal Chit for the final three months moving southwards down the Malay Peninsula had just about exhausted the old memory bank. But now the full facts were out, he realised why they had gone by train for a few hours at a time and then commandeered trucks or rickety old buses or sometimes just walked, until the single-track railway line appeared again. Could it really have been that to get Chit from the end of one piece of track to the start of the next, Giant Glen (six feet, four in his cotton socks) actually smuggled her in his kit bag? Well he did. When they walked, had they literally stepped over the dead bodies of locals left behind by the terrorist groups moving North? Well they had.

At the time, none of them, including Hanger, had any idea that they were travelling over more bones than railway sleepers, treading on more dried blood than fallen teak tree leaves and passing more ghosts of hell than in the entire Books of the Netherworld. All this whilst forming a hatred of the Japanese race that was to set harder than granite.

After eating his cheese and biscuits and swallowing two aspirins, Eugene opened his sideboard drawer and took out the Wikipedia print-out that the kind assistant at the library had found for him. Even now and after many attempts, he could still only read bits of it without welling up.

The important bits for Eugene were knowing that after the Japanese defeat at the Battle of Midway in June 1942, a way had to be found to get supplies and troops to the newly seized Burma. The sea route of over 2,000 miles from Japan around the Malay Peninsula, through the Straits of Malacca and the Andaman Sea to reach Rangoon, was becoming too dangerous due to the lurking presence of Allied submarines. The Japanese decided that the solution was to link up existing railways with the Burmese port at one end and Bangkok in Siam at the other. And so the now infamous Death Railway was conceived. Routing via the Three Pagodas Pass on the border between Siam and Burma, the line was surveyed as being 69 miles in Burma and 189 in Siam (current day Thailand). There was a historical note that back in 1885 the identical route had been examined by the British government, but due to the hilly jungle of the terrain and the many rivers to be crossed, the project was considered too difficult to take on. Eugene could appreciate that necessity in wartime, if not the mother of invention, was to be the mother of construction and at whatever cost. And cost it did. It cost misery and lives – many lives.

Construction of the railway began at the Burma end in September 1942 and in Siam two months later. For manpower and from May 1942, the Japanese moved prisoners of war northward from Changi Prison in Singapore and from other camps in Southeast Asia. Most of the construction materials, including tracks and sleepers, were brought from dismantled branches of the Federated Malay States Railway network and from the Netherlands East Indies. The railway was completed ahead of schedule in October 1943. As he read on, Eugene thought to himself that two statistics in the write-up that were trotted out quite casually, failed utterly to embrace the enormity of the project: 258 miles of track were laid and 600 bridges were built (including six to eight long-span bridges). With his experience of the heat and humidity of the land, Eugene wondered how anyone looking back could conceivably comprehend the sheer effort and human suffering that went into building the railway. There was no proper transportation available to move all the heavy materials. Spades and hammers were the only tools in use. For the workers in these killing conditions, there was a total absence of proper medication which, together with the scarcity of food, created the perfect condition for starvation and death. Figures compiled by the Australian Government suggested that 330,000 men worked on the railway line. Of 250,000 Asian labourers, about 90,000 died during construction and of 61,000 Allied prisoners of war, 16,000 died. Eugene was thinking that his own self-built house north of Rangoon was a positive mansion compared to what these poor sods were subjected to. The historical account says that the construction camps consisted of open-sided barracks built of bamboo poles with thatched roofs. The barracks were about sixty yards long with sleeping platforms raised above the ground on each side of an earthen floor. Two hundred men were housed in each barracks, giving each man a two-foot wide space in which to live and sleep. Sketches have been found that show men asleep in a standing-up position.

As his head fell against the back of the settee, Eugene's last drifting thought was that no venture under whatever pressure could possibly justify such barbaric treatment of fellow human beings. Worse, the whole thing had been brought on by a self-interest land grab. The endeavour might have been an engineering masterclass but it was truly damnable. And as for the Japanese themselves….. Eugene sank into a troubled sleep.

*

Today, Eugene is feeling like a new man – well nearly new anyway. It is early May, the sun is now well up and the air is warm under a cloudless blue sky. He has washed and had his daily shave, made himself eggs and bacon for breakfast with his customary mug of steaming hot *Yorkshire* tea. The latest tablets seem to have numbed the pain in his backside and his left hip has stopped aching – God knows why. But, best of all, Pete the postie came early for once and brought the stuff the library lady promised to research for him. His question had been, "Can you please research for me how I can get from Bangkok to Singapore cheaply by train and also, if it's possible, in style and comfort?" Actually, the library lady has a name and it's Pearl and for the first time last week, she asked him to call her by name. He is her favourite regular customer and for some months she has helped him choose books from his favoured *travel section,* but more recently he has discovered their internet research facility. Pearl is drawn to the creaking old man and he fascinates her. *Bright as a button brain inside a world weary head* is how she thinks of him. It is stupid and she knows it but when he lumbers through the library door, her heart rate quickens and she is instinctively drawn to help him with whatever the latest search request is. *What has this man been through, what have those eyes seen, those huge hands touched and what has that frame been damaged by?*

Using his trusty ivory-bone gardening knife, Eugene opens the white envelope to take out the two papers, each from a separate travel company. The first is the so-called *Cheap, Historic, Relaxed Way* and the second the *Green Carpet Luxury Adventure.* As he reads, and being in such high spirits, Eugene grins to himself thinking that whether the choice is cheap or expensive, the route will be the same and so will be the distance of 1,250 miles or so. He was reminded of the story his pal at the club had told him about his son-in-law who, when checking in at John F Kennedy International Airport in New York to fly back home, he asked by the check-in clerk if he was interested in paying an extra bargain discount fare of $500 to travel first-class as the forward cabin was pretty empty on this flight. With a perfectly straight face and in the quietest voice he could muster, his son-in-law asked, because he was being met at Heathrow, if by travelling first class he would arrive any earlier than by sticking with his economy class ticket.

Still in reflective mood, Eugene was thinking of just how these two means of travel were worlds apart for the *haves* and the *have-nots*. Whether, in the old days you were living with a ration book or able to use the black market, whether an AC2 or a Group Captain, whether a Romusha on the death railway or a Japanese General, whether claiming benefits or an investment banker, it always has been and always will be the same; there are those that are up and those that are down. Using the lowest class ticket and taking just 48 hours, the whole journey from Bangkok to the new Woodlands terminal in North Singapore can be done for about £40. But then look at this, taking the Eastern Oriental Express with exactly the same stages (Bangkok to Penang, then to Kuala Lumpur and finally to Singapore) on the same single-line track will involve three nights in a private sleeper car and four days overall. Thrown in for good measure is a tour of Penang Island via the ferry at Butterworth and a tour of the Malaysian capital. Including all meals (but, Eugene noted with a wry smile – no drinks) the price is £1,600 each with two sharing; a few bob more if you happen to be alone. Everything in life is relative.

Even the cheap way today would have been luxurious for the 1,800 of us making our way down to Singapore in 1949. Forty-eight hours, took us more like ninety bloody days! No wonder I can't remember much about how we did it, but I do remember running out of railway track, the mosquitoes and the cockroaches. I remember bartering with the locals for banana, water melons and monkey nuts for Monty. I remember how my pals corralled and concealed darling Chit and how we got away with it and I remember only too well the roof top of her aunt's flat in Singapore as they hauled me away, and I remember her screams. How I remember that afternoon. Despite the beautiful day, Eugene was down again.

If they had gone out on HMS Devonshire as boys, they had returned as men. Four years is nothing in a normal lifetime. But it isn't duration that matters but compression through enforced incarceration. Being taken from that which is known and thrust into the unknown. Who could have predicted that a butcher-boy would be required (it wasn't voluntary) to brave tropical skies and drop rice to starving people. People who should never had been subjected to deprivation and all the horrors of war in the first place? How do you survive being given, and then torn from, the only person you ever really loved? Eugene poured himself a glass of Bells and took two tablets. He hoped that this time he would sleep for ever.

FIVE

It had been a long and tiring journey back home, although a piece of cake compared to what had got him to Portsmouth. First the train to London Paddington then the Underground to St Pancras before catching the Main Line to Nottingham's Victoria Station. Finally, an hour's wait for the all-station-stopping branch line steam train back home. But all the drudgery and boredom disappeared as if by magic once Eugene stepped out of the station and began his walk home. In his new de-mob suit and with his kitbag slung over his right shoulder, this young man of the world with his upright military gait exuded confidence. As he marched across the market square, all the locals who were standing around acknowledged him and, although he nodded a greeting, he did not stop to talk. Reaching the front door of the Big House he pushed the centrally located brass knob, but to his surprise the door did not open. *What is going on here? The front door is never locked until the last one is in at night, it must be stuck, try again.* Eugene knew there was no point in knocking on the big oak door because they would all be at the back, either in the kitchen, up the yard in the making up room or in the shop. Puzzled, Eugene walked up Harper Lane, pushed open the small side gate to the house and entered the old familiar butchery yard. The yard seemed smaller than he remembered but the van was there and so was his memory of those dark cloudy nights of the secret slaughter runs.

Brother Harold must have heard the side gate as it swung closed and footsteps in the yard because he was there in an instant standing at the door of the making-up room.

'Aye-up, yung uns back and don't he look a toff. Had a good holiday have ya while we bin slavin', makin' ends meet?'

Willy appeared behind Harold and, pushing his younger brother aside, ran from the butchery door to Eugene to clasp and shake his hand.

'Welcome home Eugene. It's great to have you back and don't you look smart in that suit? You've lost weight, not that there was much fat on those bones when you left. We're dying to hear all about it, I'll get this garb off and we'll go into the house, Mam will be over the moon, she never stops talking about you. Just can't tell you how pleased we are to have you back safe and sound – Harold come on, bloody pies can wait and at least try to pretend you're pleased to have our brother home again.'

★

Eugene was thinking of how things had changed in just four years. The house wasn't as big as he remembered it and the yard certainly wasn't as clean. The buildings were all dark and drab and the clothes they all wore even browner than the bricks, just everything was so tatty. What happened to the uplifting spirit of victory? Willy, always his big friendly-bear brother, was never a skinny-ribs but now he had got fat. Fat on the pork pies, fat on the crackling, who knows? Eugene hadn't seen a fat man in years, staying alive was just about all he could envisage. After all, Willy was only forty-three for God's sake, why was he letting himself go? Was there no woman? And Mam seemed shorter than he remembered her and Dad

49

was definitely more stooped. His eyes were bloodshot with big bags underneath and he had certainly aged, in fact there was a resigned sadness about his whole countenance. In this, his seventy-fourth year, having raised a huge family and still being the head of a successful business, surely he ought to be content with his lot, he ought to be so pleased with his life? What was wrong?

Mam, Dad, Willy and Eugene were seated at the big table in the sitting room having a cup (in Dad's case a mug) of tea and for each of them a slice of Mam's fruit cake on her best china plates. Harold was not there. "Bloody sulking in the making-up I should think". Eugene was now sharp and worldly; things had changed. He had returned home to the big comfortable house with its huge Edwardian upholstered settee and matching armchairs, his mam's treasured Victorian ornaments and the Monarch of the Glen picture still hanging proudly on the wall. Yet, it was not the same. The atmosphere was terrible. This was not a home for a returning war hero in which he could relate his adventures at leisure. It was not even a house, big or not big, it was a den. He had returned to a viper's den.

*

Willy was upstairs in his room, Mam was in the kitchen knitting so Dad took Eugene into the parlour; he wanted to talk.

'There had to be changes. Rob came out of the pit just after you were called up. At least going down the mine kept him from the war and with George having been lost in Singapore, that had been a good decision – Mam would not have survived the shock of losing a second son. God preserve us, it could have been four boys away had James not had a weak chest and Harold flat feet. Harold had to be controlled. He was lording it over all of us and running Mam rigid with his constant demands. Keeping our front door locked, that was his idea; as you well know, it was always left open. Seems more like a prison now. So I took the decision to put Rob in charge. Another thing was your letters; not that I blame you in any way, you were not to know but with you talking about your girl out there, we thought you might decide to stay or, if that was not allowed, at least go back once discharged. Eugene, my eyes are failing and I know there's another problem because of the blood and I am not, absolutely not, going into hospital. When the time comes, I will die upstairs in my own bed.

'If only for the sake of peace and quiet, I've cut down to just one delivery van that Rob and Harold take out every day except of course Sundays. They still do a fortnightly run but now double up to get both the old rounds in, using the one van. It's working well. Our regulars use two weeks' worth of coupons on the one visit each fortnight and we still have access to a bit of spare meat. Willy stays in the shop and the customers like him. Molly and Eve come in on Saturdays to make the pies and sausages for the shop and the van. When they heard you were coming back home, Rob and Harold came to see me. If I let you back in, they will leave me and set up on their own and, Eugene, your mam thinks like me, we cannot keep this place going on the shop alone. I don't know what you were thinking but I'm afraid you will need to branch out on your own. And Eugene there is something else, we are both very worried about your brother James.'

Eugene was stunned. He stayed silent and let his father continue.

'As you know, James left five years ago to run his own

butchery business from a rented shop in Pincton. He saw it as his big chance to break away from the family and stand on his own two feet. But we have to admit, there was more to it than that. After all those years of working with Willy and me, he got fed up with Harold's tantrums and trouble-making. What could I do? Harold had only just turned twenty-two. Did I turf him out on his ear, and in wartime? So, James took on the lease of the shop and left; our mam cried for the best part of a week – well, you remember that don't you? Anyway, things haven't gone well for James I'm afraid. The vinegar factory closed and with it went half of his registered customers. Then, he got involved with a married woman and her husband found out. There was some kind of dust-up in the street outside the shop and James came off worse. As you well know Eugene, your brother was clean and accurate with the cattle stunner but he was no man-fighter. He hasn't asked for anything, but I know he has money troubles and Willy says the doctor has increased the strength of his heart tablets. Sorry to have to tell you all this, but you might as well know what's been going on. You will stay though won't you Eugene? Your mam has kept your room just as you left it and, you will not be surprised to hear, has been up there cleaning it every single week. I often saw her sitting on your bed with that school photo in her hand. Probably break her heart if you didn't settle back with us. Look, if Harold gets under your skin, clock him one.'

Eugene's first reaction to what his dad had said was anger. It was only days since he had turned down the chance to stay in the RAF and for good reason; he wanted to work his way back into the family business and in time take it over. He was the one with his dad's brain and business sense and what's more they all knew it. He was the one who had been called up, he hadn't volunteered for it had he? About to lash out with verbal resentment, he hesitated, why? Because looking at his dad slumped into that big chair, he recognised the serious features of the man who had guided his huge family to a comfortable living within a community of working-class people and, with his wife at his side, had seen all thirteen of them to adulthood. It was hardly his fault that at seventy-four he was losing control. The fault lay with the two sons who had pressured him into submission. Eugene knew he could handle Harold if he had to but the fact that Rob had muscled in, was a surprise. A nasty surprise. Several minutes had passed. He stayed silent. He looked into his dad's bloodshot, sad and watery eyes. Eugene had seen enough in the Far East to comprehend real hopelessness in a face. He rose from his chair in that familiar parlour and hovering over his dad, placed his hand on the old man's shoulder, squeezed it slightly and left the room.

The following morning after eating a hearty breakfast of eggs and bacon prepared by his mam (and how he had missed her meals and her fussing over him), he stepped into Harper Lane for a long walk – as he had said to her, "To clear the air Mam". They had not talked about what he had learnt from Dad but he knew she understood how he felt. It was a bright autumn morning and although the air was warm, Eugene was cold, very cold. Despite wearing his old trench coat, he could not get warm; his body seemed to be chilled like the side of bacon hanging in the making- up room. The tropical heat was still in him and the way this homecoming now felt, he wanted it to stay. More than that, he wanted to go back. He wanted Chit. Where was she, what was she doing, what were they doing to her?

Eugene was walking blindly, going where his feet took him. Down the Common Road and up the other side, over the lane to the stile and now crossing the fields, field by field, stile by stile. He was walking into Pincton without realising how far he had gone. His mind was clearing and there amongst the row of terraced houses was James's shop with, above the green painted awning, the sign "Whitby's Wish Bone". Rather good actually, a typical bit of James humour. The *Closed* sign must be a mistake as today is a Monday, admittedly not the best day for the butchery business, but still there is always somebody wanting something. Eugene pushed at the door but it was locked. Odd. Walking down the ginnel to the left-hand side of the shop, Eugene lifted the latch to open a gate and entered a small yard. Walking to the rear of the shop premises he saw what was obviously the back door and whilst expecting it to be locked, pushed against it anyway. To his surprise, the door opened. He had entered the cutting-up room. Seeing all the knives of the trade laid out in strict order of size on the spotlessly clean wooden cutting block, he smiled to himself. The old man might be sinking now but in his day he had been a stickler for hygiene and knife discipline. "If the knives are in order, there will be no mistake – no accidents". The room was small and gloomy, so where was the light switch? He looked up to the steel joist with its *S* hooks and iron pulley. That was when he saw James hanging from the pulley rope.

★

The Reverend Williams was saying that taking this funeral service was one of the saddest duties he had ever been asked to perform. The Whitby family had been associated with St Peter & St Paul's not only for many years but also for many generations. Hedley and Iris had been married here, each of their many children had been christened here and Iris attended evensong every Sunday. That a young man in only his thirty-ninth year should choose to end his own life was beyond human understanding. Only God knew why. Whatever had driven James Whitby to hang himself, and whilst of little comfort to his family, we could rest assured that he was now safe and at peace in God's hands. He wanted all the mourners to understand that the act of suicide, which in the past had been much vilified, was now recognised as the act of a soul in torment. No blame could be placed at the door of James's family and friends. Rather pity. Suicide was the curse of this post-war age. Too many services at this very church gave testament to that fact.

Joseph, being the eldest brother, gave the eulogy. Reading from a prepared script, his voice was barely audible and the words were convulsed with emotion.

Although the sixth born, James had only been eight years younger than me. That fact said everything about the closeness of the children filling the Big House on the market square. They had all grown up together and all of them had worn hand-me-downs and all of them had played with each other's toys. As they grew older, each one helped in the business, even if it was only sweeping the yard at the end of the day. When three of his elder brothers and his elder sister left home, it fell to James to work with Willy and Dad to build the butchery business, for which the family is now famous.

I ask myself what kind of person was James as a child growing up, as a handsome young man, as a master butcher and as a human being? Well, he was the practical joker in the pack, that is what he was. The sausage skin filled with sawdust, the pork pie made of wood and painted brown that one of our best customers brought back to the shop in a fuming rage, only to leave again smiling with her free half-pound of black pudding –" this isn't made of horse's blood is it?" But it seems even clowns cry. When will we all stop crying after this?'

Frank rushed forward to help Joseph down from the pulpit. They leant on each other and walked slowly back to their seats. Mam was crying uncontrollably.

Not for years had all the girls been back to the Big House at the same time but the spread for the wake was down to them and Alice, being the eldest, had pulled them all together. She and Molly had come on the bus from Norton, Eve had walked from the far end of the village and Mary from the farm in the valley. Willy brought in the ham from the making up room while Mary provided the eggs and cheese. Mam had made a huge fruit cake. It had been planned as a Welcome Home party for Eugene but like his intended return to the business, events had dictated otherwise.

True to form, Harold entered the sitting room and swaying slightly, came straight to Eugene and edged him into the corner near the parlour door. His breath stank of ale.

'Now, Eugy lad, ain't this a turn-up? You're the bright one, gud at numbers, thirteen little niggers, two gon', eh? Dus that leave eleven? So who does tha think's next then?'

Perhaps Harold didn't realise that Eugene had not exactly been on holiday these past four years, despite his earlier snivelling insinuation. Maybe he didn't realise that all war veterans had had combat training. Whether he did or not, it was too late. Eugene had his right-hand index finger under Harold's nose and, pushing upwards banged Harold's head against the wall. There was a high-pitched squeal like that of a little pig separated from the mother sow and held aloft for inspection. As in the church a mere two hours ago, it was

Frank who rushed forward to save the day; well, to save Harold anyway.

When all the visiting family members had gone and the Big House was once again eerily quiet, Frank told Eugene to get his coat, they were leaving together. Parked outside was a shiny black, four-door Austin A40 Devon with several people gathered around it. The casual manner in which Frank raised his trilby hat slightly to acknowledge the admirers of his new car, had a strange affect upon Eugene. It was a feeling he had not experienced before, perhaps a mixture of being caught red-handed after doing something not quite right, and deep-seated admiration. He had no idea that Frank was in a position to own a car like this gleaming beauty. In fact he had no idea what Frank had done for a living since leaving school. He knew that his elder brother was still in his early forties and it dawned on Eugene that there had been no mention of him in any of the letters sent from back home. Neither his mam nor his sister Mary (the two he had relied on most to keep him in touch with life in and round Huthwaite) had once referred to Frank.

Having been removed from the scene, Eugene hadn't given a single thought to how the motor trade had developed in the past four years but, he now pondered to himself, over the ten years since Dad bought his ten horsepower Ford, cars had improved in leaps and bounds. Frank caught his younger brother eyeing up the dials on the dashboard of his latest acquisition and smiled to himself.

The car park at the rear of the Conservative Club in Great Sutton had several reserved spaces. Frank drove into the one marked *Treasurer*. Having selected a key from the bunch in his suit pocket, he opened a back door that led into a small passage. Locking that door behind them, he unlocked a second door immediately to their left, leading off from the passage and marked *Committee Only*. This room oozed quality and refinement. There was a centrally located, highly polished Boardroom-type table (not teak, thought Eugene – more likely mahogany) butted up to which were six extremely plush armchairs with maroon coloured padded seats. The walls were oak panelled and the thick carpet was deep blue. There was a portrait of King George VI hanging on the far wall set in a gilded frame. Eugene took several minutes to take in the whole scene. His mind flashed back to Group Captain Bennett's tent on the Padang in Singapore – the *field* of the great decision, – and what decisions, he wondered, are taken in this little room?

Frank tapped lightly on a serving hatch half way along the left-hand wall. The hatch opened in seconds.

'Charlie, my usual please and a pint of best bitter for my guest, make it snappy will you.'

As bidden with a slight wave of his brother's right hand, Eugene pulled out one of the chairs and sat at the table. Having signed a tab handed to him by Charlie, Frank collected the drinks and sat opposite his younger brother.

'Eugene, it's time for a serious talk, it's time you and I got our heads together. I know from Mam, that Dad has given his reason for your being shut out of the family business. Well, your return has made me think hard, and after that pantomime at dear James' wake, my mind is made up. I am going to tell you the real reason for this shabby treatment. What I am about to say will upset you but let me finish before you wade in because I have a plan. A plan which, if it comes off, will get you into this room on a proper footing. Dad has told you that Rob and Harold have threatened to leave and set up on their own if you rejoin the business, right? Well that is no doubt true in its way, but what he didn't disclose is that he can't afford to buy another van and get you on a new butchery round. The reason he can't is because the two of them are fleecing him. My suspicions were aroused when I invited a few of my pals back to the Big House for drinks one night after we'd had a meeting down here. On coming back from a pee, I heard those two dear brothers talking in the back room and I also heard the clinking of coins. Before we all left, I asked Mam how much had been handed over for banking from the day's van round. Looking straight at me with that knowing sort of expression she has always had, she replied, "Nothing Frank – nothing at all". That is what set me off.

'Harold has been a little sod from the day he was in his cot – by the way, I nearly had second thoughts about saving his miserable skin earlier today – now the best that can be said is that he is a bigger sod. That Rob was involved was a shock but I've now got to the bottom of that. Major Chesterton, the bank manager at National Provincial down the road, had a drop too much the other night and said to me, right out of the blue, "Your brother will soon have enough for his deposit then" – 'course he immediately clammed up, knowing he'd spoken out of turn but, and this is the beauty of this place Eugene as you will learn soon enough, Bill Sowerby is on the committee. Pretending to be interested for myself, I asked him if there were any butchery businesses for sale round here. Guess what? Rob has approached Sowerbys asking exactly the same question and guess what again, he has got first refusal on Jones' place down in Morston as the old man wants to retire later this year.

'Charlie, same again if you will be so kind, make mine a double this time. Eugene, this is how they work it. The money Willy takes in the shop is all properly accounted for. As you know he is a great bloke and closer to Dad than ever, given what has now happened to poor James. He would have no truck with any fiddling of his takings and anyway I doubt he's any inkling of what the other two are up to. I'm pretty sure that it's the profit from the shop that keeps the Big House going but it certainly does not pay for the meat sold on the van. I shouldn't know this but take it from me that I do. Dad's deposit account is shrinking at an alarming rate and I know why. It's because he buys all the meat and other stuff and dear Rob and honest Harold keep the van takings for themselves. Simple isn't it? That is why you can't be let back in. You'd rumble it on the first day. Something else Eugene, I have told Alice what is going on and asked her to wise up the other girls. I put it to her by saying there will be nothing left when the old man dies, so do not rely on any inheritance. Molly has taken it badly. If there is to be a big family kerfuffle, it will come from that quarter. We will see.

'Eugene, I've got a plan. It will take a bit of luck and cunning to pull it off but I think it will work. Let me rabbit on for a bit longer, keep it under your hat and sleep on it. I have an office upstairs, so come back at ten in the morning, Charlie will let you in and send you up to me. If you want to go ahead, we'll flesh things out. Say nothing to anyone. So, here we go. On the far side of the market square (you know, diagonally opposite the Big House), is old man Fletcher's fruit and veg shop and I know from Bill Sowerby that he is selling up. His takings have gone down – well it's hardly surprising, the shop is old-fashioned with shelves, baskets, crates and stuff that must all pre-date the Ark. But the thing is Eugene, the building is sound. I've had it looked at and there are living rooms upstairs. Yes, it needs money spending on it and all the fittings and fixtures want modernising but the potential is there.

'On the business side of things, your average working man is still finding life hard but I can tell you one thing, this *Digging*

For Victory Campaign is already losing its appeal. Folks are going out and buying their veg again, and fruit especially has started coming in from abroad after all those years of making do without oranges and pineapples and the like. And Eugene, this is the crafty bit, you can start easing into butchery. It can be gradual, without the customers even realising that your sale lines are changing. Start with Woolton Pie and carrot cake, you'll have the fillings already. Ok, it will take a few years yet for the meat rationing to end, but it will happen and when it does, kerpow, the new Whitby master butcher will slaughter the old Whitby butchers, you'll see. Of course, you'll need a good woman at your side – but I'll leave that to you!

'Right Eugene, enough for now, we'll go into the big room, my pals will be around and I'll introduce you to a few of them. Can you play snooker? Can't remember, but tell you what I can remember – you knowing all the words to Twelve Street Rag and doing the mouth and hand movement for the instrumentals. Even when you were no more than eight or nine, we always knew when you were upset about something – there you would stand and perform, inviting us to join in. When it was over, you were your usual self again. When you've settled in, I want you to come over and have dinner with Betty and me. You haven't met her yet have you? Great girl is Betty, first clapped eyes on her at Doncaster Races a couple of years ago. Come on then, we'll have one for the road in the big room.'

Having his eyes opened by Frank may have been the second but not the last event in what was turning out to be a momentous day for Eugene. The wake for James, the business proposition from Frank and then, as he entered the yard through the side gate, there was Dad leaning against the door frame of the making-up room.

'Eugene, I wanted to catch you before you go into the house. I see you've been with Frank and I know this has been a very upsetting day for all of us but listen to me, just be careful with our Frank, he keeps some very boozy company these days and I know full well he's in with the big-wigs in town. Me and your mam – well, we don't want to see you coming back home each night the worse for drink, like he used to before he got his own place. But that's not what I wanted to say. I spoke to Newhurst's today, I've known Jack for donkey's years. They have a vacancy for a relief butcher who can step in at a moment's notice at any of their shops. It pays £4-2-6d a week and its regular work. Obviously they'll have to train you up as you'll be a bit rusty, but he knows damn well your background with us. I said you'd go and see him tomorrow.'

Eugene thanked his dad and told him he needed to think about it for a while since he wasn't too sure he wanted to be in the butchery trade now that he couldn't work in the family firm. He might even go back into the RAF as a Regular, they had asked him. His dad looked even older than at the funeral. His eyes were surely more bloodshot, his stoop more pronounced and his walk back into the big house slower than ever before. Perhaps it was the beer plus the whisky chaser that Frank had slipped into his hand before he had left the club, but Eugene felt a great sadness as he watched the old man disappear from view. None of this was his dad's fault. All his dad was trying to do was to get the last of his huge brood safely launched in life. And yet? There was only one place Eugene was going tomorrow: to see Frank.

SIX

It was obvious that Charlie had been stock-taking at the time Eugene knocked on the front door of the Con Club because the bar was covered in bottles and as he pointed to the door leading to the stairs, he handed his visitor a bottle of Bells whisky and ticked a box on a large sheet of paper. 'Take this up with you, it's replenishing the treasurer's bar stock.'

After putting the bottle in a cabinet just to the right of his desk, Frank motioned to his brother to sit opposite him and, without any preliminaries, started talking.

'Can you remember when I taught you to play chess? We had some good evenings in the parlour with Dad sitting in his big arm chair just looking on while puffing away on that ancient briar pipe, God, now I think back, I can still smell that St Bruno. That huge chess board came from Sherwood Street. All I did was ask Alice, and your brother-in-law Albert made the board in his garden shed. He's got all the wood-working tools in that shed – he can make anything out of wood, he has such a marvellous skill. No-one would ever guess. Albert, who now works as part of the council's road maintenance gang, fought all through the war you know. Took a heavy toll on him mind you. Get him talking some time, ask him his opinion of the Greeks – I dare you. Where he got the ebony from for the black squares I'll never know, and the frame is solid mahogany, no veneer in Albert's work. And then that cheap set of chess men we found on the market. Tell you what, when we've pulled this one off, I'll buy you some proper pieces made of ivory to go with the black squares. We've got some good chess players down stairs, come in on a Wednesday night. You'll soon get back into it, after all, didn't take long for you to beat me, did it!

'Eugene, there is a reason for bringing up the chess thing because just like pouring over the chess board, business is all about making moves. The first move is critical and it is one of four that has been pre-planned with care. Not that move two is set in concrete. It depends on what the man sitting opposite you does, but if he makes his move the way you anticipated, then you carry on with the original plan. If he surprises you, re-think the next three moves. Chess is best played slowly, only fools rush their moves – business is just the same. Never get flustered, never lose concentration. Chess is work, business is work, hard work. Playtime comes later when the brain rests and listen Eugene, never, ever, confuse the two. A bit of well thought-out socialising with a glass in hand is not playtime. Dad and the rest of them up at the Big House never understood. That is one of the reasons why the family business will not survive once Dad has gone. The whole set-up has been stuck in a rut for years and now it's a thieving rut – fatal. Nip down and get Charlie to bring us a coffee will you, I need to take a leak.'

'Bill Sowerby, the estate agent, persuades old man Fletcher to sell by auction. That first move is the key move. All the other variations of the opening play depend on it. That happening Eugene, is down to me. Bill wants to be elected Vice Chairman this time and he knows I can swing it. Don't get me wrong. There is good logic to selling by auction. Certain business people around here would not want to show their hand in advance by making an open offer for a set sale price. Why? Because such people have done pretty well out of the war but it is too soon to let the world know. By the way, dear brother Harold has opened an account in Jersey. That little gem stems from another indiscretion by Major Chesterton.

'Move two is the selection of an independent auctioneer. The man with the gavel must not come from Sowerby's firm. There are enough crafty buggers in these parts to smell a rat. But Bill has a solicitor he often uses who knows a man, who in turn knows a man who works as an auctioneer and is based somewhere up North. 'Move three is that Sowerby gives Fletcher a guide price of £1,200 for the building, the business goodwill, the fixtures and fittings as seen, and the stock in trade. The literature advertising the auction will stress that, while the price is a good one in the current hard times, it is not overly generous because much work needs doing to the premises, particularly the living accommodation upstairs. It will also note that some dry rot is to be expected in a property of this age (with a disclaimer that none has actually come to light prior to sale – interested parties to make their own examinations). Also, prospective owners may feel that many of the internal features need updating.

'Move four of our plan is less certain at this point since we cannot be sure how experienced our opponent proves to be when actually at the chess board. We can, however, do a little groundwork before the day, look into the recent record of the man sitting opposite and perhaps even get a little war of nerves going. Did I mention that I have been in the Masons and a member of Great Sutton Round Table for a few years? Since the war ended, the local Chamber of Commerce has got more active too. One way or another, move four involves putting the word out. You know the kind of thing – my younger brother, now back from doing his bit for his country, would like to stay in the area and set up some sort of little business. There is money to be made by getting our factories to produce the things people have earned, and are entitled to, after all the suffering during the war. Small retail shops have had their day, the big boys are taking over.

'Finally, (check mate already!) I will take you along to National Provincial. The Major has to believe you have it in you Eugene, but there will be absolutely no problem with this final move, oh and another thing – and don't come over all proud with me because it's all in the grand scheme of things – get yourself down to Hepworth's tailors. I have an account there and they know you are calling in. Order a couple of suits and matching ties, three or four shirts and some smart business shoes. Take Eve with you and she might as well bring her friend Dorothy, as two girls are better than one at this sort of thing. You can pay me back out of your first £100 profit.'

★

Eugene shivered again and turned up the collar of his brand new wool-blend gabardine coat. He smiled to himself for having stretched Frank's account at Hepworths – mainly due to being egged on by Dorothy. He rounded the corner into the High Street and walked briskly towards the *Co-operative Store*. December had opened like a lion with the wind blowing straight from the Artic, or so the BBC weatherman said that morning. He had forgotten what an English winter was like. Yesterday, how had they all survived the searing heat of Burma? Today, how will he survive these Artic gales? He had to put his mind to something to steady the nerves. When the auctioneer mounted the rostrum at 11am, it could well herald the biggest single step of his life. Or, would he want that huge concert room to swallow him up. He was to sit three rows from the front and not, under any circumstances, acknowledge his brother.

That so few seats were taken came as a surprise. Eugene had expected the room to be full, perhaps the bitter wind had put people off. He felt his palms sweating, good thing Mam had put two handkerchiefs in his coat pocket. Frank had warned him that the atmosphere in an auction room was a mixture of excitement and dread. "Think of the poor bugger who enters the ring to face Joe Louis. You can plan to Kingdom Come but then suddenly it is you versus him".

The auctioneer read out the sale particulars and hoped all interested parties had studied the plans laid out at the back of the room. He emphasised that the vendor was selling *as seen and inspected* and accepted no responsibility for condition. It did have potential and they should make no mistake on that score but at the same time there was a need for a bit of tender love and care (some titters in the room). The shop and residential accommodation was to be sold. No reserve had been set. He then asked for bids. The silence must have lasted for a good ten seconds – Eugene could hardly bear the vacuum – then a voice from somewhere at the back of the room shouted out "£200 and cash for a quick deal". It was Frank. The auctioneer looked down his spectacles in what was clearly a practised form of disdain. "Gentlemen, I am here to sell not give away – come along now – we all know times are hard but we can do better than this, surely?" Another long silence. Then, a man on the front row (Eugene thought he recognised him from the Conservative Club on the night he was introduced to Frank's pals) raised his trilby and shouted "£250, I bid £250". Another silence and Eugene's heart was pounding. It had gone exactly as Frank had predicted. He slowly, hesitantly, raised his right hand. The auctioneer pointed to him. Eugene, in as loud a voice as he could muster said, "£600". "That's better, a young man with some sense, now let's get moving gentlemen, what is this place worth?" But nothing happened. Neither the first or second bidder came back. Eugene was in a trance. Had the bit about going for the first time and then the second time actually happened? All he knew was that the hammer came down with a *bang* and he was suddenly the centre of attention as men gathered around him and shook his hand. But not brother Frank, he had gone.

★

Old Eugene hated himself for taking an afternoon nap. It brought to mind his visits to talk to his eldest brother Joseph in the *Peace Haven Rest Home,* back in Great Sutton. The brand new shiny edifice of brick and steel which, he recalled with no little irony, had been constructed on the site once occupied by the *Great Sutton Co-op.* Nothing symbolised more the change from thrusting energetic young man to well-past-it old codger than by siting the dodderers' palace of used-up bodies and minds on the spot just there. There ,where everyone once went to spend their coupons on food and clothes, hurried upstairs to be entertained (and, occasionally, to buy properties) and then, completing the husbandry cycle, to cash and spend their divi. To talk to Joseph was a misnomer because the eldest brother of the Whitby clan couldn't talk and for an ex-school teacher that was about as worthless as a human could get. The youngest brother of the great tribe would pass all the latest news and gossip to the eldest, while accepting completely that the response would be nil. Absolutely zilch. But Eugene would go every week anyway. Perhaps it helped them both.

The habits of the lonely post-Dorothy years were set firm. He always cooked a hot mid-day dinner and after washing his pots and pans in the sink, he tottered slowly to the two-seater settee to settle in his half sitting, half lying position. Before long he was in another kitchen. It was hot, humid and the large ceiling fan might as well have not been rotating for all the good it was doing. Whirling hot air is still hot air. He had just begun cutting up the papayas when someone started banging on the bamboo door. Odd. The lads often came round the back but only to talk to Monty and sneak him their leftover scraps but never to enter, in fact it was banned. Yet the banging carried on and the old man woke up with a start. Idiot, someone was at the door. Having made his usual slow progress, he opened his front door to find a young lady standing a pace or so back and half-turning as if to leave. Wearing a smart summer dress, her shoulder-length hair tied back with a dark blue ribbon and not wearing spectacles, Eugene did not at first recognise her. It was library Pearl.

'Mr Whitby, I am so sorry to disturb you but I was just passing and thought you might like this extra literature I came across. It's advertising really but rather informative for those wanting to travel from Bangkok to Singapore. It's from a firm that organises conducted tours of Myanmar – sorry Burma. Anyway I'll leave it with you because there are some really good descriptions of Rangoon and Mandalay and also of the far North, towards the border with China.'

Eugene felt his back straighten and his left side moved slowly upright. It was as if some invisible puppet strings had pulled him back into shape; almost as if he was being directed to face his visitor as a man, instead of the creaking cretin he believed himself to be. This was a tall, slim, elegant and smiling lady. A woman in her prime and confident in her place. The library assistant sitting behind her desk and hiding beneath the thick-rimmed spectacles had metamorphosed into a beauty. Eugene heard himself saying,

'Pearl, please don't go, stay and have a cup of tea, we can sit outside on the decking and talk – please?'

Pearl was pointing out the coincidence. After exploring all that the two cities of Myanmar could offer, the posh tour company promised to prove its credentials as the only real Far East specialist by taking its pampered guests into the North to meet the leaders of the Kokang region, the ethnic Han people of Shan State. But, Pearl thought, the well-heeled tourists would probably have second thoughts if they caught up with reports that such ethnic groups are currently in armed rebellion against the National Government and that thousands of the native population are fleeing to safety over the border into China. The old man was enthralled. When was the last time anyone had talked to him about a part of the world he once knew and about a subject he was truly interested in?

'Pearl, can you drop the Mr Whitby and call me Eugene'.

Pearl was off again. 'Mr Whitby,' (in a mildly mocking tone) 'do you know what the word Eugene means?'

'No, afraid not'

'Shame on you then. It has a Greek origin and means well born. Of course it is the gene half of the name that means born. Same derivation as genealogy and isn't that another amazing coincidence? At the library we have just analysed our latest customer survey and it revealed that the majority of our visitors are researching their family tree. Of course they go on to visit the Town Hall and search the local Parish Records but our library is very often the first port of call. Have you done any research into your family Eugene?'

'Again I would have to answer no, afraid not and it would

no doubt be an enormous task to take on, especially given the size of our family, never mind delving deeper.'

It was a beautifully warm sunny afternoon and the light breeze blowing off the sea added just that touch of sharpness to create what to Eugene was the perfect summer day. Exaggerated by its rarity, only here and now and in England could a climate be so perfect. That such an idyll would have passed unnoticed by a man dozing on a settee was due to random chance. No plan, however well conceived, could have created the circumstances in which Eugene and Pearl sat side by side talking like old friends over afternoon tea. But, it had happened. This was real time. The old man, however fleetingly, was in his heaven.

With an involuntary and almost subconscious movement, Pearl eased her chair closer to Eugene and leaning forward as if realising suddenly that he might be slightly deaf, said;

'Why don't we make a start? If you can find a writing pad and a pen of some sort and put your memory box into gear, I'll jot it all down, go away and type it up neatly. It would be the perfect reason for me to come back in a week or so to have a go at filling in the family bloodline. After that, who knows? I might be able to go back another generation or two and find out where an old man, who's always pestering me at the library, really came from.' Pearl crossed her long shapely legs and reaching for Eugene's left hand, looked him straight in the eye with a smile to turn rock into mush. He was hooked; she knew it, he knew it. What Eugene didn't know, as he rummaged through his tin box of treasures, was that it wasn't only a case of her giving him a new lease of life.

'You will find your fingers aching after writing all this lot down. It's hard to believe that my mam bore thirteen children, actually fourteen – one died within two days of birth – and spanning twenty-three years. What a woman (what a man some might say) and it wasn't as if they were Catholics either. As Julie Andrews sang in The Sound of Music – let's start at the very beginning, it's a very good place to start!'

Pearl's eyes widened. All she could think of saying was, 'Indeed.'

'They named the first born Joseph, and he was born in 1904 a month after Mam had her twentieth birthday. Dad had wanted that name and it would not have been a surprise to Mam, because one of my very first memories was sitting on Dad's knee while he told me the story of Joseph and his Coat of Many Colours. You know, Pearl, that famous tale from the Hebrew Bible. I have often wondered since if there was something deeply prophetic about my dad's love of the story. After all, when Jacob came back to the land of Canaan, he already had eleven sons and his wife Rachel was about to present him with a twelfth. Jacob cared deeply for the new baby whom they called Benjamin but Joseph who was then seventeen years old was his favourite. That Jacob gave Joseph a coat of many colours made his ten elder brothers jealous and thus a family saga involving twelve siblings was spawned. Did Dad in some way model himself on Jacob? Could Mam have possibly guessed what she was in for? Our Joseph was not to be the favoured son and nor was he to be thrown down a pit, but still, some sort of die was cast.

Pearl, sorry to have wittered on. I will whip through the rest of our lot quickly and I think I have this right. Jack 1905, Willy 1906, Frank 1908, Alice 1910, James 1912, George 1914, Rob 1916, Mary 1918, Molly 1920, Harold 1922, Eve 1925 and finally, if you can believe it, me in 1927.'

'That was some family Eugene. You are not pulling my leg are you?'

It was the old man's turn to move forward and he squeezed her hand,

'Wish I was Pearl.'

'And Eugene, I expect you are the only one left.'

'Ok, another surprise for you then, actually I'm not, but if I tell you everything now you might not come back to see me again and you wouldn't want to break an old man's heart would you?'

★

Eugene hadn't given much thought to Dorothy since the stilted evening at the Drill Hall the previous March. Not that sister Eve hadn't mentioned her once or twice, but asking her for a date would just be a waste of time. Eve was going steady with Stan now and the last thing they would want was another couple tagging along. In any case, after Chit, there couldn't be another girl. How he longed to have her back, teach her more English words, show her things. All he wanted was his beautiful, happy, loving Burmese girl. No-one else would measure up, no-one ever could.

Eugene had to admit it. He had been thrown a bit. When he saw Dorothy waiting with Eve at the main entrance to Hepworths in late October, he felt an instant pang. It just happened, he didn't want to be affected by her, he had to concentrate on Frank's big plan. Still, there was a stirring, no point in denying it and her giggles at the tailor's antics had lodged in his mind. The phrases; "Which side do you hang sir?" and "We just have to get the inside leg measurement exactly right sir," were not the sort of thing a respectable young lady was supposed to hear. Or so the giggle seemed to denote. Plus, along with Eve, she had been helpful. Plain, pinstriped or chequered? How was he supposed to know? Tropical white and, after rounding Gibraltar, Air Force blue and then the Burtons dark blue de-mob suit was all he knew. Same with the shirts and the shoes, without the girls he would have been lost and at the mercy of the sales assistants. As for the gabardine topcoat, that was solely down to Dorothy. She found it on the rails, forced him to try it on and somehow got it charged to Frank's account. He did think to himself at the time that, despite her giggles, admiring glances and comments as he was being measured for the suits and trying on the shirts, there was some pushiness about this Dorothy

Inexplicably, it was as he walked away from the *Co-op* that Eugene thought about Dorothy again. He needed to tell her that he was now the proud owner of a business and wouldn't it be great if she was with him for the appointment with Major Chesterton. She could hold his hand, so to speak. She could push the Major a little on the size of the loan he had promised. Yes, a good idea on this fantastic day.

The envelope was on the front doormat when he came downstairs. He stared at his name for a few seconds. It was Eve's writing. It was ridiculous but his heart rate had quickened. He had a good idea what the envelope might contain but not the answer. Resisting the temptation to discover his fate immediately, he walked calmly through the living room and into the kitchen. The smell of eggs and bacon sizzling in the frying pan was, as usual, one of the very best aspects of getting back home. "Look Mam, I have a note from our Eve, wonder what she wants". Mam never wasted words, "Open it and find out". Eugene was on edge but a quiet voice in his head was telling him to take his time. He selected one of the sharp dinner knives from the sideboard drawer and nonchalantly sliced open the flap –

She says yes but only if you take her to see King Solomon's Mines at the Tivoli on Saturday night, she says it has a good write up in the Free Press and it stars Deborah Kerr, Stewart Granger and Richard Carlson. She will meet you outside the main door at seven-thirty.
Eve.
P.S. just be sensible Eugene, she is a nice girl and I don't want her upset.

Mam said nothing but handed Eugene his plate. Her questioning look got a response, "Oh, apparently she wants to know if I fancy taking her friend to the pictures on Saturday night". "Really – what a surprise".

He had never actually seen Dorothy on her own before and somehow could only visualise her in Eve's shadow. When they were both at Hepworths it had been cluttered with rails and mirrors, sales assistants were buzzing about and the whole floor had been a hive of activity. But here she was, standing alone. He was dead on time but she was already waiting at the main door and seemed taller than he remembered. Had she really got this dressed up merely to meet him, simply for an outing to the pictures? No wonder she had been keen for him to buy the gabardine coat because her long coat was equal to it. It was a violet/purple-ish colour with a black thick-edged collar. She was holding a brown handbag with matching gloves and no longer standing still. She was walking forward to meet him.

Before leaving the Big House, Eugene had assumed he would be hesitant when they met at the Tivoli (assuming she didn't stand him up of course) and wondered quite how to play things. Would they just say hello to each other before he went to the kiosk to buy the tickets, or what? And so he couldn't understand why, just like some of the lads who rushed down the gangplank at Portsmouth to meet their sweethearts, he and Dorothy fell into each other's arms. Even beneath that thick coat, he could feel her heart pounding as she just clung to him while people jostled to get past them and out of the bitter cold wind. But Eugene, for the first time in months, did not feel the cold, but instead her warm body next to his. Her perfume and the smell of her hair made him breathless and giddy. As they pulled apart he saw her flushed face, he saw the tears in her eyes and he bent slightly to kiss her. For the second time in just over a year, Eugene knew he had been a bloody fool. All that wasted time since last March. All that wasted time.

★

Eugene had never been inside a bank before. Dad had always paid in the cheques and cash at eleven o'clock on the dot every Monday morning, his ritual from years past (with a wry smile to himself, Eugene was thinking that must now be another job less for the old man). With its grey/blue Derbyshire sandstone exterior and imposing, some might say pompous, twin Palladium columns guarding the huge oak door, the National Provincial Bank was the epitome of a rock-solid institution. More than that, it was a temple. Potential new customers, such as the likes of Eugene, were meant to be impressed, even overawed. Self-confidence on the High Street could easily evaporate on entering its portals. But that was without reckoning on the presence of Dorothy.

Assumptions can be misleading. Unlike Eve, and years earlier sister Mary, Dorothy did not work on one of the Heliot straight-bar hosiery machines at the Co-operative Wholesale Society factory off Great Sutton Road. She was in the office upstairs and in charge of the accounts payable section. Her dad was a solicitor and they lived in one of the big houses bordering *The Lawn* at the far end of Great Sutton and she had been put through Queen Mary's Grammar School For Girls. Not that the factory girl/office girl distinction had bothered Eve and Dorothy, they had been friends for years after chatting during the midday break. Had he taken the trouble to make a few enquiries, Eugene would have worked out how Dorothy had been able to track his war career. Her dad played snooker at the Conservative Club and often paired up with Frank. Her best friend was one of his sisters. But Eugene had been both wallowing in self-pity and acting as Frank's puppy dog. He could see that now. He had a girl and she was somebody and together they would take this town apart. He straightened his back and holding Dorothy's hand, walked with military precision into Major Chesterton's office.

Dorothy was explaining that as a friend and with her dad's help she had prepared this paper which they all hoped would convince the bank to support Eugene's application for a business loan. The original idea was to seek a loan of £1,300 to pay for the property and contents at the pre-sale valuation plus £100 extra to cover legal fees and a few commissions. Even though he had been lucky to buy Fletcher's business for £600, the application remained at £1,300 because following a detailed inspection, the property would benefit from two major alterations both of which would lead to an increase in sales. First, the cellar should be converted into a cold-storage room so that the pies and cakes could be kept for several days without spoiling and in due course meat could be hung. Secondly, the accommodation upstairs needed modernising so that Eugene could actually move in and literally live above the shop. While building up the trade, being on hand would be a huge advantage.

Dorothy was about to describe the ideas they had for an entirely new shop window display and signage when Major Chesterton rose from his chair and walked around his desk to where the two of them were seated. Noting the Major's ram-rod back and bristling moustache, Eugene thought to himself, *ah – here comes the military training, now we are for it.* The Major perched on the arm of Dorothy's chair and placing his left hand lightly on her shoulder he glanced across at Eugene and said, "Young man, I have absolutely no doubt that with this young lady at your side, you will build a very successful business at Fletchers – though do us all a favour and change the name – and there is no need to go through your plans in any more detail. I was aware how much the place made at auction and of course it needs knocking into shape. The numbers Dorothy has read out are most impressive and I should say it's more than I normally get from would-be business people. However, (hearing that word Eugene thought – *here we go, there is a big snag after all)* you have probably underestimated your initial in goings, especially on the working capital side of things and so I intend to draw up papers for an initial business loan of £2,000.

"As a new customer, the interest rate will be 1.5% above base and of course once you get going there will be a need for an overdraft facility, but we can leave that until later. At the end of each quarter, the bank will want to see some figures and before you leave I will give you a simple form to send in with costs and sales and spending on equipment, that sort of thing. Dorothy, you can see to that side of things can't you dear? We will send you a monthly itemised bank statement. I want to extend to you a very warm welcome from National Provincial Bank and trust we will share a happy and fruitful relationship in the forthcoming years. Oh, and Eugene one last thing before I forget, your brother Frank has signed a personal guarantee secured on a few of his properties. Suggest you buy him a drink in the club tonight".

★

The *Tivoli* was known locally as *The Fleapit*. Posh it was not. Both of the other two cinemas in Great Sutton *The Portland* and *The Kings* were better regarded. Each had an upstairs balcony stemming from the days of the variety theatre. The seats were located on each side of a central aisle, down which, walking backwards, the usherettes sold ice cream and soft drinks from a cumbersome tray hanging by straps from their necks. In addition, and as the picture-going treat of the week, the front-of-house ticket office sold *Holland Toffee* bars, tubes of *Refreshers* and for those who were really flush, a box of *Paynes Poppets Chocolate Covered Raisins* was hard to resist. None of this splendour applied to the *Tivoli*. The poor relation picture house had just one floor, no central aisle and no goodies on sale. But, on this bleak winter night, it was showing *King Solomon's Mines* and on the third row from the back it boasted amongst its patrons Dorothy and Eugene.

In his minds-eye, Eugene could see Eve's note: *be sensible,* but that was not proving to be an easy instruction to follow. One thing the *Tivoli* did have was warmth and intimacy and once the beautiful top coat with its thick black-edged collar had been removed, Eugene was feeling decidedly weak at the knees. This he knew was mainly, though not entirely, due to knees. Dorothy's knees. Hitching up her pencil skirt in order to sit on the not-too-comfortable seat, she exposed the most delicately formed ones that a certain young man had ever seen. A certain young man who was finding it hard not to get aroused and not solely due to a lady's knees. Dorothy was wearing a tight-fitting white blouse that made no pretence of hiding her well-formed breasts. After the film's credits had stopped rolling, Eugene slowly and hesitantly reached for Dorothy's hand and found it waiting. She squeezed his hand gently and looked straight at him and even the darkness of this fleapit could not hide that gaze. Eugene remembered nothing of the film; nothing at all.

After the *Tivoli* had turned out, one young couple along with a few others, walked into *The Lawn* either on their way home or merely to be together in the darkness. Arm-in-arm this young couple came to a gentle standstill. He leant against the smooth trunk of a huge beech tree and she moved closer to him so that they almost melted into one. Eugene kissed Dorothy gently at first and then fiercely and hungrily. Driven by raging desire, his hand moved inside her coat, searching, searching, but then stopped. Why had he stopped? Because this beautiful girl who had sought him out after so long and whom he had ignored with blinding stupidity, was sobbing softly. She hadn't tried to stop him, she couldn't. It was more than Eugene could bear to hear her sobs. Beneath that tree and on that cold bleak winter night he removed his hand and instead enveloped her in his arms. It was the right thing to do: it was enough. As he walked her home she gradually calmed down and started to talk.

'Darling Eugene, I do so want to be your girl. I know you had a girlfriend overseas so you are experienced but I am not. Believe me, I am not. I have had two boyfriends but in each case it finished because I would not give them what they wanted. Eugene, I am still a virgin. I want you so badly, I want to be with you for ever but I want to save myself for my wedding night. I am so afraid of losing you but please try to understand. Do not rush me.'

Eugene could sense the presence of men moving between the trees, it made the hairs on his neck stand on end. Not that, even on such a cold night, it had been his only uplifting experience.

SEVEN

Mr & Mrs H H Whitby are pleased to announce that their daughters Molly and Eve will marry Jack Brown and Stan Curtis at a joint service to be held at 3pm at St Peter & St Paul's Church, Common Road, Huthwaite on Saturday 14th April 1951. An evening reception will be held for invited guests in the Concert Room of the Great Sutton Cooperative Store. The couples are wished every happiness for the future.

The announcement in the Free Press was no more than would be expected from the family living in the Big House that dominated the market square and whose butchery business had played such a prominent role in the community over the years. And, as Harold had said to Mam, "Won't do business any 'arm either." Molly had been courting her Jack for over four years and some said he would never pop the question, but the whirlwind romance of Eve and Stan seemed to have "stuck a hot poker up 'is arse" – another Harold-ism to Mam.

The old man was very pleased with how things had turned out for his two younger daughters. They were good girls and had stayed loyal to the family business for all these years while living at home and in Molly's case even after she had moved to lodge with Alice. Each Saturday the two worked together making pies and sausages for the shop and the van and they never asked to be paid. At the reception he would present each daughter with a mantel clock just as he had for Alice and Mary on their wedding day. The walnut case clock housing a German mechanism with its Westminster quarter-hour chime, was a quality gift and one that he, as head of the family, would be remembered for.

Hedley Whitby approved of both Jack and Stan but for different reasons. Jack was a quietly spoken reserved man. He was clever and at technical college had qualified as an electrical engineer. The firm he worked for manufactured a range of sophisticated electronics, but what made Jack a blue-eyed boy in the eyes of the old man was his demonstration of a working television set, the latest wonder of the modern post-war age. He had assembled it himself and the previous week, had brought it up to the Big House with a temporary aerial and they had all watched Alan Wheatley in Sherlock Holmes. It was mesmerising: Jack was a genius and dearest Molly would soon be his wife.

Stan was different to Jack. He was outward going, a fancy dresser, a joker and Eve had fallen head over heels in love with him. They had only been going out for about nine months but the whole family felt a marriage had better take place sooner rather than later. Stan and Eve were a demonstratively tactile couple. Stan worked on the coalface and was proud of it. He made good money and spent it. Eve had the time of her life and each Sunday was whisked away in Stan's Morris Eight. Stan and Eve, a love match if ever there was one.

It was the impetuous Stan who sprang the surprise. The two couples would honeymoon together (but, he cheekily informed Jack, staying in separate rooms so he could take full advantage of Eve). Having booked the Imperial Hotel in Torquay, he was paying and they would all go down in his car; no arguments. But Jack had his pride and was explaining to

Molly as he walked her home that although he was not over the moon about the double wedding, he could see the sense in it as regards all the family coming together on just the one occasion rather than two. And, of course, it would save the old man a lot of money on catering and hiring the Co-op concert room. But, if Stan was really serious about paying for the hotel, then he must insist on the terms being bed and breakfast only and he, Jack, would pay for the evening meals for all of them. Stan might be on big money but Whiteleys Electricals paid him a fair salary and he had savings put by. And so the honeymoon arrangements were settled.

The idea came from a poster in the waiting room of Great Sutton Junction Station where they had gone for a snog after the pictures. It was the first time that Eve had let his hand reach above her stocking top and his fingers explore inside her panties. First one finger and then two entered her while at the same time his left hand was inside her bra, gently caressing her erect nipple. Eve gasped at the sensation caused by his touch and, moments later and shaking uncontrollably, was completely overwhelmed by her first orgasm. Holding her tightly, Stan knew he had his girl. It was on leaving the waiting room that he saw the poster, *Visit Torquay, Queen of the English Riviera*. It was a sign. In Torquay he would give her the time of her life.

April in the East Midlands can be cold, dark and bleak. The hedges and trees are not yet green but the crocuses and daffodils of spring have finished. Not so, April 1951. It was as if the two couples so full of love and energy had placed their special order for blue skies and starlit nights. April 1951 was very special. The two factory girls with their pork-pie and sausage-making Saturdays had known nothing like it. The Imperial Hotel was a palace, beholden with grandeur and guarded by the tall footman resplendent in his red-braided uniform. The reception staff were polite and helpful and the dining room with its red curtain drapes and mahogany panelled walls was straight from a Hollywood set, at any rate that's what Eve thought.

For the newlyweds, days passed as a floating interlude. Sublime. Perched high on the cliff top, the hotel's terrace offered daytime views over the harbour to the yachts beyond, matched only at night by the lights sweeping around the bay until they reached the Grand Railway Station at the far end. Hand in hand the two couples walked the promenade under the palm trees and through the Royal Terrace Garden. They travelled on the Cliff Railway and visited the Model Village and on the Wednesday, Stan drove them to Paignton and then Brixham where they ate fish and chips wrapped in newspaper while sitting on the harbour wall. The next day they walked to Berry Head which Jack had read about and now that they were so close, he wanted to visit the Napoleonic Northern Fort, the Berry Head lighthouse and the old Artillery Store. Afterwards, they called in at the Berry Head Hotel and Molly treated them all to afternoon cream tea. They followed the coastal path past Shoalstone Beach, strolled along the new promenade and then caught the bus back to Torquay. The whole adventure brought out the philosopher in Jack. He was saying as they climbed the steps to greet the friendly doorman that having just finished reading *The Murder of Roger Ackroyd,* Agatha Christie may have penned her mysteries here, but today had been the real thing. This good life would never end.

★

Dorothy and Eugene worked on the shop premises during what was left of the winter, through the spring and now into the summer of 1951. A summer that turned out to be one of the best on record with clear skies and warm days throughout June, July and August. A newcomer to Huthwaite in September wouldn't have known that Fletcher's store had ever existed. The new sign displayed *D & E's Superstore* and below it *Opening Soon*. The way Frank had worked it out made the refurbishment project fairly easy to follow and supervise. His own architect had drawn up the detailed plans which had been nodded through the council planning committee since there was to be no change of use. As the need arose, his skilled men came onto site; brickie, joiner, plasterer, sparky and the hours each man worked were listed on the project work sheet by Dorothy and priced up weekly. Eugene fetched the weekly wages in cash directly from the bank and drawn against the business loan account. Frank charged a 5% supply fee based on the total wage bill and, as agreed with him, the fee was entered in the name of a second joiner whom it proved unnecessary to actually bring to the shop.

The split of the supervisory work was such that while Eugene concentrated on the ground-floor shop premises and the basement, Dorothy took charge of the upstairs accommodation and the installation of a modern flush toilet. Being able to have an indoor lavatory was a particularly good idea because it meant the outside earth closet could be filled in and used as an extra storage room. With help from her mother, Dorothy was able to make sure that the living quarters contained most things that the modern couple might desire when starting married life.

Frank was happy to stay away as work on the business premises progressed being, as he put it, the ideas man and in that regard had a few useful thoughts. When the stage was reached that fittings and fixtures needed purchasing, it would be best, he said, to do this through one of his companies. That way his reputation and buying power would secure the best prices and the total sum could be charged to the business loan account rather than fiddling about with individual items. He would add 5% to the total to cover the admin. Mr. 5% he called himself. His second idea was that Eugene should also work directly for his property company whilst the project was ongoing so that he had some money coming in while at the same time gaining experience in dealing with suppliers and customers. On the subject of customers, he would nominate his brother for the Con. Club to help spread the word and in time get Eugene introduced to a few of the trade organisations.

Saturday 15th September 1951 dawned like any other day, except it wasn't just any other day, it was the day. *Grand Opening Day.* Dorothy and Eugene had worked into the small hours to make sure that the window display was just right and that the pies in the cold-storage room would be in perfect condition for bringing up to the shelves by 8.30 am. The till was brand new and sited, on the advice of the salesman, in full view of customers.

'By actually seeing the keys depressed and their money being put in the cash drawer as it flies open, they realise this is the modern place to shop and they will not be diddled – psychology young man, very important in the retail trade. Another thing, you need a good opening-day gimmick. Tell you what one of my customers did up in Yorkshire and it worked like a treat. Put in your opening day adverts and on the house-to-house flyers, that you are giving away one free banana for each child accompanied by an adult, while stocks last. That will bring 'em in, you just see. They all remember, "Oh yes, we have no bananas", from the war years. Mark my words.'

Frank arranged for the Mayor to cut the blue ribbon at 9 am and give a short speech welcoming our young war hero back to Huthwaite, one of the areas now being refreshed by new businesses to help us all get back on our feet. He was saying that the local Chamber of Commerce and the Town Council stood four-square behind the upcoming breed of entrepreneurs of which Mr Eugene Whitby was surely a shining example. The queue moved slowly forward as local people entered *D & E's Superstore,* saw, approved and bought fresh fruit, vegetables and pies and, on leaving, the children clung onto their free banana as if life itself depended upon it. There was one young lady inside the store smiling at her customers, taking their order, working the till and stopping occasionally to touch the hand of a young man moving back and forth replenishing the stock. Across the road stood an old lady dressed (unusually for a Saturday) in her best Sunday clothes. She was small in stature, was leaning on a Melaka bamboo cane and she had tears running down her cheeks. It was Eugene's mam.

★

Eugene was really surprised. Although the shop had only been open for a week-and-a-half, the routine had already been established. He opens the front door at 8 o'clock on the dot just as his Dot is turning the corner from the market square, having got off the bus from Great Sutton. But not this morning. Perhaps the bus is late for some reason but having retraced the steps she takes, he can see that the No 101 has arrived as usual. Thinking to himself that the best thing would be to telephone her, he returned to the shop to find a customer waiting. Mrs Blaby hadn't come to buy, well not first off anyway. She had some news.

88

'Mr Whitby have you heard the news? Oh dear me, awful news it is.'

'What news?'

'There has been a terrible accident at Credwell pit – men are trapped – lots of men on the night shift, your trade will be down today I should think, I'll take a couple of the Woolton Pies for breakfast and a slice of your carrot cake for me dinner.'

It was a bit like a play put on at the Civic, the timing of events was strictly sequential with no awkward gaps such as actually happens in real life. The instant Mrs Blaby left, the 'phone rang. It was Dot's mother.

'Eugene dear, I'm afraid our Dorothy won't be in today. We have had an awful night. Your Eve got us all up at half-past three this morning, banging on the door. She had run all the way from her flat and was in such a terrible state. All we could get out of her at first was, "Can't get to Huthwaite for Eugene to take me. Don't know what to do. Just don't know what to do. Can Dorothy's dad get me to the pit? Please, please!"

All three of us got dressed and after she had calmed down a bit, she was able to tell us that a deputy had banged on her door to say there had been an accident at the pit and that her husband Stan was one of the men trapped underground.

'Eugene, listen to me. You will have to close the shop and get over here. We can't do anything with Dorothy. She needs you. When we got to Credwell, there were hundreds of people at the gates and they would only let the closest relatives through into the main yard. Eve went from us and we haven't seen her since. Oh God Eugene, they are all saying there is a fire underground and the men are trapped. They can't even let the rescue men get near the pit head. What are we going to do?'

★

After Pearl had left, the old man went into his bedroom to put his tin box of treasures away and there it was, the cutting from the Free Press. The report on the enquiry into the Credwell mining disaster of 1951. In his mind's eye, he could see Stan's face as clearly as when they all met up at Alice and Albert's house down Sherwood Street. Jack would walk up from the little thatched cottage he and Molly had bought in Hall Lane and the four of them (Eugene, Stan, Jack and Albert) would play small-table billiards in the parlour. Stan always acted the cheeky chappie with his, "have you heard this one?" latest joke from his miner mates and he could down more bottles of IPA than the rest of them combined. He was the best looker too and with his neatly parted red hair and smart suits, a young man that Eve said she "had to keep an eye on – keep him out of the clutches of his admirers".

The enquiry described a number of factors involved in the high death rate. These included telephones being sited too far from the pit face, repair work being undertaken at the time on the paddy (the underground train used to convey the men to and from the lift shaft), inadequate air shafts and low water pressure in the fire hoses.

An already damaged conveyor belt had got caught in a machine causing the motor to overheat and catch fire. The fire trapped 80 men. As a direct result of the flames and smoke, they all perished. It was the serious errors uncovered by the enquiry that led to the fire not being extinguished quickly. In order to do so, the entire colliery had to be sealed to starve it of oxygen. It took the rescuers over two weeks to find the bodies of 57 men and the remaining 23 remained underground for the best part of a year.

At the end of the bland account of the causes of the disaster, and having noted the death statistics, there was one human story. A miner, who had broken his back several months before, went down the stricken pit still wearing a back brace in a vain attempt to rescue his mates. One such mate was Stan Curtis, the dashing young man who, in his brief 27 years and much like those poor sods who found themselves at the mercy of the Japs on the death railway, had done everything his country could ask during a time not of his calling. The early hours of September 26th 1951 might just as well have killed Eve too. A double wedding, a paradise honeymoon at the Imperial Hotel in Torquay and five months with her beloved Stan, was Eve's entire life. She never recovered.

With shaking hands and peering through watery eyes, the old man placed the press cutting back in his tin box of treasures. Bringing back this horror and sadness, and all because a complete stranger was curious about his family. Was it really worth it?

*

As Frank had predicted it was Molly who decided that something had to be done before all the old man's money was drained by Rob and Harold. It was the tragic death of Stan that finally tipped her over the edge. She would fight for her sister Eve. The Mayor's appeal fund had been a sincere and wonderful gesture and local businesses and individuals had responded with generosity, but a gesture was all it was. Eve's one eightieth share of the final tally would keep her going for maybe two years at the most and she deserved better. She and Eve had worked all these years making-up for the butchery each Saturday and for what? For two of the lads to cream off all the profits?

The letter Molly wrote made the following case:- Joseph

was now a well-respected school teacher. He was well out of it. Jack: the least said about him the better. Willy would be ok whatever action they took because the old man had made it clear years ago that the Big House and yard would be left in trust for Mam and then to whichever of his children was still living at home when she died.

Frank had started this ball rolling by telling her that any interest he may have had years ago, was history. He had made his own way and it was not the family's way. Alice deserved her share. Until she got herself pregnant, she had been no more than a servant and the nappy-washer in chief. Dear James has gone to a better place along with George. Mary could do with her proper share as there was little spare money down on the farm. That left herself and Eve because Eugene owned his own business and, quite wisely, had already turned his back on the Big House.

Molly's proposal was that the men should tackle the two brothers and Frank had suggested that the confrontation ought to take place on mutual ground. He could reserve the committee room at the Con Club and trick Rob and Harold into coming to "a bit of a do" where there would be plenty of food and free booze.

Albert, Farmer George and Jack, the husbands of Alice, Mary and Molly respectively, were already seated in the room when Frank arrived with Rob and Harold. Immediately he saw his three brothers-in-law, Harold turned to leave but Frank was too quick for him and blocked the door. Standing firm, Frank said,

'Right. Sorry to have deceived you both but we four are representing the whole family and need some questions answered. Neither of you is leaving this room until we get them. George, if you have to use force then bloody well do because if I personally touch either of them there will be a right kerfuffle, like all hell breaking loose. Rob, you are the eldest and as far as I am concerned the one with the most talking to do. Jack is in this room on behalf of Molly and she has written to us all on behalf of the girls. Over to you Jack.'

Jack Brown might have been quietly spoken and studious by nature but he had been so shaken by the death of Stan that he was determined to do everything possible to get help for Eve and if that meant breaking up this family, so be it. He was used to making presentations to the directors of Whiteleys and as far as he was concerned he was, once more, pitching for finance. He stood up and stepped back a pace from the table. Holding a single sheet of paper, he faced Rob.

'We know that you and Harold are working a fiddle. You must think that we are utterly stupid or else too lil'y-liv'ered to do anything about it. Well we are neither and now, especially after poor Stan was burnt to a cinder, comes the day of reckoning. But, you two buggers, we don't just reckon that the old man is being ripped off, we know: if it continues much longer there will be nothing left for the rest of the family when the time comes. For some of the lads, it doesn't much matter. They have branched out on their own or else are not concerned but for the girls it matters a lot. In their way, each one helped build the butchery business and Eve is damn near destitute. Right, you two – what have you got to say?'

With a wave of his hand, Rob signalled to his younger brother to stay out of it. Having gone ghostly pale, he turned his chair to face Frank.

'I'm really shocked at you Frank having anything to do with these accusations although I suppose I shouldn't be, knowing the ducking and diving you've done in your time and all the undercover stuff with your so-called business mates, or should we call it the Great Sutton Mafia? I take great offence at you bringing in these three blokes who've got nothing to do with the business, just blood-sucking leeches who only married our girls for what they could get out of the family.'

At this point, Albert shot out of his seat, his chair toppling backwards onto the floor, and dashed towards Rob. It took George and Frank all their strength to hold him back and sit him down again. Now Rob stood up.

'Listen you lot, this is just a kangaroo court and I'm having nothing to do with it. You can prove nothing s I'm off.'

Frank remained standing.

'Rob you prat. Do you really think I'd go to all this trouble if I didn't have proof? Do you? Last week I went into the bank with the old man and together we saw the manager and went through the bank statement. There has not been a single payment in for over two years. Not too subtle eh, Brothers Grimm? Not that you two have been buying your own meat for the van, have you? Oh no, quite happy to let the old man keep paying all the bills weren't you? Did you know that he has got hardly any money left? Did you both think it would go on for ever? Swines!'

There was silence. Rob's head dropped. Frank returned to his seat, lowered his voice and spoke again,

'While we're at it, might as well put all our cards on the table. Rob, you may pour scorn on my contacts in this town but let me tell you this, those contacts are going to land you and Harold in the clink. I happen to know there's a considerable deposit in your account at National Provincial and I also know of the first refusal you have at Sowerby's on a butchery business. And, as for you Harold, you have been even cleverer, haven't you? But not clever enough that I don't know of that little account in Jersey. What's in it, God knows, but I'll wager a fair bet it matches pound for pound Rob's nest-egg. So, you two, this is what is going to happen and Albert, George and Jack are my witnesses.

'Before anyone leaves this room, we will agree a figure that you two have stashed away. That figure is going to be split four ways for the girls, and you will both sign a form agreeing to get the money within 14 days. If you refuse to sign, we are marching you both off to the police station. As to where we go from here and until I can work out a better system, you will bring your van takings to me here at the club at the end of each day and I will decide if you are coughing up enough. I will sign for the money and the old man will do his paying-in like he always used to.'

Silence. After a few seconds, Harold rose to his feet.

'Well Frank, you organised this pantomime and have had your say and Rob has had his. You brought in the three blokes and so the cat is well and truly out of the bag. Seeing as it is, I'll tell you all what I'm goin' to do. On way tu police station I'll pop into Peacock and down a couple of pints to whet me whistle. Then I'll stand on a chair and make an announcement to all and sundry. I'll say that Whitby family 'ave grown rich by taking 'em all for a ride, raking it in on black market. All thru war years and still today and intend to carry on till rationing's off. I'll mention the part Arthur Bell and a few others played and I'll put on a little crying act as the yung un who had to go along with it but can't hide it any more. I'll say I'm really sorry.'

Harold looked at each of them in turn.

'I bloody mean it – I don't give a shit – you won't get at my money and I'll be off tomorrow, see how the precious family business gets on without me.'

George stood up. 'Look chaps, we need to give this a bit more thought. Frank, let the buggers go.'

★

Pearl had been as good as her word and was showing Eugene the chart created on her computer. Below Hedley and Iris Whitby who were centred at the top was a horizontal bar with thirteen equally spaced vertical lines, each leading to the name of a child starting with Joseph on the left and finishing with Eugene on the right. Under each name was the year of birth spanning the period 1904 to 1927. It was a work of art and the likes of which Eugene had not seen before. For several minutes he could do no more that stare at this document laid out on the table between them. It was as if it bore no relationship to him but was something that this woman from the local library had dug up as an interesting historical record. Yet, for all that, it was written proof of his generation. He had wanted so much to make Pearl feel really welcome and for the past week had thought of little else than her visit this Sunday afternoon.

Pearl felt it would be really interesting to trace the family tree back a couple of generations but actually, now they had this chart in front of them, what did he think about her trying to write the story of what happened to each child, where had thirteen children of the same blood ended up? Had their lives been similar, diametrically opposed, all ended up in the butchery trade or what?

'Ah, so you know my dad was a master butcher then? Don't remember mentioning that, then again the old memory box isn't what it used to be.'

'Sorry Eugene but yes I have done a little digging.'

She reached for his hand and shook her head slightly. 'You don't mind do you? You're not mad at me? Since I prepared this chart, one big question keeps haunting me, can't seem to get it out of my head.'

'Go on then, bet you'll be disappointed in an old codger's answer'.

'What happened to the family business? I know it's not in Huthwaite market square now.'

Eugene sighed deeply. He paused to pour tea from his Noritake teapot into the two cups, added milk and sugar from the jug and bowl of the matching set, handed Pearl a plate of his favourite ginger biscuits and sat back in his chair.

'Pearl, I do want you to know what happened and I do want you to write it all down if you can. Difficult to think where to start, my memory is not what it was and some bits will have been deliberately blotted out – suppose we all get rid of stuff we'd rather not remember. The family business probably could still be flourishing today were it not for two (perhaps more) of the original seven deadly sins being committed. Does that sound dramatic? Anyway, the two I'm thinking of are greed and envy.

A couple of years after I came home from the war, there was a terrible accident at the local pit. It would have been before you were born but it made not just local but national news. It was the worst disaster ever known in the East Midlands coalfield. Eighty men were burnt alive, trapped on the coalface. One of the men was the husband of my elder sister Eve. They had only been married a few months. You can imagine how local families were affected losing all those men. Ours was no different. Eve was devastated and never really got over it. You might say, well yes, an absolute tragedy but what has that to do with the end of a family business? The answer starts and ends with money. There was no proper compensation scheme in those days and the fund set up didn't go very far when split amongst so many families. As a result, Eve was soon pretty much destitute.

'For a time, Eve's financial situation was thought of as temporary, at any rate by her sisters, since the old man's health was clearly declining and there would be an inheritance of some sort. After all, this had been a successful butchery for many years and the family was generally regarded as of substance. What put the cat amongst the pigeons was Molly (see her on the chart) finding out that two of the three lads still working full-time at home had some sort of fiddle going on and as a result the old man's fortune was being drained away. So, in anger, concerned for her widowed sister and in a state of envy (who knows) she got her elder brother Frank and three of the brothers-in-law to confront the two on the make. But, as is often the case, things backfired. There was a skeleton in the family cupboard and one of the accused chose to rattle it.

'I should say Pearl that at the time I was working like stink to get my own business off the ground and wasn't a party to all this but as things turned out, a fatal blow had been struck. One by one the green bottles fell off the wall. Rob, one of the two brothers thought to be on the make, left almost immediately after the big bust-up. He must have had money set aside and plans made because in no time at all, he had his own butchery set-up in a neighbouring village. Harold, the other one, (and Pearl you will not believe this) just stopped working. I mean just stopped and as far as anyone knew, he never did a day's work again. He was thirty years old at the time. That left Willy who continued to run the on-site shop and who did the making up in the evenings and at week-ends, helped by Mam. The girls never went near the place again until the funerals. And the funerals, oh dear, the funerals. In 1955, Willy dropped dead in the middle of a Tuesday afternoon whilst serving a customer. He had got very overweight and still smoked his fags, but even so, he was only forty-nine. Pearl, I feel tired now. When you come next time, I will tell you what happened to the Big House, if that is ok. Will you have written any of this up?'

EIGHT

I t all started with two unforeseen events coinciding: Elaine developed breasts and the school leaving age was raised from 12 to 14. Had neither happened, Frank would have followed his three elder brothers up the butchery yard into the making-up room. But in 1920 Elaine (uniquely amongst the girls in the second year) started to change shape, and Frank overheard talk in the schoolyard. In exchange for a small present such as, it was said, a Fry's chocolate bar or a cigarette card missing from a set in her album, Elaine would let a boy touch one of her two new appendages. Frank had no idea whether this gossip was true but not being completely absorbed by the school lessons, it did give him an idea.

Any doubts Frank may have had about Elaine's reputation evaporated like the sickly milk poured by Mam over his porridge. As he successfully cornered her at the far end of the school yard, he was met by " an' wot ya got to give us then?" And so it was, from such a humble beginning, that Frank Whitby started his business career. Like all good business ideas, his proposition was simple. Frank explained to Elaine that rather than just accepting whatever bits and bobs the lads had to offer, she would do much better to ask a small price and perhaps a slightly higher one for a more generous favour. He was quite prepared to hang around and make sure there was no funny business and his gang would muscle in if the need

99

arose. With money in her purse, as distinct from presents, she could buy whatever she wanted rather than have to take what they'd got at the time. For his idea and his protection, she would let him have one quarter of what she got. A fair exchange.

While Elaine's adventure only had a limited timespan as some of the lads moved onto bigger things, it proved to be the seed-corn for the final two years of Frank's schooling. Schemes to make money were infinitely more interesting than arithmetic, in fact some of the ideas that came along demanded a higher degree of reckoning than any in the school exercise books. He took note of Elaine's interest in cigarette card albums. The commercial travellers from Players and Wills had left a pile in the shop as advertising and he could undercut other shops in Huthwaite and Great Sutton by letting the school kids have them at half price. His success in getting the latest albums out quickly, led to a second side-line; that of the adhesive-backed cards themselves. What he soon discovered was that little Harry's dad (or whoever it was) had no idea which card would be in the latest packet of Players Navy Cut Medium or Wills Woodbines. Therefore there was a chance, and Frank soon realised a very high chance, that as a series such as *Trees of Great Britain* was nearing the end of its run, the latest card would duplicate one already stuck in the album. This is where swaps came in. For a small fee, Frank offered to hold the duplicate in his bank and replace it with a missing one when that particular card entered the bank. As this enterprise developed, Frank realised he could ask a slightly higher fee when the album was short of just five cards. In fact, quite a competitive spirit developed to finish the latest album and Frank was quite prepared to cycle miles around the neighbourhood to replenish his bank and meet the demand.

It was not long before he realised that his list of cigarette card customers might come in useful for other sales ideas as they came along. And one did.

The mother of one of Elaine's friends was a supervisor on the knitting line at the *Co-operative Wholesale Society's* factory. This line produced the latest style in ladies' jumpers and, once a batch had passed through the dye house, in a variety of colours. Elaine learned from her friend that seconds were identified at the final inspection stage before reaching the Goods Outwards department,. In most cases, and to the untrained eye, it was hard to tell there was a fault in the garment. It might be just a pulled thread or a couple of loose stiches but as the *Co-op* was a stickler for quality, the label would be stamped "second" and the jumper rejected. These rejects were batched and sent to a big firm up in Yorkshire, which in turn had outlets on the markets.

Elaine was saying that if her friend's mother had the money, she was allowed to buy rejects but in batches of at least 25 and of course in any of the colours being made at the time. Many of the girls at school and in the Girl Guides would love to have a jumper in the latest style even if was a bit too big, it would still be ok because they would soon grow into it and many had elder sisters anyway. Had Frank got enough spare money so that her friend's mother could buy a batch and see how things went? He had his cigarette card customers too, didn't he? Six months later, Frank had a big tin under his bed full of paper money and both Elaine and her friend's mother were quite happy with how things had gone. Elaine was saying that it was quite a laugh really. One colour had been so successful that it had enjoyed an extended run at the factory and now the local Girl Guides were known as The Pink Princesses.

It was on one of his cycle trips to deliver cigarette cards and three jumpers that Frank spotted the hovel. The semi-derelict brick building was a few yards down a farm track leading off Wild Hill. How neglected it looked, abandoned and serving no useful purpose. He was about to re-mount his bike after pushing it up the steep incline when a horse and cart came into view. Without quite knowing why, Frank waited until the driver was alongside him and shouted to ask if he knew who owned the hovel. The little chat that followed was destined to shape his life. Always eager for a talk to break up his none too exciting day, farmer Sid Topham pulled his horse to a halt and jumping down from the tumbril said,

'Tis mine lad, why dus tha ask?'

Frank adopted the casual not overly interested approach that had proved successful in his now established little business schemes. Leaning against the handlebars of his cycle, he was wondering what use the old building could be put to if it was done up a bit, made weather proof and generally returned to what it must have been like in its heyday.

'Arr well, shud a dun it missen but if hovel was a gudun, we'd store fodder in t'summer and keep yung beast tied up in winter.'

After five or ten minutes talk about how hard things had been during the Great War and how farmer Topham had managed to help the villagers out a bit with potatoes and eggs and the like, Frank popped the question. Would good use of the hovel be worth £25? He had some strong mates and knew where bricks and timber could be found and one lad's father was a builder by trade. If Mr Topham wasn't satisfied with the final job then obviously he wouldn't pay up. The two shook hands to seal a gentleman's agreement.

Over the years that followed, Frank often relived the

handshake that had sealed his first property deal. He had also related it so often to his business colleagues that there could sometimes be heard in the various hallowed halls of power murmurings of, "Watch out, here comes the boring hovel man". But only in jest of course.

The fact remained however that as a mere fourteen year old, Frank hadn't the faintest idea what it would cost to do the job promised. Neither had be got any workmen lined up and yet there must surely be enough money in his big tin to buy all the materials needed and pay for the work to be done. Although the farm building was derelict, it still had some standing to it, well it must have since otherwise he would not have spotted it would he? And, if people passing by noticed work going on, they would ask questions such as "who is doing this job and why?" By the same token, if it turned out to be a disaster, young Frank Whitby would be a laughing stock: "he may have some little schemes underway with girls' jumpers and cigarette card albums but they are just passing fads that will die out, no permanency to them. The upstart whippersnapper will have to get himself a proper job. Maybe he could try his hand at making sausages?"

There is one big thing about business, any business, it is risky. There are loads of skilful people about and there always have been. But, by definition, workers can't take risks. If they could, they would all be Queen Bees. Frank was a Queen Bee. No-one had to tell him, he knew instinctively. His only task with the hovel job was to get some knowledge and then some worker bees. Simple. Task number one: find a schoolboy whose dad was a skilled brickie or similar and get him to plan what needed doing. Then, list the materials to be bought and from where, and supervise the work. He couldn't afford to pay him on this job but if things worked out well, there was an opening for a foreman on future projects that Frank had in mind. Because they had all done woodwork at school, his teacher would probably give some guidance on a real project and it couldn't be that difficult to lay a few bricks and tile a roof.

Then, Frank used the masterstroke he had found to work on his two existing schemes. In his mind he saw it as *giving the customers an extra, something for nothing.* For instance, he would replace a lost or stolen cigarette card album free of charge because it wasn't the customer's fault it had gone missing and anyway he needed to keep his card swapping sideline going. Same thing with the jumpers. If one got spoilt or nicked, Frank was happy to replace it at half-price provided the customer could find him just one more buyer, no sweat. Would Mr Topham like to have a double-door entrance in place of the single-door in the front wall. Frank would have to spend a bit more on the timber but it would then be easier for the cattle to enter and leave. Also, what did he think of the new door and window frames being painted a dark green colour instead of what had been a dull brown? From his visits to the Great Sutton woodyard and to the brick kilns on the far side of that yard, it was surprising how much more expensive bricks were than rough timber. His best friend had come across a tin of outdoor green paint in his dad's shed and it wouldn't be missed.

On completion, Frank's figures showed a profit of £12 8s, and that was after he had knocked 10s off the original price of £25 once Mr Topham had agreed to tell all the other farmers and dealers at the regular Saturday morning market how pleased he was with the hovel job. Also, would Mr Topham be ok with Frank showing the finished cattle house to these potential future customers? The answer was "yes": he was launched!

★

Preparing the family tree for Eugene was having an unexpectedly profound effect on Pearl. The fact that this old man once had twelve siblings was in such sharp contrast to her own childhood experience that the mere act of reducing names and dates to paper sucked her uncontrollably into a vortex of family reminiscences. It was as if a doppelganger was mentally preparing a parallel chart. A narrow focussed representation of a parallel life. A creepiness was afoot, a fateful premonition that without some drastic self-determination, it was only the passage of time between her as now and her as him on that settee in that old and worn-out state. Why was her life on hold? Was it self-pity? If it was, then she was stupid, and more self-indulgent than the upbringing she had been privileged to receive could conceivably warrant. She now saw that the chance meeting with Eugene was a signal. A signal to take stock.

Her grandfather would have been ten years older than Eugene and it must have been while on leave in 1945, no doubt believing the war was over, that he lay with his beloved Sarah to create their only child James, Pearl's father. James, perhaps due to his pedigree, and perhaps not, had had the high-flying career that no son of Eugene could ever have aspired to. After Rugby, he took an MA in Military History at Brunel and moved directly into Sandhurst as an Officer Cadet. It was at the Officers' Ball in 1970 that James met Susan. Within a year they were married.

Rising rapidly through the ranks, James was a Captain by 1973, the year Pearl was born. Sixteen years later and living in a large house with its two acres of ground, including a tennis court and croquet lawn, life for the family was perfect but, as Pearl now acknowledged with stoical honesty, a state of perfection is transitory.

On her way to visit Pearl at Roedean one summer Sunday afternoon, Susan's car was hit head-on by a white van cutting the corner on a minor road leading off the Sussex Downs. She was killed instantly. No man, whether a Colonel in the British Army or a humble shopkeeper, can replace the mother of a sixteen year old girl. No privileged upbringing, no higher education specifically designed to develop an individual's personality, no absolutely nothing can replace a good gossip over afternoon tea. The doppelganger's chart is wet with Pearl's tears.

★

Does wisdom come with experience or is it innate? Time to think was the only nugget of goodness to come from those interminable hot and sticky days journeying from Burma, through Siam and Malaysia to reach Singapore. But that nugget was pure gold. The experience put a solid floor to the value of life: it begat wisdom whether it was there before or not. There can be no sharper focus on mortality, on seeking out and grabbing the best there is while it is there, than pushing through dense jungle into a clearing in which nine British soldiers, with bound hands and feet, are hanging by the neck from poles stretched between teak trees.

It was after the lads had buried the bodies and erected the nine wooden crosses that Eugene thought of his dad who would be buried in the cemetery in Huthwaite, close to those gone before and waiting for those to come. Unlike these poor buggers, he would have had a full life, that much is true, but working day after day, making babies year after year, watching his children leave to join their own world and then in the end; in the end what exactly? Eugene knew that if he ever survived this hell-hole, he would work hard, of course he would, but not just for material things, not just to make a safe home for himself and darling Chit but for them both to enjoy what they had, to travel, to see things, to meet new people, to live. To have given and not just taken. To look back at the end and be satisfied. Mandalay Hill was only the start. They would climb together into the cool fresh air of England; their joint spirits would soar.

It was taking the right-hander on the roundabout at the far end of Baslow that snapped him out of his daydream. When would be get Chit out of his head? It wasn't her on the back of the bike, it was Dot and she was wearing the wrong clothes for the spin they had decided on a whim to take. It was Good Friday, the store was closed and as Eugene had said with some emphasis "It stays shut 'till Tuesday, we're having Easter off. We've got enough money spare, so we'll spend a bit of it, have a good time together."

When he went round to pick her up from home, she was wearing the pencil skirt again, exactly as she had done on their first date. It was a conscious choice. She knew it brought back memories and that he fancied her like crazy when she wore it. So different to her work-day store outfit. Unfortunately, it wasn't too practical and to straddle the bike she had to hitch it up even higher than when getting comfortable at the Tivoli. Not that it was unfortunate for Eugene, in fact he had sort of semi-planned it by not disclosing in advance his idea for a trip into the Derbyshire hills. When the road was straight and smooth and even though he wasn't too confident keeping the beast under control (it being only a week since he passed his test) his gloved left hand still wandered from the handlebars to her knee. And that simple act created a second beast that was hard to control.

Dorothy expected him to swing left to Chatsworth Park as before but Eugene had planned a surprise. He intended to take another right-hander at Curbar to point out Froggatt Edge, the gritstone escarpment of the Dark Peak that his Dot would not have seen the likes of before and which would, he hoped, release her mind from the business and set a marker for their future together. A future, as much of leisure and adventure, as of customers and schemes to make money. Taking a sharp left in Grindleford, they took the steep uphill to arrive at his surprise destination, the ancient and beautiful stone village of Hathersage and, crossing the road, came to rest in the car park of the George Hotel. It was here that they would spend their honeymoon; all that remained was for Dot to approve, to fix a date in the summer and choose the love nest room.

To mark the six-month anniversary of the store opening, Eugene had taken the decision to buy it, the dream motorcycle every young man wants to own. As with every purchase they made, Frank was consulted and once again, out of seeming impossibility, he found a way. Because it had been in successful production for three years and was aimed at the American market, the Triumph 6T iron-head 650 twin Thunderbird was not cheap but as Frank said, with a bit of "inside track knowledge" it was possible to cut out the dealer profit by collecting direct from the Meriden factory. He would go 50/50 on the price and Eugene could pay him back on a private basis by monthly instalments over a couple of years with the normal 5% added on for Frank's trouble (the two brothers laughed out loud – Eugene was learning). As regards Eugene's half, take some profit out of the business – check with Dorothy how much – but for the rest he could draw down the last of the bank loan and enter it in the books as Plant & Machinery for tax purposes. Anyway, what was stopping him buying a side-car later and doing some deliveries? It was this dark green beauty that attracted a small audience in the George Hotel car park and as he recalled his own similar admiration for Frank's new car, Eugene felt very happy. He had his girl, his business and a brother who knew a thing or two. He was on the way up.

Paul had been de-mobbed three months after Eugene and had got his old job back even though the departmental manager had decided that his experience helping to re-build bridges over the Irrawaddy River was "Not quite what we do here lad but useful training, useful training." He was telling Eugene (his uncle and war-time buddy) "They just have no bloody idea what we went through and Christ have they got a wake-up call coming when those Asians get their act together. Something else, Eugy, the pay is pathetic." Because he was family, because he and Eugene had developed such a strong bond, because he had learned from his mam what was going on at the Big House, but most of all because he could use some spare cash, Paul started to help with preparing the store. He also began helping Eugene collect the rents from Frank's properties and it soon seemed natural for him to get involved in the purchase of the metal beams and the rolled steel joists and later the fixtures & fittings. So much so that Frank, for the first time, started to take a direct interest in the ongoing work. He suggested to Paul that when the store was finished, he might like to take a look at some of his buildings "Bits and bobs, part-time, cash-in-back-pocket sort of thing, qualified structural engineers are bloody expensive."

It was on the evening before the grand opening that Eugene heard himself saying to Dot "With Paul turning up and Eve showing an interest and wanting to leave the factory, now you are here it's almost as if a new family business is being invented."

★

Having made an appointment to see Rev. Hudson after the service, Dorothy and Eugene attended their very first evensong at St Nicholas's Church in Great Sutton on Sunday 29th June 1952. She being a spinster of the Parish and he from a highly respected family in a neighbouring one, Rev. Hudson saw no reason why the happy couple should not be married in his church and, provided the banns were read during the service on the following three Sundays, Saturday 26th July was available for a 2.30pm marriage. When could they make a rehearsal and would they want the choir in attendance and should he contact the tower captain for the bells to be rung? Perhaps they might like to take note of the costs and decide in the next few days. Dorothy realised that it was going to put time pressure on her mum but already her whole family was raring to go. Her dad was paying for everything, of course he was, he wouldn't have it any other way. She was his only daughter of whom he was very proud. Dorothy only wanted a simple reception and as soon as possible she and Eugene would zoom off on the Thunderbird. She was so excited.

Like all weddings what had to be done would be fairly straight-forward until deciding on the guest list. Dorothy came from a small family and the invitees pretty much took care of themselves. In any case, Eugene neither wanted nor had any say in it. But his side was a nightmare due to both size and animosity. However, Eugene was explaining to Dot as once again they tried to keep their hands off each other after closing up the store, he was only inviting those he wanted to attend the wedding and that if it highlighted the family split, too bad.

As he talked, Dorothy made three lists:

List 1 – Brothers
Joseph, yes (eldest, school teacher, bachelor – invite him to say a few serious words)
Jack, no (complete stranger to Eugene and whereabouts unknown)
Willy, yes (will look after Mam as Dad too ill to attend)
Frank, yes (plus his Betty. Will invite him to say a few words, but doing his stand-up comedian bit)
Rob, no (stabbed Eugene in back and fiddling family fortune)
Harold, no (ditto Rob)

List 2 – Sisters
Alice, yes (with husband Albert – see note on son Paul later)
Mary, yes (with husband Farmer George and two children – invite 12 year-old Mable to be a bridesmaid)
Molly, yes (with husband Jack)
Eve, yes (invite to be chief bridesmaid)

List 3 – Other special guests
Paul, (invite to be best man)
Billy, (will thank bridesmaids and may want to reminisce on war)
Group Captain Bennett, (if Eugene can locate him, if he will accept and if he is not serving abroad – a long-shot but if he does attend, will be guest of honour)

Still leaning over the shop counter, pen poised to await the next name, Dorothy was too slow to stop him leaving her side and coming to her from behind. She was trapped. Eugene had his left arm around her waist and held her tightly,

'Now then young lady, and what's to stop this wayward right hand of mine slowly – like this – slowly, very slowly move up the inside of your so smooth and beautiful legs.'

Dorothy was pinned against the counter and helpless, she leant her head backwards and pushing her breasts forward, opened her legs to await his fingers. Her breathing was heavy, her face flushed and her knees buckled and started to shake. "Oh God, Eugy, when will you do me properly, oh Christ, oh Christ you've found her again – don't stop, please don't stop, oh God Eugy, my darling Eugy, oh God Eugy….. I'm wet through again.'

And it happened again on the back of the bike; they hadn't even reached Baslow, never mind taken the turn northwards to the George Hotel. Perhaps it was the excitement of the afternoon, Frank's innuendo jokes, especially about what shocks a good girl might expect on her wedding night, Billy's praise of his mate's courage in the jungle, the two sherries, the very close attention of both Billy and Paul, the towering presence of the Group Captain wearing his medals, or maybe none of those things. Maybe Eugene's wandering hand squeezing her knee whenever the road allowed, or just the jolting up and down of the ride. Whatever it was, Dorothy had an orgasm. She kept her secret for years to come until one night after an especially heavy session, she finally told him of, "Her thunderbird on a Thunderbird."

It was the head waiter's recommendation.

'Noisette of Derbyshire lamb Sir and a full-bodied Burgundy to refresh the lady after the journey.'

After he had left them, (there was no-one, absolutely no-one else in the George Hotel's posh dining room on this peak season Saturday evening) Eugene whispered to Dorothy,

'Why did it take him so long to take our order? Having

sawn up a few sheep in my days at the Big House, I'm going to ask him when he gets back and with the same degree of solemnity he used, to explain the difference between a lamb born in Derbyshire and one born in Nottinghamshire. In fact, wouldn't it be a tough little beast seeing it's got to get up this mountain at the back? When they're trained, do you think the main subject is not so much how to hold a plate steady but how to be a real-life supercilious sod?' Dorothy reached across the pristine-white tablecloth to hold his hand and giggled. She loved her Eugy and would never, ever, let him go.

Given the thunderbird experience, Dorothy assumed that would be it for the day and, as her mum had said when they were fitting her dress that morning,

'Dorothy darling, don't expect too much on your first night together, it might hurt a bit at first but things will improve with a little practice.'

Dorothy was trying to relate this to Eugene in the early hours before concluding,

'How wrong is it possible to be, my Eugy, how wrong? Can we do it again – please?'

She wasn't Chit, he knew that, but he also knew what Chit liked best and this time it wouldn't take months to get there. The lady on reception had suggested in all seriousness that tomorrow they climb Mam Tor for the sheer effort of it and to take in the spectacular view. Eugene couldn't see that happening for a day or two at least. His sheer effort and spectacular view was not of the Derbyshire mountainside.

★

Frank had a further little favour to ask of Mr Topham. Would he stand surety at Pearsons cycle shop? Although he could now afford the £8-12-6d for his dream cycle, he wanted to use the new never-never, easy-payment terms: 65 weekly payments of 3s 2d, so that his savings could pay for the materials on his next building renovation job. Mr Topham could surely understand that a businessman needs to hold onto some capital and if anything went wrong, he would work on the farm for free until the debt was paid off. Grateful as Frank was for the bone-shaker bike his dad had picked up at the cattle market and without which his hovel restoration job would not have happened, he still needed the latest model. It would get him further afield to find other building jobs but more importantly, it would impress his potential customers. Would they see any other fifteen year-old riding the very latest *Special Triumph No 21 Gents Roadster* with its 24 inch frame and 28 inch wheels? Not only that but he was going for the extras; Sturmey-Archer "Model A" three-speed gears, Middlemore saddle and toolbag, Dunlop Magnum Tyres and the inverted lever brakes. Mr Topham was telling his farming neighbours that he had never met anyone like young Frank Whitby. "Poor Iris has just dropped her tenth and from what Hedley was hinting at last week at the market, the litter aint complete yet. Wonder if some other bloke sneaked in to sire this one, he's not like tuthers, wish my lads had half his spunk. Cheeky little bugger but if he takes summat on, it'll get done believe me, I know".

And the jobs came in and the friend's dad who had lent his skills on that first building became a self-appointed foreman and over the years a surrogate second father. But the mutterings from an increasing work gang of "Butcher's boy to builder's boy." was not mockery, more respect for the "'Yung-un' that gets us work and pays well". Frank's reputation grew with the passing of his teenage years and so did his love of a pint at some remote pub found by the *Triumph Roadster,* out of sight of his dad and the rest of them at the Big House.

He was sitting outside the Old Shepherd in Teversal drinking his second pint of Mansfield Best Bitter when the next big idea started taking shape. It had been an exceptionally good day for Frank. At 11am that morning he had been summoned into the committee room at the Conservative Club in Great Sutton and elected as the youngest ever member. The proposer was a Mr Sidney Topham and the seconder was a tradesman unknown to Frank but who apparently had a daughter named Elaine. After a couple of swift halves of Stones Ale to "cement in" (Mr Topham's phrase) the new club member, Frank cycled to his afternoon appointment with farmer John Bell of Teversal. Starting out with more hope than expectation, the mid-afternoon chat in the stackyard had ended with the job of building a row of pigsties and, if that went well, the chance of refurbishing the 10-standing cow shed. Even though he was alone, this day deserved a celebration and his trusty bike would get him home. In fact, wasn't his *Roadster* the good luck charm he always knew it would be?

Walking back into the pub for a third pint to see him on his way, Frank passed a man sitting on a bench at a table with, opposite him, two boys aged perhaps eight and ten years old. These two sons (he assumed) were arguing over who had the right to the last crisp in the single packet they had obviously been sharing. His prevailing good mood and natural generosity was overwhelming.

'I'll get the lads a packet each with my pint if that's ok with you". "Good of you to offer mate but you won't – landlord's run out.'

The world is full of coincidences, of random chances; or are they? Whilst waiting for his interview that morning, Frank had read in the erudite magazine The Economist that sat somewhat majestically on the coffee table outside the committee room, an article about the rise and rise of the potato crisp market. The rise from the fryer. London born Frank Smith who was (and could this be believed?) the seventh son of a seventh son, took over from his greengrocer boss the novelty side-line of frying up potatoes. Soon he was selling to other shops and then to pubs. Within seven years and from a disused Cricklewood garage he was turning out half a million bags a week.

Adopting his by now well-polished air of nonchalance, Frank asked the pub landlord why he had run out of crisps, only to be told, "I only gets three tins full a week and they've gone in no time. It is a shame lad 'cos between me and thee, when kids have had a bag, salt in that little blue packet makes em so thirsty, they pester their parents for a second bottle of pop. And I tell you this, there's as much profit in pop as in that pint tha's just ordered. Summat else, mam and dad wants a bag these days and then they wants another drink as well. I know it, brewery knows it. Shortage seems to have come once Cardiff FC won the cup in May. Rumour spread that their footballers has been fed a daily diet of Smiths Crisps – *the finest food on earth.*"

The year was 1927 and Frank was nineteen years old. Iris Whitby had just given birth to her fourteenth child, thankfully her last. She had picked up an American magazine that Frank had somehow got hold of. There was an article about a young man who had made his fortune on Wall Street. His name was Eugene; she liked the name.

As his bike wobbled its way back home, he ought to have been sketching in his head the outline of a row of pigsties. Instead, little blue bags of salt, closed with a tight twist, were leaping from the tarmac just ahead of his front tyre and screaming something at him. At first he couldn't make it out. Then, peddling furiously up the last steep hill, his head suddenly cleared. He could make out what they were saying. There was no doubt. One by one, one after another, each blue bag was crying out, '*Everest, The Peak Of Crisp Perfection*'.

NINE

Upstairs in the big bedroom where five of the boys used to sleep, Willy was alone for the very first time and loneliness is deeper and more cutting during the long hours of fitfulness. On this Sunday morning, probably during breakfast and certainly before Mam got ready for church, he was dreading having to tell her. Each time one of her brood left home, she cried on and off for the best part of a week. This would be no different. Worse still, together they would have to break the news to the old man who had taken to his bed three days ago and increasingly seemed unlikely to get up ever again. What a mess.

Last night (was it only yesterday?) Rob had come to him as he was scrubbing out the shop after the day's business to say he was leaving. Leaving for good. There had been a bust-up involving Frank and the brothers-in-law and Harold had threatened to blow the whistle on the black market rackets going back to the autumn of 1939. Rob was off, this bloody family could go to hell as far as he was concerned. As the elder of two brothers who had worked their socks off covering two butchery rounds with the only van left, he felt entitled to regard that van as his own property and so was taking it together with his own set of knives, saws and cleavers. His only regret was not having dropped the exposure bombshell himself but in leaving it to snivelling Harold. He would be opening his own place first thing Monday morning with the meat from the old man's last order. With the best will in the world, he had given up his well-paid job in the pit to keep the family business going, (with the old man's blessing) and look what happened. As far as he was concerned, the girls had wanted an inheritance that was not warranted. Never had been. Anyone with any gumption could see that the old man had only weeks to live. And don't even think of inviting Rob to the funeral because Rob will not be attending.

Mam tucked an extra hanky up her sleeve before fetching her cane for the walk down the Common to Morning Service. She thought it best for Willy to tell Hedley. Seeing her in this state would not help. Reaching for the po under the bed, Willy went through his now familiar, three-times-a-day ritual, of pulling the old man up onto his pillows, finding his scrunched-up penis and encouraging him to have a go. Sometimes he could and sometimes no orangeade came out. It was the daily deepening of the orange colour that spelt out the deterioration. The old man would not see a doctor and Willy was certainly no medical man. But he didn't need to be. A butcher knows his animals and his dad was drifting into the stupefied state so common to the slaughterhouse. He felt very, very sad. How could this little screwed up thing he still couched in his right hand have created such a huge dynasty, one now crumbling faster even than the creator himself?

Yet, as Eugene was to relate to Pearl in his build-up story of the demise of the Big House, both brothers were wrong about the impending death of their dad. True he was in failing health and to the very end would refuse to see a doctor, true he had reached the biblical three score years and ten and true he would never leave his home again. But the old man was destined to survive another five years. Those last years of Hedley Whitby were to witness Willy's death and Rob as his own epitaphist.

*

Eugene wanted a little chat. He picked a Wednesday because that was the evening Eve came around to talk with Dot and he asked Paul to drop by after his normal midweek inspection of Frank's properties. Once the family group was seated in the living room and deliberately without any introduction so as to get an instant and surprised reaction, he read directly from an article in *Traders' Weekly*. The gist of the story was that two years earlier (1951) an ex-US Navy sailor called Patrick Galvani, who was the son-in-law of the chairman of Express Dairies, proposed the opening of a chain of supermarkets. The point of the article was that the first supermarket located in Streatham, South London, was now taking ten times as much each week as the average general store such as the one above which they were all sitting.

As far as Eugene could tell, there were three reasons for the incredible increase in sales. The main one was concept. Rather than standing at a counter to be served by someone else with a list of pre-decided items, customers picked their own goods which of course was much quicker and so saved time. Secondly, think of the temptation of seeing things not on the list and realising maybe even subconsciously, that they might as well buy that tin of peas, or whatever, whilst in the store. This new idea, from America by the way, also freed up space so more goods could be displayed, further increasing the temptation to take extra items home.

The third reason for a supermarket to beat the general

store in sales per customer, was the issue of what were called trading stamps. This was another Americanism. In effect these stamps were a sales discount: "Remember Dot, the bananas we gave away the day we opened? It seems the real trick is to encourage the saving up of stamps to hand in for a more expensive item, say for example, the new portable radios we have started to stock. Naturally, to collect enough stamps requires the customer to spend more! It reminds me of the tale Frank tells of how he got started with his cigarette card bank. The clever difference of course is that, with trading stamps the reward is not the satisfaction of completing a full set, but rather getting something back for the saving effort. Something for nothing you might say."

The silence that followed was broken by Paul.

'I think the Yanks are brilliant. They saved us in the war and now they are at it again! But Eugene, surely there isn't enough space downstairs to make this new concept work, is there?'

Eugene turned to his wife.

'Dot tell us what your dad has discovered.'

Dorothy left Eve's side to sit next to her husband and started to explain that, through the office, it was known that the boot and shoe shop next door was due to close. If they could take over the lease and then break through to create a single large floor, it would be perfect for the area's first supermarket. Eve jumped up.

'That would be just fantastic and I'll be store manager – oh, sorry Dot – got carried away.'

The two girls met in the centre of the room and hugged each other. Eugene sensed he had started to turn the iron wheel and the lock gates were opening just enough for the first stream of water to be released. If he had the strength to continue turning that wheel, then the increasing swell would surely wash away the debilitating sorrow of Eve and float her boat downstream to where Dot was waiting and a new business dawn was breaking. That much, at least, he owed to Stan.

Once eyes had been dabbed and more tea poured, Eugene continued by explaining that Dot's dad thought that, if the business was to take a new turn by expanding and acquiring more stock and staff, then it would be sensible to form a Limited Liability Company. Naturally, National Provincial would have to go along with the change and so would Frank because of his personal guarantee of the business loan. The main suppliers would also need to be told but, all things being equal, it seemed to make all-round good sense. Dot's dad would look after the legal side and was interested in taking a small stake – maybe 5%. Of course he and Dot would retain the lion's share of the issued capital, say 75%, but if Eve was prepared to work for the new supermarket full-time, she could have 10%, and they also wanted Paul to have 10% in the hope that one day he too would be fully involved. A lot more thinking was needed, much work to be done and risks taken, but having survived the war and got this far with the store, he and Dot were in the mood to go for it. So what did they think of the plan?

★

The proud puffed-up chest was surely that of the accursed spotted dove that woke him every morning to the reality of the early kitchen shift in the camp outside Rangoon. Spots could trigger the past. The three-repeat monotonous durt-durt-durt call of the dove in its teak-encased humidity couldn't conceivably be mistaken for the five-repeat complex song of the speckle-chested thrush perched perilously on the topmost twig of the ash tree. Was he calling to attract a first mate? Did he want a new mate? Was he crying out to the soul of a lost mate? Why does everything so audibly clear, so visibly clean, so constructively simple have to bring back the machinations of the past? Could we not just have and enjoy that which is? The male song thrush insisting we know that this is a wonderful day in a wonderful world. Accept it at face value.

Eugene's daydream was broken by the opening of the conservatory door and the appearance of a beautiful and elegant lady. A new day dream girl called Pearl holding the tea-tray with its bounty of Noritake china and ginger biscuits. She must order, well in advance, the clear blue skies and warm sunshine of a Sunday afternoon. Person, place and time must be synchronised to perfection: must be so. The chart spread on the table had grown, or rather developed. Pearl was pointing with her long slim index figure, with its immaculately manicured pink-polished nail, to a line traced beneath each of the thirteen names. Each line broke its journey southwards by the insertion of a chapter number and, she was explaining to the old man, in her mind the sibling would have a life-event at that point. Some detail had been filled in already from what she had learned during their last two talks and she was eager to carry on. It might even make a book one day; The Whitby Saga! She reached for his hand and as he melted into her smile he noticed that there was another document pinned behind the chart. It did not look like another family tree, more a single column timeline, and his instinctive reaction was that Pearl hadn't meant it to be there. Perhaps it was something she intended to show him at a later date. As a light breeze disturbed the top corner of the Whitby chart all he could make out on the one beneath was a single name, James.

He pulled himself together, Pearl was asking him a question,

'You promised to tell me what happened to the Big House and how the family business collapsed.'

'Yes, well, ok but I'd better apologise in advance if my timings are a bit askew, a lot of things have happened since – let me know when the boredom kicks in.

I mentioned before that immediately after the family bust-up, Rob left to set up his own business and Willy and Mam did their best to keep the on-site shop going. Indeed they did so for a year or two but even before he dropped dead at the counter in 1955 the writing was on the wall; customers who had been loyal for years started to drift away and I have to confess Pearl, that Dot and I didn't help because, just as Frank had predicted when we first applied for our business loan, meat rationing did finally end. From 1954 we started to stock sausages, meat pies, boiled ham, meat balls, that sort of thing and of course once the slaughtering and cutting-up finished at the Big House, these were just the things Willy was selling. The day he died Mam closed the shop and it never re-opened. Harold was bloody useless (excuse my French) never lifting a finger and it was his very presence that kept Alice, Mary and Molly away. A more spoilt and idle sod never trod this earth. I think Eve went occasionally to see the old couple, but that was about it. So the Big House, that for many years had been bursting at the seams with kids and visitors and, let's face it, reeked with the pungent smell of worn and washed-out nappies, became a living mausoleum.

'In 1957 the old man died. At the end he was no more than a skeleton with sockets where his eyes used to be and skin like white wrinkly stained cloth. When I went to the funeral parlour all I could see were those poor buggers hanging from the Teak trees. That image closed in like a stranger standing too close. I couldn't get past; it wasn't my dad. At the end I never saw my dad. He wasn't moving the light in a vertical figure of eight, he wasn't opening the yard gate to let the van in and he wasn't ushering me into the Big House. He wasn't there.'

Eugene was fumbling in his pocket for a handkerchief. Pearl leaned over to help and said she was sorry to have opened such a deep wound and perhaps it would be best if she left. For the first time that afternoon, he reached for her hand and held it tightly. She knew he had to keep talking, to let it all out. 'Pearl, the funeral was a very moving event. More so because all Huthwaite knew he had been ill for years and confined to the Big House, yet still they flocked to the church as if the death of some famous man had been sudden and shocking. What's more, I left feeling thoroughly ashamed. How could I have not known where he had come from? It had taken Joseph's research and excellent diction to drive home just how underprivileged the start had been and how hard were the times when he worked like a dog to get the business established and later to hold his huge family together.

Graciously, thankfully, Joseph had glossed over the latter years of a long life. Born in 1882, Hedley Whitby had little if any proper education and, in his early teens, had been sent down the coal mine. The detail of what really took place before 1900 was lost in time and never recorded, but it was known that before he was twenty years old, Hedley had three jobs running concurrently. He was managing a gang of men on the coal face, he rented five acres of land down Common Road and somehow, God knows how, he started to slaughter the beast fattened up on that bit of land. He had the butchery sheds built and, not long after courting Iris, he had enough money to build the Big House. Joseph concluded his eulogy by saying that the next generation, of which he was proud to be the eldest, could not possibly hope to match the achievements of Dad. God rest his soul. Pearl, Mam was stooped low over the front pew: she never looked up. Physically, as far as we knew, there was nothing wrong with her but within six months she passed away peacefully, in the bed they had shared for fifty-four years. To the very end she barely spoke a word.

'The final irony was that in his will, made years earlier, Dad had left the Big House and all its contents in trust for Mam during her lifetime and thereafter it was to pass to whichever children were still living at home at the time, and in equal shares. By 1958 only Harold was at home. As you have seen, no trace of the house, yard and butchery remains. That is because the lane, down which the horse and cart and then the van had carried their burden, was unsuited to the cars, buses and lorries needed for the modern era. The council demolished the lot under a compulsory purchase order for the road widening scheme. Full commercial compensation was paid to the owner – Harold.

'Pearl, I have done a lot of thinking since you were here last. Of course it is entirely up to you and I am useless at writing things down but look at this. I have been making some notes. Really it's just a list of dates and key things that happened as best I can remember them. I've tried to go right back to my early years at school and helping my dad with the business. Then being called up and where we were sent and so on. I suppose to make any sense of it, some research needs doing. I mean to say, the why of it for a start. Looking back now, what on earth was a lad like me doing in the Far East? I sometimes wish I had kept a diary or at least made more notes to go with the folder I brought back. After all, if no-one ever recorded what was happening in their time, history would be even more fabricated than no doubt a lot of it is. What I am trying to say Pearl, is that if things that were wrong die with the wronged, then the next lot will not learn, will they? Perhaps they won't anyway. Pearl, if you do ever manage to write the story, please be kind to Chit.'

What Eugene didn't tell Pearl, because he didn't know, was that soon after his dad's funeral, his mam visited their store when Eugene was at the wholesalers and handed Dot a brown envelope. It contained Hedley Whitby's most private papers that had been locked in the bottom right-hand drawer of his writing bureau.

'Dorothy dear, you are a sensible girl. I want you to have this package. Read what's inside. You can decide on the best thing to do.'

★

Frank sent a pint over to Sid Topham with a note.

*When you've won the fives-and-threes game let's have a chat in
the Committee Room, got an idea for a different sort of double six!*

Sitting opposite each other at the committee table both with a pint of Mansfield Best Bitter, Frank reached inside his jacket pocket for his fake-silver cigarette case and passed it over to Sid with a gesture to help himself. They each lit up and Frank leaned back in his chair, adopting his casual semi-interested approach to make it seem like a side-line thought that had just crossed his mind.

'Spuds.'

'What about spuds Frank lad?'

'Sid, how much land do you actually farm?'

'One hundred and twenty acres – why?'

'And how many acres of spuds do you normally grow?'

'Well, before war I'd say maybe about five – just for locals, sold from farmhouse door. But 'course war changed all that, we bumped it up to more like fifteen, lot of demand from certain quarters – know what I mean – and if thars interested, changed to main crops too like Majestic, King Edward and Red King, cos folks wanted to store and save them for winter to come.'

Frank stubbed out his cigarette and sat bolt upright in his chair and, for the first time, looked directly at the farmer.

'Sid, we know each other quite well now, don't we? You know I've got my head screwed on and my men have done good jobs for your farming neighbours, yes? I want you to think about something and keep it under your hat. There's no hurry to this. It's now early September right and I'm thinking about next March time, but what if you turned the whole farm, the whole lot, over to growing potatoes. Not only that, but you helped me persuade some other local farmers to do the same?'

'Look lad, yur bloody crackers, aint the demand, even by-passing the shops as I do, they'd all sodding rot in fields!'

'Sid, I said keep this to yourself. If what I am planning comes off, I will take every single spud you can grow and that could mean two crops a year if we get the variety and timing right – don't ask me what I'll use 'em for – top secret, top secret.'

Frank had got his first residential house job. It was to modernise a big rambling piece of Victoriana built in 1890 on the prestigious far side of Great Sutton Lawn. Mrs Lazenby wanted a new bathroom with water closet and all the latest sanitary fittings. She also wanted the very latest kitchen that eliminated the need for a separate pantry by installing a Freon refrigerator, and a new bedroom that was to have built-in wardrobes to save space. Her ideas were coming from *The American Home,* a magazine received from her husband who was something big on Wall Street. Somewhere, she told Frank,

'You ought to think about going, there's pots of money being made out there. Anyway, take this copy away, it's the lay-out on pages ten to fifteen I was thinking of trying to have installed here.'

Back at his yard, Frank tore out those pages and gave them to his foreman. That was his side of things. What caught Frank's eye was an article near the back of the magazine in the *Good Healthy Food* section. It was headed *Potato Chips – How They Are Made.* Frank remembered the two boys sharing one bag of crisps and what the landlord of the pub had said about his meagre supply. It made him think.

The main theme of the article was the evolution of the snack market. It was informing its readers that in 1925, just three years ago, two things had happened that were now turning what had been a localised cottage industry into a mass production one. The result was that potato chips (Frank was thinking to himself *they mean crisps)* were being advertised as a healthy everyday snack that anyone could afford. The first development was the invention of an automatic potato-peeling machine and the second had come about when several employees at *Laura Scudder's Potato Chip Company* ironed sheets of waxed paper to form bags. The chips were then hand packed into these bags which were ironed again at the top as a closure. The writer went on to explain how the seasonal disruption of farm-fresh potatoes had been solved. The answer lay in the application of science to the need to hold stocks during the non-growing parts of the year, principally autumn and winter. Stored potatoes were kept at a constant temperature of between 40-45 degrees Fahrenheit. Several weeks before they entered the factory, they were moved to a reconditioning room heated to 70–75 degrees Fahrenheit. After reheating, the stored potato is equivalent to a freshly supplied one.

What surprised Frank was how this article was publishing what he would have thought were trade secrets and he was further taken aback by an itemised account of the actual manufacturing process. On first arrival at the processing plant, the potatoes are examined and tasted for quality and some are punched with holes in their cores for tracking. Green edges (which are apparently poisonous) and blemishes are discarded as defective product and if the whole batch of such unacceptable ones exceeds a given allowance, then all the current supply is rejected. First-stage quality control is vital for successful batch production. A gently vibrating conveyor belt takes the potatoes to a vertical helical screw conveyor which allows stones to fall to the bottom while the good product is conveyed upwards to the automatic peeling machine. Washing with cold water then follows. Next comes a revolving impaler/press that cuts the potatoes into thin slices. These slices fall into a second cold water washer that removes the starch released by the cutting process. All the finishing processes were then described in detail including the actual frying, flavouring and packaging. Frank was thinking about the knitwear warehouse down the Common Road, vacated by the Co-operative Wholesale Society and was wondering if any automatic potato peelers had found their way over from America.

*

As Frank walked to his builder's yard the little demons clinging to his back were banging his head with rubber hammers and making his eyes smart with their poking fingers. The celebration of his twenty-first birthday with his pals at the club had gone on well into the night and had got deep and serious after news came through on the wires that something dramatic had occurred on Wall Street. There was talk of a crash and millions of dollars being wiped off the value of shares and bonds so fast that hardly anyone had time to sell out. Those that had to, to meet commitment calls, had been cleaned out. Discussing the possible causes of the market collapse and trying to assess the consequences over here had kept most of the business men drinking well into the small hours. If his head was anything to go by, Black Tuesday, as it had already been dubbed, would be followed by Black Coffee Wednesday.

Frank had come to realise that a man, such as himself, might well have the get-up-and-go spirit to make things happen and so set him apart from others but that also needed a fair slice of luck. And how was his luck playing out on the biggest decision he had taken so far? Well, he reckoned he was one up. Just seven days ago, Mrs Lazenby had made the final stage payment. But as for his second venture, he knew he had taken one hell of a risk and had done so before news of the USA crash came through. He had used most of his savings to secure the lease on the warehouse, paid Sid for his first crop of potatoes (which had been in store for a month without the refrigeration they were supposed to have) and put the deposit down and signed the hire-purchase agreement on the automatic peeling machine. He was stretched and how! He had been to the lecture given by the regional president of the Chamber of Commerce, who gave a brief outline of the then current situation.

The chief economist of the National Chamber had predicted that if the past was anything to go by, the Americans would call in their loans to other countries and put up customs barriers to stop imports. If so, the depression would be exported to Europe. It was conceivable that up to 25% of the entire working population of Britain could find themselves out of work (2.5 million). Not that this would necessarily be bad for everyone. In the south-east of England, for example, new light industries were being developed such as electrical goods and chemicals and for those in work, benefits would be felt from lower prices. But the businessmen of the North and the Midlands should not kid themselves, this was the patch of heavy industry. Of coal, iron and steel. Where was the modernisation following the Great War? It hadn't happened. There was another factor; possibly just as important. This minority Labour government, propped up by the Liberals, would almost certainly not have a clue how to tackle the inevitable loss of revenue that occurs when unemployment soars. Two things happen simultaneously. The level of income tax collected from wages drops and yet expenditure on welfare benefits is bound to increase. Now, supposing the government increases taxes and cuts unemployment pay in an effort to assuage its income shortfall problem. The net effect, Gentlemen, would be to reduce the overall amount of money people have to spend. A vicious circle will have set in. There is another temptation that the government is unlikely to resist. They might impose higher and new import duties, in a misguided attempt to protect the home trade. In fact, history tells us that this will have the opposite effect. For example, with less materials coming into the country, what need is there for our ships and our railways to get the goods to market? Finally, if they bring in a means test, then God help us all.

Frank, like the rest of them in the Chamber and in the Great Sutton Conservative Club had no idea if this academic chap was right about what the future held for their businesses. Each man would have to make up his own mind and take whatever steps he felt necessary. And, for the first time, that is what made him think as a real businessman must think. He was in this hook, line and sinker. Think, think. He needed lots of factory workers. They will have to receive the rate of pay he can afford and they will have to be flexible in the shifts he puts on – part-time working will be inevitable. Sid and his farming neighbours will come to realise that hard times are coming and to offload their entire harvest in one go at a guaranteed price will be a godsend. Potatoes, in any form, are a staple food (everyone remembers the Irish famine). In difficult times, will people give up their little luxuries such as a salty snack? Sod it. He was pressing on with this plan.

When he got to the yard there was an envelope on his desk. Not a formal business one but an embossed Basildon Bond pure white envelope. The single sheet of paper inside had a printed letterhead *The Lazenby's, Beech House, Great Sutton Lawn. Below, and handwritten in blue ink he read,*

31st October 1929.

Dear Frankie,
I have received some very bad news from my husband. I need to see you.
Yours, Mrs Lazenby.

TEN

It was three weeks after they met in the Ex-Servicemen's Club that the letter arrived from Billy. It was a long rambling letter; pages and pages of it. Pithy it was not (Eugene allowed himself a smile). Like himself, Billy's formal education had been limited and when just fourteen years and one week old, he was a junior storeman in the pencil factory in Kendal. But, the word education needs defining. A twenty-two year old disembarking at Portsmouth is highly educated. Educated in life, in death, in suffering and most of all in the placement of value. Not least in relative value. If he never took an employed job again, or if he did but it was lowly paid, he would nevertheless be the richest man on earth. He would be alive, not a half-buried corpse. He would be free to roam and think, not shackled, beaten and humiliated.

Billy's philosophy on life (post the Burma years) was the gist of the first few pages. He was trying to say to his old buddy that, during their previous get-togethers over the years, they had talked of how life had treated each of them, what they were doing at the time and why, etc, etc. But the revelation about Chit had affected him profoundly. He was trying to express in words his understanding of the other old man's heartache. He had wanted to include Eugene in the reunions but knowing of his old mate's business success back in Huthwaite, his busy life, his happy marriage and tight-knit family, things drifted.

Even if they had been prepared to take him on, Billy had

no intention of returning to the factory. He needed space, open air, vistas like those from the DC3 over the steaming jungle. It was while striding over High Borrans looking down on Windermere that the idea hit him. He would contact as many lads as he could, those he had been with after Eugene went north to Mandalay, and organise an annual get- together in Kendal. His notes of their experience would be the fulcrum for appreciating the life they had now and for never forgetting those less fortunate. One of the blokes became a well-known poet and last time they all met he handed over a poem composed especially for them. Billy copied it for the letter:

From his airless compartment of sweat
A collection of cheeps can be heard.

It's a tumble of cries that is yet
A sweet tune, unmistakably bird.

When he opens the door to outside
He is bathed by the new and cool breeze.
And he sucks in the air deep and wide
Sweet relief from the night of unease.

While the breeze and the birds satisfy
At one level, the need is still there
For a sign, for a hint, of the why
Is his life still so full of despair.

But the song dies away and the air
Starts to bake; daily life carries on
With canned music, aromas of fare.
Mood abandoned, depression forgone.

Ben Banes (a sergeant at the time) hadn't made the reunion but it had been his birthday on the day the invasion of Singapore began. He recalled how his regiment, The Cambridgeshires, never retreated whilst under attack and they were all astonished when the order came to surrender. They felt they had been holding their own and had no thoughts of throwing in the towel. It was reckoned that a quarter of the British soldiers taken prisoner in Singapore did not survive their captivity and some 50,000 Chinese residents of the Island were massacred by Japanese soldiers after the surrender. The exercise became known as *sook ching*, meaning *the wipe out*.

Before he died, Flt Lt Leslie Paine used to bring his medals to each reunion. Medals awarded to him for saving his Dakota after it flipped during a severe monsoon in Rangoon. Miraculously, he managed to right the plane before successfully completing his mission to drop supplies to the 14th Army.

Henry McTavish, then a young army lieutenant, who had recently died only a few months short of what would have been his 100th birthday had, even when meeting up with old colleagues, extreme difficulty discussing his experiences. He used to say that, once he arrived back home, talking to people proved too difficult. That included his wife who had always been very supportive. "She simply couldn't understand and I often felt she wondered if I was making some of it up – I learnt to keep quiet."

But his story did come out. He arrived in Singapore on 6th February 1942, two days before the Japanese invasion. He and the other soldiers hadn't even unpacked their kit bags when it became obvious that the task of holding the Island was futile. The battalion was ordered to surrender without a shot being fired. "Japanese tactical brilliance and British incompetence – a lethal combination."

The reign of terror started immediately. British and Australian soldiers were herded into makeshift camps, caned, berated and shot. Some were decapitated, others bayonetted. Henry was forced to lead a team that cleaned up the Alexandra Military Hospital where staff and patients alike, including several actually undergoing surgery, were bayonetted to death. His next job was in a group told to build a wall around the Kempeitai, the Japanese secret police. "Each day was made unbearable by the screams of those being tortured inside."

Six months later, some 60,000 survivors were crowded into railway cars and moved north to Siam (modern day Thailand). He used to say, "The books written about the death railway will tell you the rest. Is it not extraordinary that the 45,000 survivors of the Burma Railway were not honoured, or even acknowledged after their eventual release? After I disembarked in Liverpool in October 1945 I was left to get on with my life as best I could. There was no welcoming band, no advisers, no nothing. Even our wives were asked to stay away. And do you know, compensation was not offered by Japan until millennium year, 2000, and of course by then most of the poor sods had died either of their injuries or just old age."

Group Captain Peter Knowles was part of No 134 Squadron in Burma and in December 1943 was operational on the Arakan front flying sorties against Japanese positions. His Hurricane escorted Dakota transport aircraft supplying the 14th Army. He told the story of his plane, in February 1944, diving on and killing a Japanese "Oscar" aircraft. "It started smoking and crashed in the jungle". Later, and by then equipped with the American built P-47 Thunderbolt, he was again supporting the 14th Army as it advanced on Rangoon.

Billy ended his long letter by pointing out to Eugene the irony, given all that has happened since, of the Soviet Union staying neutral throughout the horrors committed by the Japanese until their surrender on September 2, 1945 and only declaring war on Japan and invading Manchukuo after the United States had dropped the first atomic bomb. Like the Americans coming to the aid of Europe, what a difference it might have made if, much earlier, the Russians had had the intent and the forces to march east as well as west.

Eugene thought long and hard on the contents of Billy's letter. He had read it over and over. He started to think that the so-called reunions had not actually occurred. Some of the men mentioned would have been ten or more years older than Billy and himself. How did he contact them? How did they get to Kendal? Another thing, why had he not been invited? The explanation at the start of the letter hardly held water; they had met up several times over the years. His supposedly busy life hadn't stopped them getting together, so why not for the Old Colleagues Club? No; more likely the wartime stories were gleaned from obituaries which started to appear in the daily papers as the years passed and as the various anniversaries of the events and atrocities occurred. Still roaming those mountains above Windermere after his lifetime as a shepherd, Billy's mind could have wandered with his boots. He could have created meetings that had not existed, but he wished they had. He could have wanted to meet the Bens, Leslies, Henrys and Peters. But he never did. Or, up in his lofty world where unseen things may soar, perhaps he did.

It was only after Pearl left that Eugene remembered where he had put Billy's letter. It was in the Burma folder he had handed to her.

★

Dot was not herself. It hadn't affected their weekend away or the enjoyment of the two walks, but still she was not the confident, giggling, bubbly girl he had married three years earlier. He had managed to book one of the upstairs courtyard rooms at the Castle Hotel in Castleton where they now preferred to stay on these Derbyshire High Peak bike trips. It wasn't as posh as the honeymoon hotel in Hathersage but the buzz from fellow riders, walkers and climbers made for a more relaxed stay even though there was no head waiter to make fun of, only oodles of staff dashing to and fro serving the speciality pies and fine Robinson's ales. On the Saturday they had walked up the steep path to Hollins' Cross and turned left to follow the high ridge to Mam Tor, before descending past the entrance to the Blue John Mine. It was in the shop guarding the entrance that Eugene bought her a banded purple, blue and white fluorspar bracelet. Dot had chosen it herself and always referred to it in later life as her "Blue John special." Yet, even on the descent past the Treak Cliff Cavern, with the jewel safely stowed in her rucksack, there was something not quite right.

What really surprised Eugene, in fact what was starting to upset him, was that the business was flourishing and until recently Dot had been nothing short of ecstatic. Not only had they opened their second supermarket in bustling Chesterfield, but Eve had taken charge of it. This meant that with Eugene now managing the Huthwaite original store, his Dot could concentrate on the office side and, in effect, return to the paperwork she had been trained to handle at the Co-op factory. Furthermore, Paul had researched the newly arrived electronic point-of-sale machines, replacing the old mechanical tills, so the profit margin on groups of sale lines could be identified and the stock balance reduced instantly on making a sale. So good was Dot proving to be at interpreting this sales analysis that the overall margin on all sales was gradually creeping up. With Paul getting more and more involved on the practical side of things, their family business seemed all set for rapid and successful expansion.

It was when they closed on the Thursday after the weekend away that she broke her news to him. Almost certainly, they would never have children. She had not had a proper period for over six months and whilst at first she had assumed it was because she was pregnant, she now knew the truth. She had kept it from him until the test results confirmed what Dr Graham had suspected. Cysts had developed in her ovaries and whilst, in themselves, these cysts are harmless, it had been explained to her that such things are underdeveloped sacs in which eggs develop. Because they are unable to release an egg, this in turn means that ovulation doesn't take place. The doctor had asked if she was an only child and, on confirmation, said that probably explained how the problem had arisen since the condition often runs in families. Just as her mother only had one child, so it was possible, but unlikely, that she might get pregnant. She told Eugene she might as well get all the bad news out of the way, this condition can lead to complications in later life: the most likely being type 2 diabetes.

So now Eugene understood, and as he held his sobbing Dot, so he felt himself sinking.

★

Pearl's last two years at Roedean were an emotional rollercoaster. She missed her mummy so terribly much. All through her teenage years, the two had been more like sisters than mother and daughter. Unlike most of her friends, Pearl had not gone through a rebellious phase. She had played tennis with her mummy, they had gone horse-riding together and, at every opportunity, had gone up to town for the fashion shows and to check on the latest that Oxford Street had to offer. Now she was alone and by inclination had stopped going to church. God had deserted her mummy and that meant her too. It was all too awful and there was worse to come. In 1990, just one year after the accident, Daddy, newly promoted to Brigadier, was posted to the Middle East as part of the British response to the invasion of Kuwait by Iraq. That meant no weekends back home and no visits. He had resisted on compassionate grounds but to no avail and Pearl's loneliness was profound.

People tackle grief in different ways. The extremes vary in degree from going off the rails to losing oneself in work. In Pearl's case it was the latter. A combination of the character-building ethos of Roedean and climbing out of the abyss of loss by dedicated study, put her on the road to a different degree. She was awarded a place at Somerville College, Oxford to read English. In one of his last despatches before completing the assignment on the Bosnian front, Daddy had written that his attendance at her graduation ceremony in the autumn of 1995, was the happiest day of his life. He had ended his letter by saying that it was such a shame that her granddaddy was not there to see her receive the 2.1 degree. The Group Captain had passed away the year before, three days after his 77th birthday.

The five years leading up to the millennium left an indelible mark on Pearl's memory. She and Daddy were reunited and sharing his grace-and-favour apartment overlooking the Thames. He was now seconded to the Foreign Office and she was a sub-editor on the Financial Times. Pearl acted as her daddy's escort at the high-ranking military functions he attended and together they would go to first-nights on the

South Bank. On Sundays, if the weather was fine, they drove down to Brighton in his Jaguar XJS R 6 4.0 and after parking somewhere near the Royal Pavilion, walked westward on the promenade as far as Shoreham-By-Sea. They usually took lunch in a little seafood place just off the front. Poor weather would find the pair back at the Imperial War Museum ("coals to Newcastle", he would say) before eating at one of their favourite haunts in Soho or holding off until the inevitable "Darling, we'll have a spot of dinner at the club."

It was that one incident that took Pearl aback. It stuck in her mind because of the surprise – almost shock. In the *Flying Mackerel* he had reached for his glass of Chablis for the ceremonial "Bottoms up Darling" when that resolutely steady right hand jerked and knocked the glass over. There had been a bit of fuss at the table what with the mopping up and the waiter making too much of bringing a fresh napkin; not helped by some jumped-up clown of a buffoon staring at Daddy with eyes which implied *you shouldn't be in a nice place like this if you cannot hold your drink.* Fact was he never drank too much and in any case, this was the first drink of the day. Her one slight irritation was his rigidity in all physical movements and always doing exactly the right things in the right way. But, if the officer cadet training at Sandhurst was to blame for that, so it was to be thanked for his outstanding career thereafter. Nothing is perfect, of course it isn't. Let's forget it.

A few weeks later, the walk back from Shoreham was interrupted when he inexplicably missed a step when descending to the final stage of Brighton promenade. The stumble was corrected quickly and nothing was said but Pearl was, as with the wine glass, taken aback. Daddy never slipped, never. Months passed, spring turned to summer and she had long since put the two little accidents behind her. Then, and in the same week, a red light started to flash in Pearl's head. She had returned from One Southwark Bridge after an evening shift and casually thrown her coat on the settee and kicked off her shoes, when he shouted at her.

'Hang that coat up and put the damn shoes in the rack where they belong!'

Not once in her twenty-eight years had Daddy shouted at her and instantly she burst into tears. He apologised saying he had no idea what came over him and that it would not happen again, but the final clincher for Pearl was what happened after breakfast the next morning. There were never enough pots to bother with the dishwasher, so he hand-washed them in the sink. As she was about to leave, an extraordinary thing occurred. As she started the walk to the office, her first reaction was that she was mistaken. But then, how could she have been? He had filled the bowl with warm water as usual and added the washing-up liquid but, and yes she was absolutely sure, he started putting the plates away whilst they were still in the after-breakfast state. That is to say, without washing them up.

Even before checking her email inbox, Pearl started her research. It took less than ten minutes. She was certain. Daddy's symptoms were of Huntington's disease.

★

Mrs Lazenby lay on her back with her legs open and asked Frank to put his right hand between her legs so that his thumb just touched her pubic hair. He was not to move that hand until she said so. It had been a long time and she wanted the feeling to develop slowly; he would know when the time was right by seeing her moisture. She hated the word sex, which was all the rage now, she loved her Frankie who was all man, and she was going to teach him how to love her properly. Her, a real woman. A woman who had longed for him since the project started. Actually, he was why it had started. It had been so long since a man had touched her. Her voice was becoming deeper in tone, her cheeks rosier and he noticed her nipples were erect. She had been about to join her husband in New York but of course that wouldn't happen now. He couldn't even afford to send her the tickets and, instead, was stuck on The Exchange desperately trying to get back into the market. She was saying something else but the words just seemed to get sucked back into her long, slim neck. All that came out was a kind of gurgling sound.

Frank wasn't used to taking orders. He was the one who decided what to do and he knew that she knew that. He did leave his hand where she wanted it to be but drew his thumb slowly up and down her lower lips and as he bent over to lick her left nipple, she started to groan with a deep throaty sound he had never heard before. Her abdomen and pelvis were suddenly thrust upwards towards him as she craved his erection.

'Oh, for Christ's sake Frankie, make this stallion mount his mare, split her in half, do it, do it. Don't stop, yes, yes – oh God Frankie, oh God. I knew you'd do it for me, I knew, I knew, I knew.'

It was three-thirty in the morning when he finally got home. He had walked for once. He just had to. Although he had read about it, he did not believe it; romantic twaddle. He wouldn't wobble on rubbery legs; it could not possibly be that being so physically exhausted he could scarcely think never mind put one foot in front of the other. But he did remember the champagne and what she did with it and he did remember her animal smell and her sheer energy. What a woman. She had blown his mind and blown everything else as well. He had thought business was a buzz. Mrs Lazenby was a super-buzz. What had he done to get into this? Frankie was a lucky boy. A super stallion lucky boy.

In between their engagements, Frank and Mrs Lazenby did some talking, not much, but some. He about making crisps and she about selling them. She knew about selling; hadn't she sold a New York Stock Exchange proposition to her husband? Impressed by Frank's body, impressed by his mind. That seemed to be the message even if, on occasion, the former was prone to overrule the latter at the most unexpected times and in the most unexpected places. The idea of manufacturing crisps was brilliant and his timing was spot on. And from where, she wondered, had come the brand name *Everest* and the key advertising phrase *For The Peak Of Perfection*? So clever. My beautiful stallion Frankie. But she would take it from here. He was going to make oodles of money, enough to buy one of these grand houses on the posh side of *The Lawn*. Perhaps even this one!

★

It might be a male-members only club but that didn't stop the gossip. It was not a female prerogative. When a young and thrusting member starts to miss appointments, people talk. If it was a one-off appointment that could not be met, then that was quite understandable. Obviously something more important took precedence. They all knew that. But with Frank it was different. He had missed a morning committee meeting, an early evening snooker match in the knock-out tournament, and now he had backed out, at the last minute, from a day trip to the races.

Sam Turner had a wholesale greengrocery business. Three days a week he left Great Sutton at four-thirty in the morning for the market in Nottingham. On two of those mornings last week, he had spotted young Frank Whitby leaving a certain house on the far side of *The Lawn*. That did it. They all knew who lived at that house.

Frank assumed that the nudges, winks and little asides he was now getting "Knock this one back Frank, it'll help keep your strength up," would result in him being excluded from the card and domino tables and even lead to him being blackballed at the next committee election. Strangely, the opposite was happening. He had heard the men talk about the change of atmosphere when matron did her rounds at the General Hospital. A sort of quiet deferential respect, with those otherwise in authority drifting into the background as the dominant character appeared. Obviously, it wasn't really like that when he now walked into the big room of the Conservative Club. And yet, somehow, it was. Men he barely knew started sounding him out on one subject or another. The real state of America was suddenly a favourite topic.

It was the same Sam Turner who made the first move. He knew Frank's reputation for discretion.

'Come along to a bit of a bash at my place. It's to celebrate a piece of tasty business I have pulled off against all the odds. Only a few of the chaps know but I have offloaded a whole ship full of grapefruit in one go and at a bloody good price."

'What?'

'Not being in my trade Frank, you wouldn't know but grapefruit were first bred in Barbados in the 18th century and, as they are now in season and as the upper-crust have started eating them for breakfast, I took an enormous risk and commissioned a whole shipment from my import agent.

We're having a party because up until last week, I honestly thought I was wiped out.'

'What?'

'You'll have read that the dock workers in Southampton have gone on strike? Well, after just five days or so stuck in that dock my few hundred thousand grapefruit would have rotted and I would have gone bust. So listen to this one Frank. My agent found a wholesaler in Rotterdam and, God knows how, he got the ship diverted in time, so it chugged its merry way up the Channel, over the North Sea and, would you believe it, grapefruit fetch more on the continent than they do here; not that I knew that when this caper all started. Keep it quiet. It's just among us lads, but Frank, I am rich, bloody rich – are we going to have a night of it, or what?'

And that wasn't all. Over a few drinks sitting together at the far end of the bar, Sam was saying that there would be a few other chaps at the party who Frank would not have met, mainly because they were not members here (by the way, there would be wives and girlfriends there and did he want to bring anyone along?)

'Make a few notes Frank and I will introduce you on the night before they are all plastered. Number one is Roger Slaney. If you are staying in property development as well as the factory you have just got hold of, then he is your passport. Don't be a shrinking violet with him Frank, he likes to see confidence; a touch of arrogance won't go amiss. Mr Slaney is a district councillor – more relevant is that he's chairman of the planning committee. He stands as an Independent and that's why you won't find him in here. I heard you were thinking of building some proper butchery sheds on your dad's yard, well that idea is a good starter for you. Another thing, I have heard on the grapevine (he chuckled) that if and when this bloody depression is over, the boys on high have the idea of throwing up thousands of what will be called Council Houses. They will be financed by the local authority and rented out to get rid of the slums. You see Frank, these new houses will have a standard design but use proper materials so anyone who can get a foot on that ladder is going to rise quickly; get my drift. For Christ's sake don't mention that rumour to Slaney but make damn sure he remembers your face!

'There's another bloke in my circle who again you won't see in here simply because he is red-hot labour. By the way, if you do chat to him, make sure you praise the working man and say how the bosses must put up wages once the jobs return. Like me, he's in wholesaling. His lines are biscuits, sweets and fags and he is as crafty as a cartload of monkeys. Between you and me, before each Budget he holds back his smokes and then stocks up the shops at the higher price – plus a bit for his trouble. Believe me, his network around these parts is enormous. I've got plenty of customers but he must have twice as many drop-offs as me.

'Thing is Frank, if what they say about you going into crisps is true, cultivate Harry Carter. Sod the political stuff, if he can't get your crisps out, no-one can!'

★

After the three children had gone to bed, Mary and Farmer George sat in the front room of Red Roof Farm to ponder on the day's events.

George was saying that there was nothing quite like a funeral to pull you up short, to make you think about death and for that matter life itself. At least they were happy and pretty much self-sufficient. They might not have much compared to the Big House but provided he could keep up the mortgage payments to the National Westminster Bank, they did have their own place and land now the tenancy had been bought out and most important of all they had each other and the rascals upstairs. He was saying that there seems to be a succession of funerals on her side. "Must be, what, four years since Stan was killed, (wasn't Eve in a state again today?) and six since James committed suicide: now Willy's gone. And isn't it amazing that your dad still hangs on and your mam is still keeping that house and the shop in one piece? Should have been that bugger Harold in the box today. Noticed he never lifted a finger again. Snivelling, idle little sod.

'Mary, don't you think it's amazing that after that huge family, the next generation have, so far at any rate, had so few children? If it isn't too upsetting, take me through how things stand now".

'Well George, it really is so sad about Willy. He was such a nice chap and so good with the children on the few occasions we went back. They still make those rabbit things out of folded handkerchiefs just as he showed them and it was through him they started the paper folding and did those magic tricks. Poor Willy – he was only forty-nine and I suppose the shop will close now without him. You are right about the lack of children. He was the third born and none of the eldest four of our family have had any. Joseph seems to have been quite happy with his books and his teaching, Jack – well Jack, none of us even knows where he is – he wasn't there again today. The fourth, Frank, well it's a mystery why he hasn't fathered any. That Betty is as lively as they come and back in the thirties he was rumoured to have a girl-friend, although from what I gathered from Willy, she was not so much a girl as an older woman. I went through all this with Eugene this afternoon and he was trying to take some notes – he said he keeps some sort of file of events, can't imagine what for.

'So we come to Alice who only had Paul and then none again with James, although I suppose there might have been after that woman he got tangled up with. Poor George was killed when so young and I suppose after all these years we've tended to forget about the baby. Apparently as he boarded the train and handed their little bundle back to Daisy, his wife, the very last words he spoke were "Look after our little pet". And that is what Daisy christened her. Like so many war widows, poor Daisy couldn't stand being at home without George and so she applied for, and got, her emigration papers for Australia. No-one could blame her for not keeping in touch, in her circumstances I doubt if I would have done. I was only thinking the other day that baby Pet will be about sixteen years old now and probably a typical down-under blonde beauty being chased on some beach by a bronze hulk of an Ausie boy. How the lives of her and me will have been so different. Her George never to return and my George who never leaves my side – except to milk the cows that is (not for the first time that day, Farmer George held his wife while she sobbed quietly. Not this time sitting in the front pew of St Peter & St Pauls' church but in the front room of Red Roof Farm; after a little break Mary continued her recollection). Rob seems to have been too busy building his business to care about a family.

'And that George gets us to our three. I know Molly and her Jack are trying but nothing has happened so far. Harold, as you say spells trouble. Who would have him? Even if he wasn't too mean to treat any likely lass. The last two, well Eve couldn't have had children anyway. As a child she was very ill and I've heard Mam say she was lucky to be alive. We were never told what the problem was but they took away whatever she needed to get caught. Thank God Stan never knew that. Last, our Eugene. Mystery there too. He and his Dot seem well suited but it's now three years since the wedding and no show yet. So as at today, and from all thirteen of us, there are just five children and we have three of them!'

'Mary, when you put it like that – what a saga. I was one of seven and have enough trouble keeping tabs on what is going on with our lot. It has been such a sad day for you and all the Whitbys. Let's lighten things up; what about making our personal contribution to this second generation up to four?

ELEVEN

It was 8.35 am on Monday May 7, 1956 and Dorothy called out from the office, 'Eugene, there's a man on the 'phone wanting to speak to you. He won't give his name and he sounds a long way off. Says it's personal and urgent. Insists on you taking his call. Sorry, I will take over from you.'

'Damn, I'm just setting up this till. Ok will come and grab it, expect it's another rep.'

'Hello, what do you want at this early hour and make it snappy.'

'Am I speaking to Mr Eugene Whitby?'

'Yes.'

'Mr Whitby, my name is Clarence and I want to know where your brother Jack is and don't say you have no idea because he left here ten days ago to see you about some family business or other. I am his friend, his very best friend. He promised to call me every day and hasn't done so. I'm worried sick. What's going on?'

'Listen Clarence, or whatever your name is, I haven't the bloody time for your messing about, we have a shop full of customers here. How the hell would I know where Jack is? None of the family has heard from him in years. He left from around here years ago and just disappeared. Anyway, how would he know my address and how have you got this 'phone number?'

'Another member of our group comes from your neck of

the woods and he gets the Free Press sent to him. It didn't take Jack long to work out it was your *New Concept Supermarket* that was advertised and if you don't want 'phone calls then why put your number in the advertisement? I can tell you this; Jack is damn near broke and he reckons there's money in the family and some of it ought to have come his way.'

★

At around 6.45 pm on Thursday May 10, as was their custom, Dorothy and Eugene sat in the café built into the corner of the supermarket with a pot of tea and to reward themselves with whatever cake was left over. This evening they were lucky.

'We'd better polish off this strawberry and walnut cream cake Dot, won't last till tomorrow.'

They smiled knowingly at each other. The routine was to tot up the till-rolls and for Dot to enter the day's takings in her sales book. She had devised a system whereby that figure could be compared with both the total of the previous day and the same day of the previous week. It was her flash report on how we are doing (Dorothy was rather proud of her invented phrase). It was because the figures were good and she could tell that her Eugy was happy with the way things were going, that Dorothy reached for his hand and started the little speech she had been rehearsing in her head all day.

He, like her, must have been wondering what that strange phone call early last Monday morning was all about. Was he a crank? Did he really know the older brother Jack? Might he come back with some sort of blackmail threat? No, she wasn't being over dramatic; she was frightened. Had Eugy picked up on that sort of lisp in his voice; that reference to friend and our group. Of course he must have, her Eugy was as worldly

153

as anyone. She pleaded with him not to be mad with her but she had spoken to her dad, having made up a cock-and-bull story about some flashily dressed effeminate bloke coming into the shop and asking for a brand of cigarettes no-one had ever heard of.

'I asked Dad if, from a strictly legal standpoint, we would have been in order to serve him had we stocked what he wanted or would we have been within our rights to refuse on the grounds we did not want his sort in the shop. As I anticipated, he had a good laugh at my expense saying he thought it unlikely the man would be active in the store. But you see Eugy, that gave me the chance to find out what I (we) really need to know. I asked him straight out what the legal situation is with men who seem to be of that sort. Please don't look at me like that, I have been thinking about that phone call at lot this week and it bothers me.

'Last night my dad handed me this note that he had his secretary type out. Read it in full if you like, but the legal background note refers to that case two years ago when Alan Turing, the cryptographer who helped to break the German Enigma Code, was victimised for his homosexuality. He was charged with gross indecency and had to choose between prison or hormone treatment. He lost his job and his death was treated as suicide. Apparently, this and other cases led the government to set up a Departmental Committee under Sir John Wolfenden. My dad says that the legal profession expect the findings to argue that homosexual behaviour between consenting adults in private should no longer be a criminal offence. But the point Eugy is that the report is not expected to be published until later this year and even if it does recommend change, it is likely to take years to come into effect.'

Eugene let go of Dorothy's hand and stood up. He was trying desperately to keep his temper but could feel his face becoming flushed and in a voice that ought to have been steadier than it was he said,

'Dot, I just hope your dad hasn't seen through the real reason for putting you wise on the homo thing and that he doesn't pick up on the innuendo that there is a practising homosexual within our circle of contacts. And, now I think about it, if he or anyone else for that matter suggests or even hints that a brother of mine is that way inclined, then I tell you now, I'll be bloody furious – and that's swearing. Look Dot, act your age. If that clown thinks he knows my brother Jack, who could have died years ago for all I know or care for that matter, then why, oh why, has this elusive man not turned up here asking for whatever he thinks he wants? Come on, we'll lock up and go home, have some supper and I'll take you to bed. If I can't make you forget the whole sorry incident in the time it takes you to get your knickers off, then my name is not Eugene Whitby. Silly girl, come here, let me have a little feel before we leave.'

★

On Saturday, May 12, the fingers of the big clock on the wall pointed to 3.20 pm when Sarah, one of the shelf-stackers, came into the office with an envelope.

'Mr Whitby, a lad has just given me this to hand to you.'

Written on the envelope in black ink was: "Eugy boy – personal." Eugene knew the handwriting. Using his silver paper knife (a birthday present from Paul) he slit open the envelope, pulled out a single sheet of writing paper and read:

The Big House, Huthwaite.
May 12, 1956

Eugy boy,
In the interests of brotherly love, I thought it only right to warn you
that our Jack turned up out of the blue a couple of weeks ago. Said
he had poked his head into your shop but as it was heaving with
customers, decided instead to pay us a visit here. I refused to let him
upstairs, just the sight of him would have polished off the old man.
Mam, of course, welcomed him like the long-lost son he was and I
asked her if she normally hugged and shed a few tears over an old and
scruffy black sheep. He started to come over as the big brother who
had missed out and wanted his share of whatever we had. I took a
knife out of the kitchen drawer and faced him up. Like all bullies, he
soon backed off and started whining about his lost life or something
similarly stupid. I told him to look at what was left in the Big House,
bloody nothing. No butchery and since last year, after our Willy died,
no damn shop either. I told him in no uncertain terms to sod off back
to wherever he had come from. I said there was only three of the tribe
who had got anything and if he thought he could get any dosh from
smart-arse Eugy boy or spivvy Frank, he had better think again. As
for Rob, that blood-sucker who left us all in the shit, well, I gave him
the address and more or less bundled him out. I wasn't even going to
bother letting you know he was around but then, with you having
all that stock and a beautiful wife who we wouldn't want harming, I
thought better of it. Eugy boy, I know we haven't always seen eye-to-
eye but take a tip from me – watch your back.
Harold.

Eugene probably wouldn't have shown Dorothy the letter but
since Sarah had already told her that one had arrived by hand,
he had no choice. She read Harold's letter slowly, carefully
and having reached the end, started all over again.

'Eugy darling, you ought to keep this so put it in your folder. Call it woman's intuition if you like but I smell trouble. He will have made a copy for himself and who knows what mischief he might be planning for the future. I realise now I was being silly over the homosexual thing and was putting two and two together and making twenty-two, but obviously that Clarence chap was telling the truth and since he hasn't 'phoned again, maybe your Jack has gone back to him. But can we be sure? Eugy darling, I really am quite frightened. Why don't you go over and talk to Harold and the two of you go and see Rob. Sort something out even if it does cost us a bit. Nip it all in the bud.'

Eugene continued to stand by his desk leaning slightly forward with his arms straight and the palms of his hands flat to the desk top. He looked at his lovely young wife and nodded his head slowly as if indicating he both understood how she felt and agreed with her logic. What Dorothy did not read in his countenance was the attention he had to pay to a little voice speaking deep in his head and saying: *who really is this silly, stupid woman I married who sees practising homosexuals performing their criminal acts behind our shelves, who imagines an old tramp coming at me hatchet in hand and who would ravish her if only he wasn't a pouftah? She can't even give me a son. Would I want one with her anyway? Christ, this thing called sex drive has a lot to answer for. Oh Chit, my beautiful Chit, please come and save me from this nightmare.*

Eugene reached over the desk and took her two hands in his.

'Yes darling, I will give it some thought, you are probably right as usual, all just a storm in a teacup I expect.'

★

The police house was just outside the village on the main road from Morston to Thansley. Sergeant Attenborough was not best pleased. Behind locked doors he had been in the Red Lion drinking and talking with the locals well into the small hours and now at a godforsaken time of 6.10 am on this Wednesday morning May 16th someone was knocking five bells out of the front door. It was Nora. He knew perfectly well who Nora was. He made it his business to know everyone living on his patch. He also had a good idea why she was in this state. She was only half dressed, still had her pink coloured slippers on and her red mop of hair was all over the place. Still in his dark blue dressing gown and feeling like death warmed up, he placed a hand on her shoulder and led her gently into the kitchen,

'Nora, just sit down in that chair and take a few deep breaths, try to calm down while I make us both a pot of tea. No need to rush, just collect your thoughts and over a cuppa you can tell me all about it and I'll take a few notes.'

Nora's story (which he would later paraphrase at the inquest) was that she and Rob Whitby had been courting for over three years, more or less since he took over the butcher's shop. They planned to marry next year. Because he spent long hours building up his business and she had two jobs, one serving in the local Co-op and the other behind the bar at the Travellers Rest, they were not able to be together very often but he always took her out somewhere on a Saturday night. But not last Saturday. She was ready for the dance by 8pm as they had arranged but he didn't show up. She had been mad. She was not used to being stood up. She stayed in and washed her hair and on Sunday (just to show him she didn't care) went with Alma on the Mystery Bus Trip before her evening shift at the pub. But then, as the Sergeant would know, the butchers' shop didn't open on Mondays. That made her upset thinking he had gone off somewhere without telling her, but then she knew trade on any Monday was poor. Of course, that was the answer, he had gone to Mansfield to buy her an engagement ring. By Tuesday everything would be back to normal. Except it wasn't and the shop was still closed and several in the village had seen the wholesaler's delivery van driver knocking on the door and eventually go away. Rob would never not open his shop for two days running and never not contact her. Last night was the worst of her life. Sorry about the state she was in. She hadn't slept a wink. She pleaded with Sergeant Attenborough to find her boyfriend.

The policeman finished making his notes.

'Nora, we'll have some breakfast together, then I'll get onto it. Work has probably got him down, it does that to all of us sooner or later. He'll have gone off for a break. Don't you worry, we will find him. And Nora, when we do, he will have me to answer to – can't have a pretty girl like you upset. I'm on the lookout for a new girlfriend you know.'

★

Farmer George and May had a routine. It had started as soon as they were married and aside from when she was heavily pregnant or on her periods, it had continued ever since. On Sundays, and this June 3rd was no different, after the roast lunch, they went to bed. It worked well because Sunday was the day of rest on which only essential farm work was done. When each of the three children were at the baby-to-toddler stage, they were having their afternoon nap and as they grew older were either out playing or with their school friends. The seventeen years of marriage had not dented their need for each other and despite his little jokes about dominating the Whitby daughters' breeding programme, the family size was well under control. George had his three sources. First and easiest was Randall the Barber with his left-hand bottom drawer and "something for the weekend sir?" Second was the medical shop on Clumber Street in Mansfield, which he had to visit periodically to replace his surgical bel. He needed it to control the hernia sustained as a young man straining to spread muck from the cart in winter. Finally, and more latterly, was the plain envelope supplier who advertised discreetly in each week's Derbyshire Times.

George came downstairs at just after four o'clock and pulled on his working boots and whistled Darkie from his kennel. He crossed the stackyard on what was another cool and dull day to start his chores. The cows' mangers had to be filled with the turnips he had ground that morning. He fetched more from the pit and, having thrown them into the grinder, did the same for tomorrow morning's feed. He added a little flaked maize to each manger to balance the diet and finally one spoon of black treacle from the drum. With Darkie at his side, he set off.

The season was late. February had been perishingly cold and March, April and May were cool and overcast for the most part, just like this afternoon. Because of the lack of early grazing, he hadn't turned out the beasts until well into April and now there was precious little grass left. He was worried that the hay would not last out and even if Arthur Bell had a surplus, he had no spare money to buy it, nor any young beast to swap. The last one went to market last week. His farming worries came to a rude halt when Darkie, instead of running round the British Friesians at the end of the Wharf Field, had disappeared into the ditch at the extreme far end. He cursed under his breath. This meant a walk of another fifty yards or so to do the round-up himself. Stupid dog.

As the cows got into their customary long straight line to plod up the hill for milking, the farmer heard his dog growling, though still out of sight. There had been talk amongst his neighbours of a feral dog around and George ran back to find Darkie. He was ready with his stick. It was not needed. Darkie emerged from the steep bankside dripping wet from the brook and gripping in his jaws a human arm.

★

In all other respects June 7th had been a normal Thursday trading day at the Huthwaite supermarket. That is why Dorothy was taken by surprise by the urgent-sounding three-tap knock on the external office door. The door only accessible via the private path down the left-hand side of the supermarket. Only the shift manager was allowed access to the office by this entrance and then only in an emergency such that the other staff were not aware something was awry. Standing there in her smart summer dress and holding her son Adrian's hand was Mary. Dorothy's instant reaction was that her sister-in-law looked bewildered, almost as if she had found this backroom office by mistake or perhaps she was taking her youngest son to the doctor's for what might prove to be a worrying diagnosis.

'Dorothy, I'm sorry to butt into your busy day but is there anywhere Adrian could go to play for ten minutes while I speak to our Eugene?'

Mary had only ever been to the shop once before and, like his wife, Eugene had no idea she was aware of their private entrance to the office. So, as Dorothy explained the situation, his instant reaction was that a crisis had hit the farm and he just hoped to God his dear sister had not fallen out with George;

161

and just in case that had happened, he had better ask Dorothy to sit in and hear what had gone off. For a start, how had she got here? She never left the farm on a weekday, especially with the two other children coming home soon. This query was soon settled with Mary saying she had picked Adrian up from school at 3.15 pm and caught the 3.30 bus up to Huthwaite. George would meet the two older children as they walked down the lane after school.

There are times in everyone's life when, in order not to make a big mistake to be regretted for evermore thereafter, it is vital to think fast. As Mary's story unfolded that mid-week afternoon, in that most incongruous of backroom places, Eugene sensed this was one such time. Mary was telling her brother that for the past three days the farm has been flooded with police and so-called experts, though what those two men and one woman in white coats were experts in, she and George had no idea. It all started when George (and you won't believe this) took a human arm wrapped in a sack-bag to the local police house last Sunday afternoon after he had finished milking the cows. The arm had been found by the dog in a ditch down the fields. The ditch was at the far end of the Wharf, Eugene would know where she meant – close to the footpath across Topham's field leading to the road which goes up the hill to Huthwaite from Blackton. Darkie had had a good chew at the limb before George could stop him and so it was all a bit gruesome. Of course they hadn't told the children.

She had to say that the police and the others who came down over the past days had been extremely discreet. They were only on the farm when the kids were at school and, as Eugene again would remember, that field is not overlooked by any neighbouring farm. They had been told to lock Darkie up, mainly because they had two dogs of their own sniffing about. Mary's point, and why George had asked her to tell her brother before news of the discovery of the body part became general knowledge, was that she (and of course now George himself) was sure whose arm it was. Eugene was concentrating like mad and fearing the worst.

'I helped George wrap it up in one of our old potato sacks. It was a right arm – you could tell just by placing it with the fingers pointing upwards. I may not have done the cutting-up myself but having spent enough time up the yard at the Big House, it was obvious despite the congealed blood that the arm had been removed carefully having found the joint, just as a butcher removes a lamb's leg. It had not been hacked or sawn off. The index finger was bent slightly inwards at the tip and on the upper arm were several dark black marks, and you know as well as I do, that all the miners have them. It's caused by the coal and stone falling when they are using the pick or loading the trucks. His finger got trapped on that shift when there was a roof fall and although it was bandaged and put in a fingerstall at the pit-top before he came home, he was supposed to go to outpatients at Queen's Mill Hospital to get it set, but he never bothered. When the bandages finally came off, that index finger had set wrong. It was bent at the tip. Suppose all that could be a coincidence but on the third finger was a signet ring. It was gold and just like the ones Dad gave to each of his sons when they became 21 years old. On the face of the ring were two letters intertwined. Three weeks ago to the very day, Sergeant Attenborough from Morston called on both our Alice and our Molly to see if he was staying with them or if they had heard from him. Don't know why, but he did not come down to the farm, perhaps he had just spoken to the constable in the village who had been down that morning to check on the dog licence, and decided there was no point.

'Anyway, Eugene, there is no question of it. That arm belonged to our Rob.'

★

On what had turned out to be the most extraordinary Thursday either of them could ever remember, Eugene and Dorothy had finally got to bed and as she turned off the light, Dorothy said,

'Eugy darling, it couldn't have been Jack who did it. He wasn't in the business. He disappeared.'

Eugene thought about not answering at all; or he could just sigh and say something like, better get to sleep after all the drama of the day. Instead he heard his voice, almost as if coming from an echo chamber, or from some stranger talking too loudly in the next room, producing some words,

'Dad was determined that every son would enter the butchery trade. They had no option after leaving school but to go up the yard and into the making-up shed. On the one and only occasion I tried to ask him about Jack, he said his second-born was a skilled cutter. Perhaps a dad is prone to over sentimentalise about a lost son, who knows? But he told me Jack was the best of the lot of us. Very gentle with the carcasses, very delicate, he seemed to have feeling in the knife. In fact, he saw him as an artist at work. Good night sweetheart, God knows what will happen next.'

Days had passed and on Sunday afternoon July 1st they were all sitting in Dorothy's and Eugene's back garden and Dorothy was saying that, well, it wasn't exactly a Buckingham Palace setting but at least, now that the wall had been built on the three sides behind the supermarket, the lawn laid and a few ornamental trees planted, it was private and surprisingly quiet. Today was George's birthday and Eugene had wanted his sister and the family to have a roast lunch, feasting off the joint of top-side of beef he had cadged from the wholesaler, as a thank-you gesture for the trade he was now placing with him. It had taken a while, as Frank had predicted, but now two years after rationing came off, the meat trade was almost back to pre-war levels and not least due to the foresight of the authorities sending prime bulls to Argentina in return for an assured future supply of beef once the war in Europe ended.

For once during this awful summer, the weather had been kind and the family group of Dorothy and Eugene, George, Mary and the three children was in high spirits. Eve had come over too, helping to prepare the roast potatoes (supplied by George from his first-early Arran Pilot plot in the kitchen garden), carrots and new season Greyhound cabbage. At last, thought Eugene, that awful business down at the farm was drifting into the background. They must have all been making a mountain out of a molehill. There had been no more police around and nothing in the local papers.

It was just as George was saying that he must be leaving to walk back down the fields to fetch the cows in for milking and would return later for Mary and the children when, quite out of the blue, the phone rang.

Eugene said 'Leave it Dot, it's Sunday afternoon and we have company. Whatever it is, it can wait till tomorrow.'

But it was too late. Eve was in the kitchen making more lemonade and had picked up the handset.

'Eugene, there is someone called Clarence on the line, should I ask him to call again later or tomorrow?'

Eugene looked at Dorothy and she nodded.

'No it's ok Eve, I'll take it. Sounds like we might have a problem with one of the supplies for tomorrow.'

'Mr Whitby, I just had to ring you. Things are alright again now. Sorry I was in such a state a couple of months ago.'

'Why, is he back, have you seen him?'

'Well no, not exactly.'

'Bloody hell man, what do you mean, not exactly.'

'Our group have received some money in the post, enough to keep us going for another six months at least. When I say not exactly, I mean the dosh must have been sent by him. He has done this sort of thing before. Gypsy in his soul – expect you are a bit the same. He didn't put any note with the cash but of course it is from him.'

How the stink do you know it's from him?'

'Come off it Mr Whitby, who else would know where to send it? We don't advertise to the rozzers where we are, do we Mr Whitby?'

'Clarence, I have a feeling you will not call me again. Look, it's my turn to say sorry. I am jumpy talking about our Jack. We have people here and I can't stay on the line, but can you tell me anything at all about why he deserted the family and in what circumstances?'

'Mr Whitby, you are no doubt a clever and worldly chap. You can put two and two together I am sure. One day the law will change, but until it does…. If it helps, I know how he first left your area. He was very young and not at all cut out (no pun intended) for the family business and when the travelling fair came onto the market square, well, the young virile lads working on it – I've said enough. Just wanted you to hear the good news. He'll be away from me for a while but will come back in his own time. Oh, and by the way Mr

Whitby, just to say I am on the mild side. There are some here who are not. Best keep your trap shut. Good afternoon.'

★

Eugene was thankful that all that nasty and upsetting business concerning his brother Jack was well and truly behind them and that he and his Dot had not allowed the mistaken worries of Mary to disrupt the trading which was romping ahead. On this early evening in the third week of September, just as they sat down to their meal, there was a knock on the door and Dorothy returned with two men.

'Darling there are two policemen to see you, something about contraband cigarettes circulating in the area and can they have half an hour or so alone with you since it's all a bit detailed and I'll no doubt be bored to death.'

'So, it's Mr Eugene Whitby – is that correct?

'Here are our warrant cards. I am Detective Chief Inspector Hooton and this is Detective Sergeant Clarke. We are from the Divisional Office of the Notts and Derby Constabulary. Nothing to get alarmed about Mr Whitby, just want a little chat about your family. If actually you are palming off fags, we'll deal with that another time. We had a long chat to your brother Harold this afternoon and since then he has kindly been into the station and signed a statement for us. Correct me when I go wrong but from what he has told us, you came back from the war expecting to re-join the family firm, but found no room. His elder brother Rob had sort-of taken your place. Bloody complicated rabbit warren of a family you had as I understand it. Thing is Mr Eugene Whitby, you must have been understandably a bit miffed. I certainly would have been. Slogging your guts out for King and Country to come back and find they have shafted you. Still, we've had a few of our people over the past few weeks looking at your three supermarkets and from what I hear, you're doing very nicely now, thank you very much. But then again, to see the old firm going down the plughole must have grated and then, sod me, this Rob goes and sets up on his own. If I'd been you, I'd be thinking, where did he get the brass from and what with the shop shutting and the old man on his death-bed – yes, one can feel the family bitterness.

'I'll come to the point Mr Whitby. For the first time Sergeant Clarke interrupted with "Thank God for that CI, I need to get the kids to bed, can't stay here all night" and he looked straight at Eugene. A human arm was found on your sister's land back in early June. She must have told you about it. It had a few distinguishing features. Miners' bruises, but then there are bloody thousands of those around here, miners I mean. By the way, we had one in the nick last Saturday for hitting one of the girls down Mansfield. Seems she said to him something along the lines of; "you bloody miners come to me with pricks like cigarettes and have the cheek to tell me I have a big one". (This time Clarke laughed and said "Hey that's a good one CI"). Then another thing, the index finger on the hand was bent. Now that gets us a bit closer. Your brother Rob had a bit of a knock, it's in the accident book. But then again, it's a common enough thing down that black hole and so is not getting it straightened properly. Still, it's starting to point us towards this brother of yours and then we strike lucky. A signet ring with the letters RW intertwined. Of course, there must be loads of RW's about, even though a signet ring would be hard to spot with a bloody right arm missing. Can't help noticing you have a similar ring on your right hand Mr Whitby. Take a look Sergeant. Sergeant Clarke came over to Eugene and grabbed his hand somewhat harder than perhaps he needed to. "Well blow me down CI, this ring's got a EW intertwined". The more senior of the two men carried on talking.

'Got to admit Mr Whitby we're a bit lost on this one. One arm but no body. No fingerprints, no footmarks in a muddy field and the dog is refusing to talk. Sergeant Clarke laughed. What we do have is a missing Rob Whitby, master butcher, a grieving girlfriend and worst of all a local Sergeant Attenborough from Morston with a stain on his otherwise unblemished record. When this case was laid at my door and after my lads had done some ferreting around, I started to think Mr Eugene Whitby, that you were a little shit". At this point Sergeant Clarke put on a stern face and looked directly at Eugene. Now that I have more facts and not least the statement from your brother Harold, plus a few bits and bobs he told me off-the-record, I think you are a big shit. However, just to let you know that there really is no need to worry. We have absolutely nothing to link you to a crime. Still, as I said to my Sergeant here, I'll bet my pension you slaughtered your brother and I never give up Mr Whitby – never. One last thing before we leave. Do you know of anyone who might have killed Rob Whitby? Any other master butcher, such as yourself, who might have so cleanly separated one arm from one shoulder?'

TWELVE

I t was as if the perfection of the weather on this, the fourth Sunday of September, served to exaggerate its distinction from each typical day of the sub-Summer now, thankfully, drifting into oblivion. Eugene had, at last, got Frank out and onto the mountain. The difference this time was that the tone of his pleading was not of the mild mocking: "know you won't come but I'm asking again anyway", kind so much used in the past. It was an urgent, almost desperate: "Frank, I need to talk to you and far away from here, somewhere quiet where we can truly be on our own and able to think clearly – please". His elder brother, supporter, sponsor and financier, agreed instantly. Frank didn't even own a pair of walking boots and never walked further than from his parked car to the club. None of which mattered a jot. The one stipulation Frank made was he was not riding pillion on that Thunderbird. He would drive them both. Forty miles was nothing for the Ford. Paradoxically, in the six years since Eugene came back from the war, Frank had become his surrogate father whilst, at the same time, so close a brother as to contradict the nineteen years that separated their ages.

The journey to Edale Railway Station car park was made in silence. Eugene appeared deep in thought and Frank concentrated on driving along the twisting steep roads so typical of the Derbyshire Peak District, taking them through

Shirland, Tansley, Matlock, Rowsley, Baslow, Hathersage, Hope and finally, the sharp right-hander leading to Edale. Frank knew that his brother came this way often and yet none of the picturesque villages and surrounding countryside attracted his attention or comment. Even the George at Hathersage was passed in silence.

By one-o'clock they had reached the point where Grinds Brook falls away from Kinder Edge and starts its perilous descent to the valley far below. Eugene, still lean and fit in his late twenties, had made the climb with little effort, but Frank was suffering. Since his mid-forties, he had put on weight and his lifestyle, to put it mildly, was not conducive to climbing to 1,500 feet above sea level. Nevertheless, he had hung on grimly to the ever-upward footfalls of his brother, stopping whenever necessary to prevent his lungs from bursting and being thankful that Eugene's backward glances caused him to pause and wait.

Having walked the mile or so from the carpark to Edale village, Eugene ignored the Grindsbrook route straight-ahead but bore right for the steep ascent up Oller Brook to reach the clough. At that point, a left-hand fork over The Nab would have been the easier option but instead Eugene headed forward to scramble and climb over the very steepest crags to reach Ringing Roger. He wanted to punish his body: he hoped Frank would make it: he had to get his head clear.

Eugene had no appetite for the sandwiches and cake Dot had so lovingly prepared. His appetite was the view and his words. Far, far below and to their left were the steep slopes of the grass meadows where they had climbed just two hours earlier. The two brothers had a single thought which Frank voiced,

'You know Eugene those sheep, so at peace with each

other and their lofty world, so harmless and yet the lambs, now the size of their mothers, will already be missing most of the males. Gone for slaughter. *New Season Fresh British Lamb.* And, in our time, we both did it. Not a modicum of emotion. Just a job: make a few pennies for the family. How did we do it? Their short life gone for ever. Gone to feed our bellies. What right did we have? Bloody hell Eugene, it sort of gets to you up here doesn't it?'

Eugene was still not quite ready. No clouds in the sky, the air clear of any industrial muck and the sun behind them, already starting its move to the West.

'See Frank pretty much straight ahead, that's the peak of Mam Tor and just to the left of that is Hollins Cross. Me and Dot have climbed up there dozens of times having left the motorbike in Castleton over the far side. And isn't it amazing how, with hardly any machinery, they built the railway line down there? Weaving its way round these huge peaks west to Manchester. Think of the journeys before that with the pack horses and their burden of cotton and the like actually making the tracks behind us as we sit with our back to these rocks. See that peak immediately to our left past the valley, the railway line and the river, well that is Lose Hill and behind it on the same bearing is Winhill Pike which shelters Ladybower Reservoir beyond. Next time I get you up here, we'll walk to its head and onto the Snake.

'Frank, I've had the police visit me. I honestly don't know what to do. It's about our Rob and our Jack. Mary has written to you hasn't she? She is absolutely convinced the arm found by the dog on the farm is that of Rob. She would swear on the Bible if they asked her to and let's face it, he has completely vanished. Disappeared off the face of the Earth. We know from our customers that his abandoned shop is the talk of Morston and villages for miles around. Of course the gossip is that he has either run off with a woman, apparently a red-head has been seen hanging about lately, or else got himself into money trouble and simply scarpered. Thing is Frank, as you well know, there has been nothing in the papers so the locals have no idea that he might have been murdered, had some sort of terrible accident, or something else. I mean to say, there was no love lost between us and him and Harold but still, he was our brother and I keep wondering when and what we tell our mam and the old man. They are going to hear from someone sooner or later. But that is now the least of my worries since the two bobbies came around last Friday night. There was the Jack thing and now they are trying to pin whatever happened to Rob on me. Christ, what am I going to do?'

'What do you mean the Jack thing and trying to pin what on you?'

'Frank, let's start walking back down to Edale. It's a bit rough to start with and then very steep so watch your step with those shoes. I'll fill you in on Clarence and Jack and we'll have a couple of pints in the Nag's Head and you can tell me what to do. Sod the bloody world. Wish I was one of those sheep – preferably a ram! How the hell can I joke, must be the Japanese lurgy kicking in again.'

Over his first pint and a packet of *Everest Salt and Vinegar* crisps, Frank could do no more than recover and rub his left knee which had started to swell up alarmingly. Half way down his second pint, he opened up.

'Are we talking about Hooton and Clarke? (His brother nodded). Thought we might be. They have built up quite a reputation for hard cop, soft cop and that Sergeant Clarke is bloody smart – going places he is. But, without a body, they are in the proverbial and it won't make them look too smart to announce they've been handed a body part but lost the trail to the whole. I have a pretty good idea where they might be snooping. 'Course, a frightener on the family might just yield the info. they're after. Listen Eugene, I know the Super, Roger Tate. He's in our Lodge. I'll have a word, tell him to pull his dogs off. There's a couple of favours we can call in. Every now and then, Rog needs a safe house. I usually have one of mine between tenancies that he can use – matter of fact, Paul deals with it now. Secondly, our Joseph coached his lad privately for the maths he needed. I tipped Joe off not to charge; never know when a debt is worth building. He understood, there's been a few rough buggers through his hands over the years.

'Eugene, we've had a great day out and thanks for fixing it. I did try hard to keep up with you and one of these days, I'll cut down on the booze and get rid of this belly and, old as I am, you see if I don't beat you to the top next time. A couple of things before we leave, I'm off with Betty tonight to a secret game of poker at a horse trainer's place.'

'Do you know for sure that Harold has kept a copy of his letter to you?'

'No, afraid not.'

'Did the plods actually show you the statement they said Harold had given them?'

'No.'

'Ok – Eugene, between you and me, and it will never, ever, go any further; did you kill Rob and leave his arm where you knew it would be sniffed out and expect the blame to fall on Harold. And Eugene, did you kill Jack as well?'

★

As Frank was hobbling, Eugene had to slacken his normal pace walking the mile downhill to the car. There was an uneasy silence as they passed the Peak District National Park Visitor Centre on their left and then Edale church on the right, Eugene's mind was in a turmoil. Did Frank ask the first question to test whether Harold's letter might be the only written evidence that Jack had visited? Another thing, could he really have thought that Jack had actually been to see him at the supermarket first, and that between them they had agreed that Jack would lie to Harold saying he hadn't seen Eugene. That way it might seem later that Jack and Harold were plotting against Rob and thereby keeping Eugene in the clear. And that second question. Had it crossed his mind that he, Eugene, might have lied about the police saying Harold had made a written statement. A lie deliberately intended to make Harold the villain. Eugene was beginning to view his brother Frank in a different light.

More surprises, revelations and shocks were to follow. When they reached Baslow, Frank pulled into the carpark of the Wheatsheaf.

'My knee is killing me, I need a drink. Get a couple of pints in and I'll give you the gist of how I made my money. You've always wanted to know but never asked. I respect you for that and I know I've upset you. This thing about Rob and Jack. I need to think it through. Need to test a few theories. Reputation is hard won Eugene. You know that now as much as I do. And it's bloody easily lost. This lot could blow us both sky high.

'After I got going as a kid, I had two big breaks. They were as different from each other as chalk and cheese (and I haven't worked in either! – come on laugh you little bugger, Frank always comes up smelling of roses, you'll see).'

Frank took a long draught of his pint of Mansfield Bitter, leaned back in one of the armchairs they had found in the far corner of the snug and his story started to unfold.

'There was this bloke called Slaney. That I had been introduced to him at all, was a fluke. In fact it came about after I'd done my first residential property job. It was the same episode that was to make the second break a success when it could so easily have been an unmitigated disaster – but I will come back to that.

Slaney invited me to join him for a spot of lunch at the Perform Club in Nottingham. Well, I tell you Eugene, there are parts of the Masons and the Con. Club that are a bit, what shall I say, toffee-nosed, but his club was something else. We were met at the door by a footman-type chap in uniform who, cool as a cucumber, took Slaney's car keys and, blow me, went off to park his car. He nodded to the girl behind the reception desk, and that was something else too – not your tatty melamine stuff – it was genuine mahogany with a leather inlaid top, I suppose to stop anything as grubby as keys or coins spoiling the polished surface. Anyway, he led me up the central staircase to a bar area all done out in red velvet and with deep brown leather sofas. We had a couple of dry sherries and chatted about this and that and when the waiter came along he waved away the menu and said – and I remember it so well – "Mr Whitby, I am going to recommend the sautéed kidneys with Bordelaise sauce. Best thing they do here and can't be found anywhere else outside Town." I worked out much later, after we became buddies, that by "Town" he meant London.

'I tell you Eugene, when you enter a place like that and taste a dish more delicious than anything you've eaten before, then it is hard to escape a feeling that this is a world you'd quite like to be a part of. And, for the life of me, I couldn't work out why I was there. Aside from the décor and the quiet ambience, it was the little things that seep into your conscience. For example, if he wanted to order another drink or decide on the next course, he just seemed to glance into the distance and a smartly dressed waiter would appear from seemingly nowhere and the two would enter into a sort of whispered secret conversation. A bit different to yelling across a crowded smoke-filled bar room, "another pint Charlie and a packet of salted peanuts!"

We'd got to the brandy stage and he had just finished telling me about the snooker room upstairs that, he was keen to stress, had a direct wire link to the bookies in order, on race days, to place bets whilst playing. And as for the casino in the basement it was, "The only properly licenced one in Nottingham and that makes it pretty exclusive." Then he came out with it. Can't remember exactly how he broached it but it was something on the lines of: "Frank, Mrs Slaney belongs to a ladies' lunch group and one day they got chatting about one of the houses on Sutton Lawn which your lads had fitted out with all the latest space-saving machines and gadgets using designs now in vogue in America. In fact, she thought she overheard one woman saying that the owner was actually over there working as some kind of dealer on Wall Street. His poor wife had been left behind to spend his money! Bloody bitchy some of the girls are you know. Anyway Frank, it got me thinking. If we could do something similar with our place, it would earn me brownie points – get my drift? So, I was wondering if there was any chance you could arrange for me to have a look around her house and maybe suggest something along the same lines, so that I could give a whole package, you know – design and new-fangled devices – to my girl as a birthday present. Incidentally Frank, there is something I wanted to mention. As head of the Planning Committee, I get advance notification of Government thinking on the nation's housing stock which, following the Great War, is in poor condition.

Of course, much of what blokes in my position get is hush-hush, for fear of putting the wind up people and the press going bonkers, but let me do a bit of anticipating and we'll forget where the thinking might have originated. He raised his eyebrows which was sufficient to order another brandy apiece. Suppose this awful situation with the Germans does lead to war, God forbid. Then suppose our dear country gets bombed in a scatter-gun way intended to break the spirit of the ordinary man. That is to say, not restricted to the big cities but, for example, to take out all the coal mines and rail links around our patch. Well, if as a nation we come out on the other side as victors – granted not looking likely as things stand today – then what is likely to happen is an intensive push to rehouse those displaced by the bombing and a final push to clear what is left of today's slums. Take The Rakings off Common Road for example.

You see Frank, I've had a blueprint of what will become known as Council Houses. They will not be flimsy things like the Prefabs thrown together after the last war. That lesson has been learnt. Rather a typical house will be semi-detached, have three bedrooms and be built on a square grid that is seven yards on each side. Compared to what went before, that is a lot of space and furthermore, each property will have a garden front and back. And think of this Frank, for the first time Council House tenants will have indoor toilets, private bathrooms and hot running water. One final thing, and for God's sake keep this to yourself, any idea that these new properties are intended for the working man will be abandoned. I'll give you a quote that came down the line: the working man, the doctor and the clergyman will live in close proximity to each other."

'After his little speech we left the table and I've no idea how the bill was paid – suppose it just went on his slate – and then went upstairs into the snooker room. He found two corner sofas and ordered a couple of cigars. After we had lit up, he started again. He was saying that with my experience in property and a good reputation in the area, I should gear up for what was likely to come. Not by spending money, because it might not happen the way the planning people expected, but instead by preparing a business plan. He could let me have a sample plan when the time came. Basically, in the event of a big new housing programme being approved for our part of England, I should list the number of men I intended to employ by skill type. Then the machinery I would buy and the business premises I would anticipate acquiring. Nothing too elaborate, but demonstrating that the firm intended to grow if an opportunity arose. As an appendix – and he said this could be the deciding factor for getting on an approved builder list – I should be pricing up a property and suggesting a selling price to show that the council is not being ripped off, because only a modest profit margin had been added.

As we drove back from the club, Slaney suddenly said "Frank, if things go well with that viewing you might be able to arrange for me, I can probably let you have a sample costing for a semi-detached house and a hint of the sort of price we in the Authority might be allowed to pay a local builder. Such info. will not come from me but someone else and needless to say, I will deny any knowledge if the balloon goes up in the future. I think we understand each other. If you do make a bob or two in due course, fancy being put forward for membership of the Perform?"

'One weekday afternoon about two weeks later, I was just bringing her to a third orgasm when I suddenly stopped. She was gasping and groaning as much as ever. Hey, listen to this Eugene, she had had four pure white sheepskin rugs stitched together and in the afternoons we almost always did it on her lounge floor on that mass of white wool – she said it felt like being outside in the field but with home comforts! She cried out "For God's sake Frankie, put him back in". But, for a couple of seconds I held back, just managing to croak "Mrs Lazenby (oh bloody hell, I've blurted out her name now, didn't mean to do that) I need a little favour". She said, "Frankie boy, anything, anything, just don't stop, please don't stop". Later on as we both lay flat out amongst the soft fleece, I told her about Mr Slaney but missed out the boring bits – there having been enough boring for one day – and she turned on her side and looked at me in that way that was already making me ache again. "Frankie, do you want me to be nice to your Mr Slaney? I will do anything for you." She reached down to take me in her hand again and bending her long, slim and beautiful neck downwards said, "On one condition, that you make a peep hole and watch. When he has gone, you show me how it really should be done".

'Eugene, what a woman, what a woman.'

'We had just finished the Garibaldi Estate when you arrived back from the war. Let's move on and I'll fill you in on the second big break I had.'

It was reasonable to assume that they were on their way home and certainly Dot would be expecting him, but three miles off, Frank pulled into another pub yard, this time The Thack at Old Blackpost. Frank was saying something about it being his secret drinking hole that even his Betty didn't know about. Eugene was caught in two minds. Yes, he was by now pretty desperate to get home but on the other hand he wanted to learn about the second bit of his brother's business history. What really surprised him, as if there had not been enough special events for one day, was how Frank was welcomed. The landlord, a chubby red-faced man of medium height, was saying 'Usual Frank and the chaser?'

Eugene had thought Frank's drinking was done in the Con. Club but obviously this was another watering hole and one he visited regularly. This early in the evening, the pub was empty and once he had settled down for the third time that day in a quiet corner, now a whisky alongside his pint, Frank began to relate his second story. Looking back it could have, and probably should have been, a complete disaster. Following events in America, a deep depression had set in. Yet, despite this, he had started a brand new business manufacturing potato crisps. All the money he had saved had been sunk into the set-up, plus he had to borrow heavily and take out hire-purchase for the key machinery. Whether he could have pulled through anyway given the trade contacts he had made was a matter for conjecture but what saved the day was a certain Mrs Lazenby.

'You see Eugene, this is years before the property side took off in a big way and by the way Slaney wasn't big. She used a tape measure on me to demonstrate the shortfall and we laughed and laughed till our sides ached. It's amazing really, we still write to each other. I'm forty-eight and she is in her early sixties but she's still asking me to come to New York. Tragic really, her husband worked like the devil to get his money back and then had a stroke. He's still alive and every day she takes him round Central Park in a wheelchair. If anything happens to upset my thing with Betty, I swear I will go over and, if I'm not a Dutchman, we will continue where we left off – at any rate so she keeps saying in her letters.

'The difference Mrs Lazenby made was flavours. Ok it's taken for granted now but when I got started all crisps were plain flavour with salt in a little blue bag that had to be searched for in the packet. Pinching the idea from America, she decided we must be the first in England to experiment with different flavours. Ironic really. She was pumping her husband for the latest snack trends in New York and I was pumping her. You could say it was a mutual benefit society. But, my Lord, how it took off. We started with salt & vinegar, then cheese & onion and finally smoky bacon. I regret it now, the impetuosity of youth, but success went to my head and I sold out to Walters who were building a nationwide business. What they wanted was the brand name, the machinery, the customer base and the flavour recipes. The production was transferred to their main factory and I had to get rid of all the workers.

'By this time, things were picking up and I sold the lease on the factory at a considerable premium. In fact, back to the Co-op. They had started to manufacture nylon stockings – yet another imported American idea.

'So Eugene, in just five years I had made enough to retire to the South of France or somewhere. I was still only thirty years old and had a mistress any red-blooded man would have died for. But then the Slaney thing came up and I was in no rush to move away. I could do some careful planning, and I did. As properties came onto the market, I bought them for renting out. In the spring of 1939, Mrs Lazenby left to join her husband. On the quayside she clung on to me like we were just one person. She was the very last person to board and waved from the deck for the next hour until the ship left. She had always been the emotional one but now I wept like the baby I was. I had no idea just how much our parting would mean to me. For at least the next year I was broken. A wreck.

My one consolation was her house. I bought it. It no longer had the sewn-together white sheepskin rugs. They went on the liner with her. She had been right all along. It had nothing to do with sex. It was love.'

*

They were sitting side-by-side on one of the dark green wrought-iron benches that had been installed earlier in the year, in time for the tourist season. Utilitarian in design, the bench was nevertheless comfortable enough for whiling away an hour or so. Although she said nothing to Eugene, Pearl was thinking that despite the so-called wind of austerity whistling through the halls of local authorities, it had not prevented Brighton and Hove Borough Council from commissioning the entwined civic crest within the back bars of each seat. The sheer hubris of the tin Gods within the Council Chamber never failed to astound her. Her daddy would have written to the local rag about the waste of public money. Poor Daddy, he so loved this place.

It was late morning in early autumn. The air was cold but crisp and there was only sufficient wind to allow the sea to lap gently against the pebbles. Apart from the occasional person walking by with a dog on its lead, they had chosen this spot well. They could enjoy the morning air together talking or in silence as the mood dictated. What had surprised Eugene was not her arrival since she had 'phoned the previous evening but rather the fact that for the first time, Pearl had not arrived on foot. Taking his arm, they walked towards a very smart, gleaming, jet-black car.

'So, Mr Whitby, you didn't know I was a car owner did you? Her name is Florence. Florence the Ford Fiesta – sounds good doesn't it? She's only small but beautifully formed and furthermore, packed full of technology. The sort of gadgets that an old codger like you couldn't possibly understand.'

She squeezed his hand and opened the passenger seat door.

'If I am such an old codger, how is it that I can contort myself sufficiently to climb into that tiny seat and also, how is it that you set my old heart racing? Miss Pearl, tell me that.'

For their seafront lunch Pearl had packed sandwiches, a flask of coffee and two slices of his favourite ginger cake.

'There is not the slightest chance of me breaking into the delicious meal I have prepared for us until you have satisfactorily answered my question Mr Whitby. A question that has been burning me up for over a week now. Your sordid little life has got me in its grip.'

She reached for his hand and looked straight into his eyes. Eugene was gone. Gone to a place of long ago and oh so far away. A place with no complications, no history to spoil things, just two people together in their own kind of heaven.

'Go on then, ask away.'

'Some of the way I put things may be different to how you see it because I have had to place my own interpretation on your notes. But dear Eugene, what I need to know is what on earth happened after what I will call the Ringing Roger Day? I mean to say, one senses a sort of watershed. What I'm trying to say is, both you and Frank were learning things about each other and wasn't that going to affect your relationship from then on?'

'One thing I have learned from our little talks is that you pick things up quickly. Yes, of course you are right. I think we both tried to be as before – he, my backer, supporter and guide through a new and at times treacherous business world.

Me, his admirer for the business acumen, for beating his own path away from the Big House and perhaps most of all for his ability to carry all sorts of different people along with his ideas. His personality, I suppose you could call it. But it didn't work. Some instinct told me to put space between us. If the supermarkets were to be successful, then it had to be through my efforts and those of Dot, Eve, Paul and all the other staff. I no longer wanted Frank around.

'All the family were brought up as Christians but it is hard to forgive someone who questions whether you have committed murder. Me, who had seen what I had seen in Burma and Siam and read what Billy had picked up from the blokes stuck in Singapore at the wrong time. How could I have risked being slung in jail for cold-blooded murder after the things me and the lads had been through? And there's more. Should he have allowed himself to be seduced by an older woman whose husband was abroad and presumably doing his best to set them up for life? And the corruption behind the property deals and the abandonment of his staff at the crisp factory simply because of a juicy offer. Did he have no feelings of loyalty towards them? Well, I was no paragon of virtue but even so, at a time when something really horrific had been done to Rob, when Jack had once again done his disappearing act and my Dot was finding out about not being able to give us any children, my priorities were at home. They were not in gloating over a fortune made and crying over a love lost. Blimey, Pearl, that is quite a speech isn't it? And to think that when we first met I could hardly string two sentences together.'

'Eugene, I can't help feeling pleased with myself if I really have made your brain tick over again. Before I've finished with you, there will be an Open University degree waiting.'

A young lady and an old man sitting on a bench watched a dog on the beach chasing its tail. They looked at each other and laughed aloud.

'Come on old codger, I'll treat you to a Stilton cheese and pickle sandwich washed down with my finest ground coffee and if you are really good, maybe there's a piece of cake afterwards – but I'm not promising.'

'You want to know what happened to him, don't you? Our Frank would tell anyone who would listen – and I suspect they were getting fewer in number – that he peaked early. Some thought that expression came from his advertising slogan for the crisps, you remember *The Peak Of Perfection*? Anyway, two years after the Ringing Roger Day, he threw a party at his place. His fiftieth birthday party. Sad to recall, it was obvious to all that his peak certainly had passed.

I have to be careful not to sound like a snob, which I am not, but the tone of that infamous evening was set by his Betty. You see, from what we were told about Mrs Lazenby (putting to one side her personal habits – and I have to say Pearl there was only ever Frank's version of events to go on and he was prone to embellish his stories a bit) and what I know for certain about my Dot, our Eve and the rest of the Whitby girls, they were all brought up as ladies. Given their limited means and bearing in mind the hard times throughout the pre and post-war years, each one dressed well and knew what good manners were. Betty was obviously from the other side of the track. I suppose she would have been about the same age as Frank, and some might say past her prime. She had put on weight so it was hardly the time to wear a tight-fitting skirt that was far too short, and a frilly blouse that was far too revealing. Our mam would have called it mutton dressed up as lamb. But the thing that couldn't be hidden by face powder was that she was very clearly a drinker. The ruddy complexion and the watery eyes gave it away. And, her language was hard and coarse. As you have probably guessed, I took an immediate dislike to this Betty woman.

'And that Pearl, brings me to the crux of the matter. The matter with our Frank that is. In a word, drinking. I should have picked it up much earlier, not least from that Ringing Roger Day. But, I suppose, listening to the stories of how he made his pile, sort of blocked everything else out. When I thought back on it though, three stops for booze before getting back home and especially the final pub tucked away on his doorstep ought to have told me everything. Drinking to drown his sorrows over that woman is one thing, we all go through bad patches, but when it gets a firm grip, when it turns what should be a good lifestyle into a bad one, then that is quite another. Not only that, but as it transpired later, he had a second monkey on his back. Remember my note about the dodgy local politician introducing him to the possibility of a posh casino? Remember how he was on his way to a poker game with Betty's circle of horseracing friends? His second big weakness was gambling.

'Just after his fiftieth birthday party got under way, Frank fell flat on his face in the kitchen while holding a goblet of brandy. The goblet shattered and shards of glass became embedded in his face. Even though he was unconscious for a while and an ambulance was called, the whole thing was hushed up. But, although no-one knew it at the time and he kept his powder dry until it could be used for a bigger explosion, there had been a journalist at the party. Our Frank was lucky not to lose an eye. But his luck didn't hold. A couple of years later there was the business of the Big Race at Doncaster and the dead cert that a trainer mate of Betty had given him. Then, to recoup his losses – the poker game. Pearl, somewhere back home I have a press cutting. Don't know why I didn't put it in my folder but it's between the pages of one of my books. I'll dig it out and hand it over next time you come to see me. That journalist did some real thorough digging and his piece is a sort of amalgam of obituary and "Poker Game Of The Year" as he kindly called it. It did a lot of damage to the Whitby Family's reputation, as did his later story called "Who Butchered The Butcher?" I think I can find that second press cutting too, if you would like it.

'Seven days after the poker game, Frank fell down the stairs at his home, landed on his head, fractured his skull and died instantly. He was fifty-two years old.

THIRTEEN

Eugene called them all together. As before, is was a Wednesday evening because it was convenient for Eve and Paul. The one difference this time was that Dot's dad, as a 5% shareholder, was there too. What they had to decide was the order quantity for the main lines of Christmas stock. He realised that on this the last day of October, it did seem ridiculously early but, if they recalled, the failure to predict demand last year left them short of a number of items. Particularly embarrassing was the lack of Christmas Puddings and (he had to admit, as much his fault as anyone else's) the new line in luxury Belgium Liqueur Chocolates. Then again, how could they have predicted that only eleven years after the war ended, people around here would have bought rather than made their own puddings, as had been the custom for generations? As regards the chocolates, well obviously the period of austerity was over.

But, before they got into the detail of forward ordering and whilst Dot's dad was with them, they were to think of this initial discussion as a board meeting (sorry if that sounded a bit grandiose). The fact was that in just three years since the idea first arose, they had opened three supermarkets. And, what was crucial was that he and Dorothy felt confident to delegate. Ok, it had to some extent been enforced by their decision early on to have time to themselves. To bike into Derbyshire whenever the chance arose and to get their boots on for a stiff hike. Also, they had been so lucky having Eve to manage the Chesterfield branch. But, the key point he was trying to make was that businesses grow by having confidence in the staff and by training good managers. It's all very well having one store right under your nose and watching every single transaction, but doing that risked getting bogged down in minutiae and not seeing the trends. Not recognising the way the wind was blowing, so to speak. The big thing about their approach to the other two stores was that they could take an overview. In particular, Dorothy had all the sales lines on her graph and the different profit margins. So, for example, if Eve gave too much shelf space to a line that was not selling well or to a product that failed to make their profit target, it could be pointed out with proper figures. No-one got upset, everyone a winner!

Eugene was seeking approval for two strategic moves and he looked directly at Paul.

'Paul, I know I don't really need to ask you but I, that is to say we as the Board, need your assurance that what I am about to raise will be treated in strict confidence. It concerns our Frank. As our business grows, and that's the second subject I want to move onto, I propose that we sever our financial links. Not that we aren't grateful, it's more than that. Without our Frank taking me under his wing when I came back from the war and playing his contact cards to get me this first place, together with the absolutely vital introduction to the bank manager (which I might add would itself have been a lot tougher than it actually was, had I not had a certain rather attractive young lady by my side), God knows where I would be now. Probably kowtowing to some small-time butcher in a neighbouring village I suppose. But, having said all that, I would like to see that initial business loan paid off such that the bank will automatically release Frank from his personal guarantee. I would feel much safer if that happened because if, heaven forbid, anything ever happened to his business world, at least it would not rebound on us. So, if Dorothy and I can do some figures to show how an increased level of repayment to the bank could be managed, even if we pay ourselves a bit less for six months or so, can I take it you will go along with the plan?

'My second idea is to go for bust. Not literally of course. What I mean is, let's see if we can get three more supermarkets up and running over the next two years. The projected increase in total sales as the next shops come on stream will demonstrate how we can afford both to pay off the original loan and justify a new bank facility – by that I mean overdraft – covering the business from all the supermarkets. Time for me to shut up. What do you all think?'

Paul started the ball rolling by saying that no member of the Board need have any doubts about his position. Like Eugene, he was extremely appreciative of everything that uncle Frank had done for him. True, it had all started rather slowly. He had to be sure he really had the courage to go it alone and abandon his engineering career and clearly uncle Frank had to be careful who he set on since, well let's face it, some of his deals were a bit on the shady side. But, what he had discovered was that doing a variety of jobs suited him very well. After being out in Burma, settling down on a production line wasn't really his bag. It was strange but although you never knew where the next month's work was coming from, somehow jobs always turned up. As it happens, just as he was doing more work on the supermarket side, so uncle Frank's property rental business seemed to be tailing off a bit. It would suit him very well if more shops came on stream; the more the merrier as far as he was concerned.

Eve thought that provided Eugene and Dorothy could make the numbers stack up and get support from the bank, she couldn't be more pleased. She had forgotten that Frank still had a financial link and she was all for the idea of paying off that first loan. Taking over the new Chesterfield store had given her a new lease of life. How could she have got through the last five years without Stan, if not for Eugene and her very best and lifelong friend Dorothy?

The little group seemed to sense that Eve needed a few minutes to regain her composure and Dorothy took the hint to fetch the tea and cakes. Eugene too was grateful for the interval. He had won. From now on it would be plain sailing. He could make distance from Frank a practical reality. If it took longer than he had said for the next batch of stores to come on track, so be it. Then Dorothy's dad spoke.

'Dorothy and young Eugene, a son-in-law of whom I am immensely proud, this is your business and you have both worked very hard to make it the success it is today. Far be it from me to dampen your enthusiasm in any way but I've got to be honest and express a few words of warning or, let's say, introduce a note of caution.

'I've been a solicitor now for more years than I care to remember. My firm has seen quite a few businesses, young thrusting ones like your own, overstretch themselves. Of course, my time in the legal profession has covered the great depression, the stressful pre-war period, the war years themselves and this post-war time of damn near famine and extreme deprivation. One could argue that looked at from one perspective such times were exceptional, and yet it's funny how often exceptions turn out to be the norm. Indeed, as I think it's now well recognised, there were those that did very well out of both the depression and wartime. The point I want to make to you good people is that business is, and always has been, risky. Markets come and go, fashion and tastes change and right now for example we hear talk of The White Heat of Technology. Quite what that means is uncertain, but as this country moves towards the 1960's, what it doesn't mean is that the items produced now and the way they are manufactured, will stay the same. By all means take this company forward, but with caution. Taking Eugene's ideas for the immediate future, yes, certainly seek to pay off that first loan and free Frank from his personal guarantee. That makes sense. But hold your horses on expansion. Make sure you can really handle three stores before going for more. Do your research on the products coming on stream and how best to get them onto the shelves efficiently. Be certain that new techniques will not catch you out. Keep a constant vigil on competitors. Interestingly, our firm has just been invited to tender for the legal conveyancing, on a national scale, for an American outfit determined to break into the UK supermarket sector by building huge out-of-town stores. It is not mind blowing stuff but once again it is mimicking what is going on over the pond, where many people now have a car at their disposal and actually like the idea of travelling to an all-in-one store. In a nutshell, walk before you try to run.

'Anyway, Eugene, Dorothy, Eve and Paul, having said my piece, I will go now and leave you to the Christmas planning. Hope I haven't put a downer on things. Just wanted to give you the benefit of my experience. As Eugene was saying earlier, there is often merit in being able to stand aside and view things from above, so to speak. That is what I see my role as. Dorothy, would you like to see me out? Ah, nearly forgot, your mum said I was to be sure to show you our new car. Come and have a quick look, won't take a minute. It's a fabulous thing, Wolseley 15/50. She said we should come and take you and Eugene out for a spin when you can both get away. Make a nice change from clinging onto the back of that motorbike. Well, goodbye all – no need to get up.'

Eugene rose from his chair and shook his father-in-law's hand.

'We are all so very grateful for your wise counsel. It's at times like this when I miss being able to talk to my dad. In his day, he too was a shrewd business man but now he just lies there like a zombie. Not like you Sir, still in your prime and with thoughts as clear as crystal.'

As they waited for Dorothy's return to the room, Eugene was thinking: *well this is a fine thing. I have the people who actually do the work and can make it all happen on my side. Eve and Paul are rearing to go and now this jumped-up arsehole of a bloody solicitor has the effrontery to tell me how to run my business. I should think in the cloistered chambers of his hallowed office, he hasn't taken a real risk in his life – what right does he think he has to stick his oar in? Answer me that! It's all my fault, I suppose. Giving him 5% of the business – stupid, stupid. Why did I do that? To keep Dot sweet, that's why. Dot who, as it's turned out, has no gumption either. Just imagine what would have happened if I'd taken her advice and gone to see Harold and Rob about Jack. The whole sodding pack of cards would have come tumbling down. And on cards, perhaps Frank has been right all along, go all out for a full house and bugger the rest of them. To cap it all, he just has to swan off and show his beloved daughter his brand new and expensive car. Suppose that was to humiliate me in front of them all.*

'Ah Dot, you're back. Great chap your dad; given us all something to think about. Right, let's get down to the Christmas stuff.'

★

They had just returned home after the old man's funeral. Eugene was saying to Dorothy that he dreaded to think what would now happen to Mam, stuck in the Big House with just Harold left. They didn't need three guesses to fathom who would be running around looking after whom. Even though he had been bedridden for what seemed like for ever, she would still be absolutely lost without him. Had Dorothy noticed how frail she was getting and somehow smaller, almost as if she was literally shrinking? He was wondering if they could take her under their wing and leave dear Harold to stew in his own juice. There was the spare room after all.

It had been a sad day. Everyone at the wake at one stage or another had taken up the theme of the end of an era. A time of reflection; of appreciating what one had; of being grateful to be alive and carrying on. That is what made Dorothy's reaction so surprising. Instead of even a pretence of sharing Eugene's empathy for the immediate future of his mam and without a moment of hesitation she said "Eugene no, definitely not. You know as well as I do, that room is for the baby."

Eugene thought, *what is she talking about? We both know there's not a cat-in-hell's chance of her conceiving, no matter how much I give it to her. To think that even on a day such as this, she can't go along with me out of sympathy. Even if, eventually, we both realise it will never happen. What is this woman thinking?*

Eugene was about to speak when the phone rang. Dorothy made no move to answer it but sat staring at the floor. Eugene picked up the receiver,

'Sorry to disturb you, this is WPC Forester of Lynton Police Station, could I speak to Mrs Whitby please?'

'Dot it's for you.'

I'm not speaking to anyone.'

'Dot, don't be silly, it's a policewoman.'

'What?'

"Mrs Whitby, it's my unfortunate duty to let you know that there has been a road accident and I need you to confirm a car registration for me. Do your parents own a current model Wolseley 15/50, number plate TFG 44?"

'Yes – why?'

'Mrs Whitby, I have very few details at present but now you have confirmed the vehicle plate, expect a visit from officers of your local police force. That should be in two to three hours' time. They will have more information. My job at this stage was to confirm a name and telephone number in a pocket diary we found in the vehicle in question. Try not to worry, everything may be just fine. Our officers are dealing with the incident as we speak.'

The funeral and use of the spare room were forgotten. Eugene did his best to comfort his Dot. He was saying that her parents knew Exmoor National Park like the back of their hand, they were always going down to Devon and walking the trails. Her dad was an excellent driver and all that would have happened is that, during their return to Lynmouth, some idiot of a tourist probably misjudged one of the bends on the A396 or the A39 and glanced the side of the Wolseley. Almost certainly it would mean them staying down there longer than planned while the car was repaired, but that was no bad thing given their love of the Countisbury Cliffs and Foreland Point. The firm would cope without him for an extra week or so and as regards her mum, the ladies that lunch would just have to manage with one member less for a while.

Nothing Eugene could say helped. For Dorothy, the next four hours were purgatory. Why did the mantel clock tick so slowly? Why were the police so inefficient? It only needed a 'phone call to pass whatever the Devon police knew to our lot. Too damn busy drinking tea in their nice warm Station to bother putting one insignificant mind at rest. The fingers on that mantel clock pointed to ten past ten when the door knocker sounded. Dorothy sprang up from her chair, rushed to the door and flung it open. What a relief, they had come at last, two hours late but they were here. Here to confirm that the Wolseley had been damaged as she had been told over the 'phone but that her mum and dad, although naturally a bit shaken up, were unhurt, just a few cuts and bruises and likely to call her in the morning, after some treatment at the local hospital. Thank God for that.

'Mrs Whitby and Mr Whitby? I'm Inspector Waite and this is WPC Selby. Sorry to call at this late hour. Can I suggest we all sit down? As you will have heard from an officer in the Devon force, we believe Mrs Whitby that it is your parents who have been involved in an accident. Apparently, it happened at around 4pm this afternoon. Their identities will have to be confirmed by you but, and I am afraid there is no way I can soften this news for you, I am so sorry to have to tell you that they were both fatally injured.'

'What do you mean fatally injured, that's absurd, you stupid bloody policeman, you can't just barge in here and tell such godforsaken lies, bugger off – Eugy ring the real police – get the sods out of my house.'

Dorothy fell to the floor, she was shaking uncontrollably and started to shriek,   'Mum, Dad, where are you, speak to me, oh God, oh God.'

She banged her head on the carpet once and then again before Eugene could grab her to him and hold her tightly as she shook and shook. She beat the floor with her two fists and wrenching herself out of Eugene's grip, pounded his chest over and over again.

'It's all your fault you bloody Whitby, you never liked them, you never liked them.'

WPC Selby knelt on the floor next to Dorothy, took her head in her hands and she too started to cry. Eugene and the senior police officer both dropped to their knees and tried to comfort the newly orphaned Dorothy. But Dorothy was not there. She was sitting in the lounge of her home on Sutton Lawn, it was her wedding day and her mum was brushing her long hair, time and time again. "Dorothy darling, don't expect too much on the first night."

★

The service manager was telling his senior mechanic that he had better make a full report to the Wolseley people. This was the new model and there were not that many on the road yet but still that ought not to matter because the rack and pinion steering mechanism was pretty much unchanged from the 4/44. It was the engine they had updated. He had never seen the locking nut for the adjustment bolt on the splined shaft, slacken like this one had. The big puzzle was, if this mechanism had left the factory with a slack bolt, it was sure to have been picked up on the PDI at the agency. Bill the mechanic chipped in,

'But boss, this car isn't brand new – look it's done over 5,000 miles. If that nut hadn't been tightened properly when the car was delivered to the customer, the steering would have failed long before now. That steep descent into Lynmouth hadn't caused it to work loose, in fact a hill, up or down, would have no particular effect on it, would it?'

'Yes you're right, in twenty-five years in this trade, I've seen nothing like this before. Poor bugger turns the wheel for the left-hander into Harbour Street and the Wolseley goes straight ahead. Straight into the stone wall of the prom. Not going very fast either, according to the police. Let's face it Bill, who in their right mind would not be breaking hard on that incline and as we've seen, nothing wrong with the brakes, nothing at all. Get the report out as soon as you can; car's a write-off. What a sodding shame. Somebody, somewhere is going to be very upset tonight.'

★

Looking back, it was the innocuous visit of the sales rep. that started it. Mentally, he would compare it to the Thunderbird. Not the thing itself but rather what having the thing led to. The bike meant getting away from here; getting to the hills, meeting different sorts of people, picking up their accents, listening to their life story. Entering another world. No different in effect from the journey to, and the experience in, the Far East. The fact that one was enforced and the other stumbled on by chance was incidental. The mind was broadened, the gypsy spirit fed. The commercial representative from IBM was always going to stand out from the average pusher of fancy cakes. The charcoal grey suit with its sharp trouser creases and turn-ups, the blue spotted tie and patent leather shoes cried out business class, and with an American twist.

Yes, it was a novel idea and yes it would probably fall flat on its face but nevertheless it could be worth a try. "If it's ahead of its time, so be it. Give it ninety days in its own space and even if the locals just come in to gawp at it, could be worth it to you Mr Whitby. Tell you what, if it hasn't sold, I'll knock it down to you as a demonstrator – can't say fairer than that". And that is how a third new world opened up. Not on the other side of the world, not in the Peak District of Derbyshire, but in the spare bedroom.

Whilst it was never going to sell in the supermarket, it found pride of place in what was fast becoming, if discreetly so, Eugene's private office. The IBM Selectric Typewriter, with its replaceable golf ball shaped typing element instead of the type bars and moveable carriages, and with the facility to change fonts, was the perfect motivation for Eugene (for the first time in his life) to sign on for night classes at the Old School down Common Road. The course on touch typing was coupled with Pitman shorthand. After the winter sessions, he was sufficiently accomplished in both to have his regular notes taken to a higher level. In fact, just as the Thunderbird had done ten years earlier, the new toy and his skill in using it was leading him astray. He no longer felt merely part of events but that he was able to rise above them; no longer just taking actions but thinking about consequences and getting those inner thoughts down in writing. The most pressing was Dot.

The tragic accidental death of Dot's parents could not have come at a worse time as far as their relationship was concerned. Even by then, the marriage was not what it had been. They both knew it and yet neither made any special effort to do anything about it. And this inaction came easily to cover the cracks. Eugene's delegated style of management allowed more and more time away from the supermarket with Paul seeking out possible sites for the next three stores. In turn, this meant Dorothy devoting much of her time to dealing with suppliers, organising shelf space by studying the profitability of the product lines and generally mechanising the main office. She felt she had to be fully prepared because, if they did actually open more stores in the near future, notwithstanding the well-intentioned advice from her dear dad, then they had to be geared up.

The new development plan showed that a substantial overdraft would have to be serviced and there was no guarantee that the larger purchase volumes would actually drive down the buying prices to the degree that Eugene had forecast. She was the finance person and it was her worry.

Eugene was perplexed. Why should a mental void lead to a physical one. Yet it had. At any rate in their case it had. Certainly it had started with the news that they were most unlikely ever to have children. But he couldn't blame her for that – and he didn't. Maybe he couldn't father children; it hadn't been, and now never would be, put to the test. And yet, some button somewhere had been pressed that day with that devastating news. The mind was asking the body whether there was any point. Then came the business over Jack. If one'wife cannot understand the risk to their business of the past being brought into the daylight, what sort of partnership was that? And she didn't side with him when her dad did his level best to kibosh his development plan. That alone had kept him off her for at least a month.

It is money, real hard dosh that tests a twosome. Eugene had been certain of Dorothy's support when he had pitched for the initial business loan, indeed it had been her figure work that had presented the case. Of course that was before they were married and still in the heady days of courtship. Even so, she had not balked at the numbers since and there had been some tight months and the shenanigans with Frank. So why, oh why, had she flatly refused to bring her considerable inheritance to their company? It had been a terrible shock, the likes of which could so easily have bent the mind of a person stronger than her. Yes, he accepted that and he accepted the full year of mourning as a no-go period for mentioning anything remotely connected to her newfound wealth. But, with the potential three new premises he and Paul had found, being available to purchase outright rather than rent, and given the now-understood need to stock many more lines in a much greater store space in order to meet the competition from the incoming big boys, new capital was vital to making the business fly.

Dorothy did not agree and the simple fact of her being financially independent seemed more and more to be the bedrock of her position. Her parents' joint estate, willed entirely to herself, had amounted to £44,450 after all duties. Each item liquidated had carried its own emotional anchor. First, the sale of the beautiful family home on Sutton Lawn, then the life policy with the insurers demanding their own investigation into the failed steering mechanism, then her dad's fellow partners contesting the accountant's calculation of his share of the firm's goodwill. Finally the heartache of establishing the insurance value of the Wolseley itself. The manufacturer carried no blame; the fault was a one-off occurring long after delivery, and in no way due to a production or design error. The steering mechanism had been tried and tested on the previous 4/44 model and no recall was justified. Neither they nor the sales agency could be held liable for whatever had caused the locking nut to slacken off.

Eugene could sense the bitter irony of Dorothy now owning 42.5% of the supermarket company compared to his 37.5%. The 5% she had inherited from her dad, plus the assured support she knew she could count on from her best friend Eve, meant that with 52.5% of the equity, her ownership and Eve's allegiance would carry the day in any contested strategic move. To her mind, Dorothy's fortune was going to give their child the best education money could buy. So, all-in-all, Eugene surmised, none of her warped thinking would bring much to the bedroom tonight.

And the fuss she had made over the casual visit of Harold.

He had only wanted a half-hour or so alone in the upstairs office. He agreed it was odd that he'd come calling after all this time and after all the bad blood of the past. But he did seem genuinely pleased that their supermarkets were back into fresh meat and actually employing a proper butcher. After all that had gone on, a re-establishment of the Whitby butchery business. The old man would have been pleased with his youngest born. No, they wouldn't be seeing Harold again. Forget about it love, forget about it.

★

The first signs were sporadic. In fact, completely unnoticed until some form of pattern eventually emerged. Dorothy had put it down to the new heating system. She had argued against its installation on the grounds of cost, but with more and more complaints from customers that the supermarkets were cold compared to the new Co-op store, she relented. The average temperature now reached 65 degrees and surely it was this dry air that was causing her roaring thirsts. She seemed to be spending half her time refilling her glass at the cold water tap. Not that Eugene noticed. That is, until the disturbed nights. It hadn't actually bothered her, nature was nature and who knows one of these times he'll get aroused as she returns to bed, just like he used to. But her Eugy was starting to complain. "Dot, have you thought of not drinking at all for a few hours before coming to bed? This getting up and going to the lavatory every two hours or so, is getting a bit tiresome, not to mention tiring". Eugene was right. Sleeping for no more than a couple of hours at a time must be the reason she increasingly seemed to be yawning constantly. Eve had noticed and was starting to ask if anything was wrong.

The two friends went together. Dr Graham was the same sympathetic listener she recalled from the time he had delivered the devastating news of her being unlikely to conceive. Having heard about the thirsts, the frequent visits to the lavatory during the night and the daytime tiredness, he asked a question that took Dorothy completely by surprise. Had she experienced any deterioration with her vision? She hadn't given it much thought but now he mentioned it, she had replaced the electric light bulbs in the office with a higher wattage. Not because of any difficulty with reading but with the figures she now had to pore over every day. Definitely the numbers didn't seem to jump out at her like they used to, she found herself squinting quite a lot. But having never needed glasses, she certainly wasn't about to start wearing them now. Why had he asked? Dr Graham, pushed back his chair, rose and came from behind his desk and walked to where Dorothy and Eve were seated. He pulled the only other chair in the surgery towards the two of them and said,

'Mrs Whitby, I am going to take a sample of blood from you and send it off for analysis. No need to be alarmed, routine these days. Come and see me again in a week's time and we'll talk about what, if anything, it shows up.'

'Doctor, do you mind telling me what you think might be wrong?'

'Dorothy, I can call you that can't I? It might be that you are just a bit rundown: too much time in that office, not enough exercise in the fresh air. In which case, I'll prescribe a tonic for you. But it is just possible, and we'll have to wait for the blood analysis to come back, that what you have described to me are the symptoms of Type 1 diabetes.'

FOURTEEN

Pearl had to get the article into tomorrow's edition. It wouldn't be exclusive but the science editor was pretty sure that only The Times along with themselves would lead with the story. The time pressure was normal. Charles, the science correspondent would submit his copy an hour late, he always did. Pedantic Charlie was her mental name for the learned colleague. As usual, she would have to cut about 250 words to fit the space allocated, besides polishing up his English, grammar and syntax. What was unusual was that she couldn't concentrate. How was she supposed to with her dear daddy's strained expression staring despairingly at her from the computer monitor?

There were perhaps three options. She could just come out with it, face-to-face. Tell him of her suspicions arising from the three incidents. The trouble with that approach was that it surely risked him subconsciously employing one of the symptoms and, well, shouting at her for being so stupid. She wouldn't be able to bear that. Secondly, she could persuade him, on some pretext or other, to go and see their doctor, maybe mentioning the slip on the promenade and asking for a thorough medical check-up. That, at least, would lend itself to a more professional explanation and perhaps save some angst. Or, she could go and see this long-time medical man herself and find out what the initial step to handling the situation was. Actually, she wondered, was there a fourth approach; her going directly to a Huntington's disease specialist.

At the end of her shift and having finally got the article past the science editor so that the breaking news would hit the City desks the following morning, *Human Genome Deciphered,* Pearl had taken her decision. Her method of moving forward would be none of the options she had first thought of but a different approach.

'Daddy, on Sunday I want us to go to Brighton whatever the weather and, for a change, I want you to let me drive so that you can be the main look-out. I was thinking that instead of parking up and taking our usual walk on the front to Shoreham, we might tootle inland a bit. Take a look at the pretty villages nestling beneath the South Downs. I'm sure you must feel the same as me, why don't we see if there's a cottage for sale, of course, not within earshot of that awful A27. There is no need to rush things but we ought to start thinking of getting out of London. You're fifty-five and I know a number of people here in Town who are using this millennium to take stock. In fact, I've been getting quite excited about the prospect of you taking that generous pension now, rather than when you are too doddery to enjoy it, only joking darling, and as for me, well I could jack in this job any old time. The world of newspapers has been good experience but, to be honest, it is a teeny-weeny bit male dominated and what I really want to do is to write.

Sorry Daddy to foist this on you but, let's leave the Smoke and vegetate. What do you say?'

The more Pearl read about the disease, the more it became apparent that her father posed a management task and the less he knew he was being managed, the better. Wasn't the real skill of management, the stealth? Bending someone to your will, without them even knowing it was happening? She had managed the death of her dear mummy, she had managed her studies whilst being so very sad and so very lonely. Well now she wasn't alone. She had her daddy to look after. She would have time to think, maybe even to write. Maybe even to plot a future. They would ride out his gradual debilitation in their own way, in their own time.

The irony was hard to escape. One of the last articles Pearl had worked on had included a conclusion that the genome could be thought of as a book with multiple uses, a history of the development of a species over time. And now, this disease she was destined to work with was a neurological condition caused by the inheritance of an altered gene. She realised that an altered gene cannot be unaltered. It works its evil by damaging the brain through progression. A slow process of deterioration and her daddy would, understandably, be frustrated by his increasingly chronic illness and would almost certainly fall into bouts of deep depression. Was there a point to deciphering the human genome when a single gene cannot be repaired?

The way she felt now, and no doubt would always feel, was that the name was just too romanticised. Mrs Tiggy-Winkle's Cottage, Honeysuckle Lane – God. Daddy hadn't turned into Peter Rabbit yet and nor was he going to. But then, as the first year passed in Upper Coketon, so it seemed to matter less. The cottage had stood its ground for a hundred years, a few more would make little difference and all the locals knew the address. They also knew she had a problem but were much too polite to enquire, realising that time itself would tell its tale. Country people are patient with incomers; all things are revealed in due course.

★

There were times during their first year of hibernation, as he called it, when Pearl questioned her right to transplant her daddy from his workplace, his social scene, his whole life scape, to a quiet backwater. Was the lack of stimulus a poor trade-off for the exercise and fresh air prescribed? But when more dramatic symptoms occurred, those doubts disappeared like a puff of smoke from the kitchen garden fire which he would sit and stare at for hours on end.

Any man promoted in the British Army to the rank of Brigadier by his forty-fifth birthday is special. He initiates, gets things done, motivates those below him. Using modern parlance, he is a go-getter, a mover and shaker. Such a man, battle-hardened by the wars in Iraq and Bosnia, understands the absolute necessity of forward planning, of prioritising and of the logical sequencing of events. He does not stay in bed in the morning until a loving daughter enters the room, draws back the curtains, throws open the window, pulls back the bed clothes and issues the first command of the day, "Up we get Daddy, off with the jammies. 'Pause and wait, no more talking till done. "This way Daddy, now do a pee.' Pause and wait, no more talking till done. And so on. Later the verbal commands are reinforced using large cards showing large letters. Nor should that man be staring at the TV no matter what daytime drivel is showing or helping with the jigsaw only once Pearl has made a start and asked him to find the straight-edge pieces.

What a man in years three and four following a move to the country will do is refuse to speak whilst eating and, after the passage of six more months, think nothing of spitting out food because he has put too much in his mouth at one time. He will be unable to answer a daughter who asks simply, "What would Daddy like for lunch today?" And he will get irritated over all sorts of little things. Just because he can't finish a sentence, does not give his daughter the right to do so for him. Eventually, a man may not be able to speak at all. Even so, the daughter must imagine he still can.

Pearl sometimes wonders if angels are born or are made. By the year 2010, it matters not. She is alone.

★

They are back in the sitting room. No more taking in the salty air from a prime position seafront bench for a while. Outside a bitterly cold east wind is blowing and even the resident robin has taken to sheltering beneath the eaves of Eugene's potting shed. But in here they are warm and cosy and on the coffee table is laid out Pearl's family chart.

'You can see I've made quite a lot of progress but there are still many loose ends; missing story lines I'd still like to draw out of the old man before his memory finally gives up the ghost. When it's finished, and it doesn't matter if the dates are not correct, I'll be really proud of what our little chats have led to, and you my good man, will have a picture of what happened to this huge family that Hedley and Iris created. I think it will come to be seen as the basis of a family saga – or is that all too fanciful my dear friend?"

Eugene stared at the chart as if it was some gold-embossed blueprint, hidden deep within some ancient mystic book of unknown origin. He fumbled in his pocket. Pearl got there first, dabbing his wet eyes with her silk-embroidered handkerchief. They sat side by side for several minutes without speaking. Then, very gently, she placed her right hand on his arm and pointed with her left hand to the left edge of her chart. Eugene took a deep breath and started his monologue.

'I never really knew Joseph. Suppose that's not altogether

Pearl's Chart - First Draft
The Whitby Family Tree

Hedley 1882-1957

Married to

Iris 1884-1958

Joseph 1904 School Teacher Bachelor	
Jack 1905 Probable Homosexual	**Willy 1906** Butcher Bachelor
Frank 1908 Businessman Bachelor	**Alice 1910** *Married to* **Albert**
James 1912 Butcher Bachelor	**George 1914** *Married to* **Daisy**
Rob 1916 Butcher Bachelor	**Mary 1918** *Married to* **Farmer George**
Molly 1920 *Married to* **Jack Brown**	**Harold 1922** Butcher Bachelor
Eve 1925 *Married to* **Stan**	**Eugene 1927** *Married to* **Dorothy**

Questions I must remember to ask Eugene:

- What actually happened to the Big House?
- Why did the family business collapse?
- When did his Dad die, and what's more, how had he got started?
- How had Frank become so important in local circles?
- Was his own business venture a success and what happened to it?

surprising given the twenty-three years and all the other children between us. I mean, it's a whole generation in itself isn't it? I've often thought how odd it must have seemed to Mam and Dad having this full-on energetic life and their first-born apparently having no obvious interest in the opposite sex or, come to that, any sex. He was your archetypal bachelor. I never knew how he came to be a school teacher. How he escaped from the butchery yard to a school yard as a teacher is a mystery, especially as it must have been just after the Great War. Somewhere along the line he would have attended night classes and got a teaching post. Maths was his subject. You may remember me mentioning how Frank used him to help with a Superintendent Roger Tate, pulling the detective dogs off me, at a time when I was under suspicion after brother Rob's arm was found (or so they claimed).

'Joseph was just a humble secondary school maths teacher who, as far as I knew, never even left the area. Content with his lot I suppose. His thoughts, his books, his numbers. Over the years, I've pondered a lot on what his life must have been like. Given what the rest of the family got up to, it does seem extraordinary that a life can be lived in apparent contentment with little or no external stimulus. Perhaps he was a throwback to the quiet academics of the nineteenth century; minding their own business and just pleased to pass on their knowledge to the next generation. When the old man died in 1957, Joseph was in his early fifties and maybe that's the best time of life to take a rounded view of one's father. It was Joseph's eulogy for Dad, as head of the family, that really brought home to me what a privileged household we had all been brought up in. Created out of the sheer sweat and determination of one man. I think it was the effort put into that life story that drew me to Joseph at the end. In early 1978, Dot had only been gone a few months and my deeply felt grief needed an outlet which I found in those weekly visits to the Peace Haven Rest Home. The stroke that had put him there had taken his voice but, they assured me, not his hearing. So, at the last, I unburdened myself of the guilt of our marriage deteriorating and he, listening to that, along with all my other gossip and drivel, sank peacefully into the bosom of the Whitby family, of which he had been the nominal head for the past twenty years. At least I hope so.

'Pearl, I don't see how I can continue with the family saga without doing my best to explain how I came to lose Dot. In 1977, two things occurred pretty much at the same time. It was to be the twentieth anniversary of Dot's parents' tragic car accident and her own fiftieth birthday. The extraordinary thing was that on each previous anniversary of the accident, she had always asked me to go with her to revisit that fateful spot on the Devon coast as something of a mournful ritual. I had always declined by saying that she needed to be on her own, at peace with them. This time, it being two decades on, I said we would go together and couple it with a weekend in a nice hotel on the coast somewhere nearby to celebrate her half-century and, granted a bit late, our silver wedding anniversary. But, she insisted on going alone as usual. She said we hadn't thought to make much of our twenty-five years of marriage as it had passed and so why now? As regards her getting to age fifty, well, what woman wants to be reminded of that?

'The thing was that she always packed her walking boots and did a "memorial trail", as she called it, on one of the off road routes she knew her parents took when they were on Exmoor. One year it might be to Alderman's Barrow, another year the climb up to Dunkery Beacon or the stroll to the Hoar Oak Tree, all of which can be accessed by parking the car somewhere on the B3223 or B3224. So why she changed her routine in 1977 is a mystery. Having checked into and left her car at a B&B in Lynmouth, she told the landlady of her plan to walk the first stage of the Two Moors Way. If she did intend to do that, well that in itself would have been astonishing. She was in no physical condition to walk the best part of four miles, all uphill, to reach the edge of Exmoor and then another fourteen miles to the first place she could have booked a room for the night or called a taxi to get back to Lynmouth.

She must have known that; she must have. But the most damnable thing of all was that her insulin and needles had been left behind in the B&B. When she hadn't returned that evening, the landlady in Lynmouth contacted the authorities and a full-scale search started at dawn the following day. It was in the early afternoon that her body was found. It was way off the long-distance trail she had claimed to be tackling. She was just lying by a fast-flowing stream, as if asleep, and about half-way up one of Exmoor's typically steep hillsides. The Ranger who found her said at the inquest that it was just as if she had chosen a spot to rest a while and then, without her vital injection, had simply drifted into unconsciousness. There were so many unanswered questions. Why would she forget her needles? It had never happened before. Why would she go off-trail? It is clearly marked and she had her compass as usual. Why had she not booked a room at the end of day one of the Two Moors Way walk or enquired about transport back to Lynmouth? There was no answer to these and many other questions. As the years have passed, there never will be.

'Death: what a terrible, terrible thing it is.

'In your young life Pearl, you probably haven't known its icy grip; its numbing, deafening, blinding, all conquering effect of taking you over, of rendering all else meaningless. Casting you down into the deepest, darkest pit from which there is no available escape route. And Pearl, even today in this world where everything is available to everybody instantly, there is nothing known about death. It comes as a complete and utter shock. It smacks you in the face and says, "right Mr Clever Dick, didn't see that one coming did you? Thought you were worldly didn't you? Thought you were on top of everything didn't you? YOU WERE WRONG. Now try getting out of this one. Try jabbering nonsense to your friends, try making sense out of anything, and I mean anything. Can't, can you? Why weren't you prepared? Where was your armour?" The death effect has no words: it is silent. On a wildlife programme you will have seen how a herd of elephants encircle the dead one. They mourn and stare in silence and stay that way for days. Immobile. Lost in grief. Unable to understand? Who knows? All I know Pearl is that's what death is. Whether Elephant or man is of no consequence. A life has gone and it will not return. And that means for eternity.

'God knows, our marriage wasn't perfect. Probably like all others, it had its phases. It was lust-at-first-sight, we went at it like buck and doe rabbits, until the blows started raining down on us. No children – ouch. No leaking the family secret – ouch. Fatal car accident – ouch. Type 1 diabetes – ouch. We think that time heals, we think that just by living one day at a time we will get through, but Pearl, we are bloody well wrong. Oh God, Pearl you're crying, I didn't mean to get carried away – you have been through it, haven't you?

'Pearl, I really am so sorry to have upset you, I just didn't realise. I thought I was near the end too before you came along. Look, I'll make a pot of tea and see if there are any ginger biscuits left. These reminiscences are not doing either of us any good.

★

'I feel better for getting Dot's tragic end off my chest and I know, when you are ready, you'll feel able to unburden at least a part of your past to me. Let me finish off your chart as best I can remember. As we started with Joseph, I can work from left to right as you suggested, that is, first to last born. Well what about brother Jack? Other than what you already know, there really is not much more I can add. That mysterious stranger who contacted me reckoned to know how Jack came to leave the Big House in the first place and, quite out of the blue, he turned up again seemingly wanting a slice of the so-called family fortune. Apparently he toddled off to see Harold and maybe Rob, I honestly never knew whether they actually met. And then promptly and true to form he disappeared again as if in a puff of smoke.

'Turning to our Willy, well, you will recall from my notes, he was a lovely man. Everybody liked him. He was the worker as Harold was the shirker. Towards the end of the business as run from the Big House, it was Willy who kept the customers coming. But he must have been an innocent at large. He seems not to have known what treachery was going on under his nose and for whatever reason he let himself go bodily. He got fat, took no exercise and paid the price. It was the year before Jack made his one and only appearance. Poor Willy was only 49 years old when he died. What a wasted life.

'And then Frank. There is probably more in my notes about Frank than any other individual. Given he had had no education to speak of, you can only say he was a brilliant business man who started at a very young age. The thing was with Frank, he had these great ideas and somehow was able to take on the risks involved in developing them with a matter-of-fact attitude that defied belief. But more than that, he had this knack of knowing how to cultivate contacts. No-one else in the family, as far as I knew, ever thought about joining clubs and trading bodies and kowtowing with councillors and such. He was in amongst the local mafia (so to speak) from a very early age. Perhaps the greatest debt I owe my brother Frank was how he took me under his wing after I returned from the Far East and got me started. Heaven only knows how I would have ended up without him. But, you know Pearl, I often wonder in relation to Frank, what life is really about. Does it follow that if you have exceptional qualities, in his case being able to make money and get on with people – even to the extent of using people – that an unseen bogeyman defies you to stay on the straight and narrow? I mean, just because you have made money, does excess naturally follow? He liked his drink and he liked his flutter on the nags; but did those twin evils have to get such a firm hold? Did they have to destroy him? Or, was it simply that he loved just one woman and when that woman left him, despite his attributes, he chose to find consolation in two of the loneliest pursuits known to man; boozing and gambling?

'Then, at last, at the fifth attempt, Hedley and Iris created a girl. They called her Alice and just think Pearl, the fifth child in six years! You know, our mam had real class; more than anyone at the time gave her credit for. There was a grand piano in the parlour and our dad bought it solely for her. How she originally learnt to play, I have no idea; no-one else in the family could. And she read a lot. I am not saying it was heavy stuff but there had always been the popular classics in the Big House. Black Beauty, Treasure Island and the rest and she was especially fond of Lewis Carroll. I had heard it said, and there was probably some truth in it, that his books were the inspiration for choosing the name of her first girl. And I suppose, without wanting to sound overly sentimental, the Big House would at that time have been a wonderland. A wonderland of drying nappies and noisy toddlers if nothing else.

There is no question that our Alice, from a very young age, was destined to be a substitute mother. Once the children kept on coming, so Alice was child cleaner, house cleaner, child minder and I would think probably the youngest fully-fledged cook in town! My guess would be that she also did her turn up the butchery yard. But of course, all that changed the year I was born, 1927. She was seventeen and pregnant by her Albert, so the young couple got married and moved to a rented house in the next village. That is how their child, my nephew Paul, came to be born the same year as me and of course how – and what are the odds against this occurring? – we met as young men in Mandalay and became close friends. A friendship that ultimately led to him being my backbone in the supermarket business. And Pearl, I'm going to tell you a story that goes to the heart of human worth. What I mean is, true worth as distinct from perceived worth. Sounds very grand doesn't it but during the many and lonely years since, I've had plenty of time to mull all this over and come to a conclusion.

'Our Alice's Albert was a labourer. He never had what was regarded as a City & Guilds trade, which was due entirely to a humble birth-right and lack of opportunity. Certainly, it wasn't to do with his skills at working with wood. In his shed up the garden in Shirley Street he could make anything you wanted out of the raw timber he got hold of. I wouldn't say our dad was a snob but he certainly regarded himself as a tradesman, let's say a successful businessman. As such, the likes of the Alberts of this world were somewhere below him. Workpeople and customers he fed and fed off. So, Pearl, this is the point I am coming to. Why did Hedley Whitby, on his deathbed, call for Albert? He could have asked for Farmer

George, or our Molly's Jack or even me, after all we were all close family. My theory is this. He knew that both George and Jack resented their wives for not having any inheritance from the family fortune. As such, they would take any confession by him as merely an attempt to justify his own arrangements in making sure only the lads got a share of his assets. As regards myself, he may have had some slight suspicion that I was on the fringe of what he wanted to divulge to Albert. Whatever, he must have found out that it had been Albert who stood out as the strong man when Frank decided to face up to Harold and Rob. I also think that the old man had an unspoken but deep admiration for this British Tommy who had gone all through the Second World War and come out the other side as the same ordinary bloke who had made his beloved daughter Alice so very happy over the years.

'With what proved to be his last words before he slipped away, Hedley Whitby told Albert that he had known from the very start that his two sons Rob and Harold were robbing the business. He knew that the van takings had slowly declined until finally ceasing altogether. At the same time, he was still signing cheques for the meat supplies. He felt powerless to act. Harold would have broadcast the black-market trading to all and sundry and a huge family bust-up would likely have been the death of his dear wife. So what could he do? He wanted Alice, Mary, Molly and Eve to know of his sorrow that they had missed out on what had been rightfully theirs. He even put a price on it. He told Albert that each of his daughters should have inherited £2,000. He had been hoisted by his own petard: his wartime black-market greed. Pearl, I realise this deathbed thing is a morbid distraction from your family chart but at last I've got it off my chest. Now it's just water under the bridge, so to speak; suppose you might say that it was murky water at that.'

'Oh Eugene, what a sore I've opened up. Perhaps I shouldn't have started all this. Skeletons in the family cupboard. Do all families have them? What happened to Albert and Alice?'

'Ah well, nothing dramatic really. Sad but not dramatic. She had a heart attack, you know how unhealthy the diet was back then – fried breakfast every morning, no doubt with Farmer George's fresh eggs and my best bacon – and Albert, well one morning whilst doing just that, frying his breakfast, he fell onto his gas cooker and the burns were too much for his body to cope with. He had been all through the war, North Africa, Greece, Italy and he ended up burning himself to death in his own home. Blimey Pearl, what a morning, let's have some lunch and then we'll carry on going through the second half of your now famous chart. Better get it over with whilst there's still air in these ancient lungs. We mustn't part until you have Part 2!

'James was the one who left the Big House to start up on his own and somehow got into a mess. A mess that was never satisfactorily cleared up. One theory was money trouble but I doubt it because he left no debts to speak of and no creditors came knocking at the Big House door. Certainly he got involved with a married woman but then again, once the fisticuffs were over, surely he could have carried on trading. They say there is no such thing as bad publicity so maybe the salacious gossip would have brought a few more customers onto his registered list. Perhaps a few more ladies looking to play away! Sorry Pearl, didn't mean to be flippant. Anyway, it fell to my lot to find him hanging in his own making-up butchery room. Thirty-seven he was when he committed suicide. In other circumstances he might have been the start of a new Whitby butchery dynasty, he always seemed to have it in him. Poor James. He and Willy taught me all I ever knew about the butchery trade and they let me in on the excitement of the secret night-time adventures.

'My brother George was killed by the Japanese when they swarmed over Singapore in 1942. I was only fifteen years old and yet remember when the fateful letter arrived as if it was yesterday. Mam cried her eyes out. So did thousands of other mothers up and down the country that year and in the three years to come. I suppose if there was any consolation it was that he left behind a beautiful baby girl and one can only hope that his widow Daisy and little Pet eventually found peace and happiness in Australia. It would be wonderful to think there is another Whitby clan on the other side of the world. Now, there is a challenge for you Pearl. A real-life search down-under! One final thing before I forget. Young as he was, it will be George Whitby's name that will be recorded for posterity. His sacrifice will be known long after all the rest of us have drifted into oblivion. His name and regiment is recorded in marble at the breathtakingly beautiful war memorial at Kranji on Singapore Island.

'Ok Pearl, that leads us to Rob and you know all there is to know about him. About his return to the Big House and elbowing me out and his scheming with dear Harold and then finally – what a word I've chosen – his murder. Well, supposed murder. They never did find a body. Of course, if he were here and relating this story instead of me, the whole episode would be presented differently. Of that I am sure. Though I never could be certain, I do not think he actually shied away from being called up. Being twenty-three years old when the war broke out, he was just about the perfect age for action and the young men at that time marched off actually smiling. The feeling at the time was that the war would be short-lived and they would all return as heroes. But the fact was that our mam faced a real prospect of four of her boys taking up arms and he, no doubt reluctantly, agreed to go down the pit, a reserved occupation.

Rob would have known from his mates that the coal-face was no bed of roses. Accidents were commonplace and anyway just working the coal would have been thought of as a step down from the butchery trade. Then, when the war was over and he escaped the dust, up I pop as the young whippersnapper back as the war hero and raring to take over. But, as we know, he had already colluded with Harold to make his own money from the business. He shouldn't have done that, it wasn't right, no matter what sense of injustice he harboured at having to work harder than when the whole lot of us were able to pitch in. One thing you can say in his favour when the balloon went up was that it wasn't he who threatened to grass on the family. Still, all the signs were that he was going to hang onto his money stash at any cost. Was it that that cost him his life? Pearl, we will never know.

'Even with this huge brood, we're running out of names but not before reaching the lovely, calm and contented Mary. I have to confess, she was always my favourite. Not that her life down on the farm with George was easy. There could never have been much money around, he didn't have enough land for that, but working as the team they always were, somehow they got by and raised three children in the process. It's almost impossible to believe now but conditions in that old stone farmhouse were basic in the extreme. For years and years after their marriage, there was no indoor flush toilet, no electricity or gas supply and just a single pipe bringing water from the nearest village. A supply that she said often failed due to a leak that George had to spend hours seeking the source of. By that I mean literally walking the route of the pipe and every foot or so pushing down his spade until he heard the squelching sound that indicated the leak was in that vicinity.

'But Mary and George were undoubtedly happy with each

other and Pearl you have to wonder if, in this so-called modern world, we haven't somehow lost a lot of things along the way. You know, simple things, working with your hands, struggling to make ends meet, having to be as self-sufficient as practically possible. Being human. Sorry, just my sentimental drivel. I will answer your next question before you even ask. Farmer George died first. He was in the bath one Saturday afternoon having done his routine of collecting the hen eggs from the outbuildings. He must have had a blood clot or something of the sort, anyway he never climbed out – he was dead. Mary sold up and lived alone for the next twelve years in a small bungalow in the village. She was often lonely, always sad and never stopped talking about George. In millennium year she had a stroke from which she never recovered.

'The story of our Molly is a strange one really, well strange from my perspective. Somewhere along the line she was involved with Harold and yet she must have felt the same resentment as the other girls about not getting any money from the business. It was Alice who kept me and Mary informed about Harold's visits to Molly's house and she even hinted that he had helped out financially, especially with one of the children who turned out to be very bright and had quite a lot of private tuition. But really it was all a mystery and Molly more than any of the others kept her distance from me and Dot and I never fathomed out why. Not once did she and her Jack visit our shops – come to that neither did the children. That's another odd thing in its way. I mentioned before that there were very few offspring from the second generation Whitby clan and the pattern seemed set for Molly and Jack. No children for the first seven years of their marriage and then, who would have believed it, four came along in quick succession. According to Alice, Farmer George – who I might say was very fond of Molly probably because she was so like Mary in many ways – used to tease Molly by saying something like perhaps she needed a new sire.

'Anyway, Molly's Jack was a good'un. The old man had taken to him from the start not just to do with his clever electronics but, I think, as a gentleman really. Which he was. He stayed with the same firm all his working life and, as far as anyone knew, was a model husband and father. He reached his three-score-years-and-ten and then, almost as if this conventional man with his conventional life had run its course, died in his sleep. No trouble to anyone. Molly lived on to a great age. In fact she died only recently in a rest home. I wanted to go to the funeral but there was no-one to take me. Well, her four children were still alive, but not one of them volunteered. See what I mean about some kind of strangeness on the Molly side?

'Look back at the chart Pearl, aside from me there is only Harold and Eve left to tell you about. Ever since the old man took to his bed, I doubt Harold has done a day's work, and he didn't do a damn deal before that either. We know how he got his original money and then there was the sale of the Big House but, unless he has been a shrewd operator on the Stock Market or something similar, it's a puzzle to work out how he has funded his lifestyle over all the intervening years. Notice Pearl that I use the present tense and that is because, to the best of my knowledge, he is still alive and living somewhere close to where we were all brought up. He has always been a pain in my side. He bullied me as a kid, bossed those still at home until they left, manipulated Willy into doing all the work whilst the butchery shop was still open and, worst of all, morally blackmailed us all into silence over the wartime trading. As a final act of vengeance against me personally, I am certain it was Harold who in the mid-eighties set off rumours that it was me who had used the family fortune to get started with the supermarkets. As it happens, that little episode backfired on him because the tittle-tattle reached the ears of Broughton Groceries, one of the emerging big boys, who were looking for more stores to knock out local competition. In 1987, we sold out to them. The price we got was sufficient to pay off the bank and leave enough spare so that both Eve and Paul were comfortably off from their 10% shareholdings. It was yet another of life's cruel ironies that not long after our Eve got her just reward for managing the Chesterfield store that she was diagnosed with ovarian cancer and died within six months.

'So there we have it. I was sixty years old, retired and determined to leave the Midlands for good. And that is how, all these years later, I came to be hobbling into a certain library, in a certain town on the South Coast, attracting the attention of a beautiful young lady without whom I would now be lost; if not dead. There is a moral in all this; stick around long enough and your luck turns.

'Pearl, here is a suggestion. I will make us another pot of tea, which I am still capable of doing by the way, while you do your notes and gather your thoughts. After that, can I persuade you to do some talking? Tell me about how you came to live in the Brighton area.'

★

It was not the piece from *The Free Press*, dated Saturday 4th February 1961 and entitled *Poker Game Of The Year*, that used a belated write-up of the business career of Frank Whitby to emphasise the insane call he made at a poker game when all his remaining assets were at stake. Nor was it an article by the same journalist dated Saturday 10th March 1962 under the banner *Who Butchered The Butcher?* A piece of so-called investigative journalism that sought to establish that at least one, and possibly two, of the local Whitby clan had been murdered in order to prevent some terrible family secret from being revealed and furthermore that the physical evidence pointed to the work of a skilled butcher. Rather, of all the press cuttings Pearl found in Eugene's folder, the one that affected her most was dated much earlier. Within the article written by Lt.-Gen. H. G .Martin for the Daily Telegraph and dated Wednesday , 20th June 1945, she was struck by the following few paragraphs:

Gen. Slim was with our forces in Burma in the campaign of 1942, which ended with the retreat to India. He took over command of the 14th Army on its formation. Having thus seen a great deal of the Japanese soldier, he knows his virtues and limitations.

The Japanese, according to Gen. Slim, is properly to be regarded not as a man, nor as a beast, but as an insect. He is like the soldier-ant who, obedient to an irresistible urge to go from A to B, will persist in going, not knowing why, but destroying everything in his path or being himself destroyed.

The Japanese soldier, acting in obedience to orders will attack time and again with blind persistence until he is killed. He will defend his position to the last man and the last round.

The 14th Army has killed about 100,000 Japanese but has taken only about 300 able-bodied prisoners. The soldier-ant does not surrender; it must be killed.

Although Pearl had no idea how and when this press cutting had found its way into Eugene's folder, she now understood clearly why he and the other lads called up soon after that article had been published, had been sent to what was then

Burma. And why, of the Three Services, the RAF contingent was selected. It was because, as she read later in the article, it was air-power that had swung the Burma conflict in favour of the Allies. The ground forces mopped up afterwards. She also now understood what Eugene and his colleagues faced in relation to the straggling Japanese soldiers still lurking in the tortuous jungle terrain.

It was the content of the piece by Lt.-Gen. Martin coupled with what Pearl had learnt from her talks with the aged war veteran, that caused her to take the decision.

*

'Dear Eugene, your quite wonderful description of the effect Dorothy's death had on you has stirred deep feelings in me. I may be much younger than you but I've been in that icy grip, as you called it, twice. If you will allow me, there is one aspect you missed, or perhaps I should say one thing that hit me more than all the rest put together: the infeasible instruction: the first four words of the greatest poem of lamentation ever written. W. H. Auden's *Stop All The Clocks*. The fact is, they won't stop, or better still, move backwards. To everyone else, nothing's happened. Events just roll on. Minutes, hours, days. They just pass like they always did. The death of one human being amongst millions means nothing. It was yesterday, last month, last year. Eugene, you and I know that the clocks kept on ticking. They all scrambled away on the surface, going around in their circles, living their tiny lives. But you in this dark pit below, from which there is no escape, are as cold and numb as the lost one. If only the clocks would stop, even if just for a little while, just long enough to fathom what has happened, long enough to say a proper goodbye.

'And Eugene, I'll tell you something I know for absolute certainty. It makes no difference if the death was sudden or long and lingering. In one instant in time, things change. Never to revert.'

With a large and calloused right hand, Eugene threw a log onto the open fire and it was the crackle and upsurge in sparks that brought Pearl back to the present in the cosy sitting-room.

'It was my daddy's lingering illness and my need to nurse him that brought me to Brighton, or rather the little village nearby. But dearest Eugene you do not want to hear of my losses and anyway it is too painful for me to go into detail.'

She moved her armchair closer to his and took both his hands in hers. Looking directly into his eyes, Pearl continued,

'I came to see you today because I have two surprises for you. The only thing is, I hope the shock from the first won't kill you off before I have time to voice the second.'

Pearl giggled in the way that was now familiar to the old man and that melted his heart, already reduced to mush.

'Mr Whitby, Daddy finally passed away in 2010 and he was 65 years old. Even someone as decrepit as you can probably work out that consequently he was born in the year the war ended, 1945. My daddy, James Bennett, had been a very senior military man. He retired with the rank of Brigadier. At the time he was born, his father, who was also a military man but not Army – he was RAF – had been sent to the Far East to lead a group of young men. They were helping the locals who had suffered terribly at the hands of the Japanese Army.

'Dear Eugene, my grandfather was Group Captain Bennett, your wartime boss, mentor and, as I have learnt, the senior guest at your wedding. What a mind-blowing coincidence.'

Eugene sank deep into his chair, his jaw dropped and his

eyes stared as if seeing Pearl for the first time. So that is what the chart headed "James" had been telling her.

'Now for my second surprise. A week today, I start my big adventure. Via Dubai and Bangkok I am flying to Mandalay. I intend to bring back a story for you. The story of what happened to Chit.'

FIFTEEN

I t was a difficult decision. In fact, if logic was applied, an impossible one. A good and satisfying decision is based on information; the more comprehensive and qualitative that information, the easier the decision. But the information was sparse and, no doubt, weathered by time and human faculty. That was why Pearl was struggling. She could go to Singapore and start in the Queenstown District, making enquiries about the aunt that Chit had sought out and stayed with.

The big advantage of the now independent Republic was that by reputation it had a first-class civil service whose records, even going back to the late 1940's, were sure to be in excellent order. Nevertheless, Pearl was still wrestling with a two-pronged dilemma. First, would there be any records? Assuming that the aunt was Burmese or of Burmese extraction – and it was hard to envisage, if she was a proper blood aunt, her being from any other Asian race – how had she got to an Island which prior to the Japanese invasion had been under British control as part of the greater Malaysian Colony? Unless, of course, she had been taken there by the Japanese army. The more Pearl thought about the tiny piece of information Eugene had supplied, the more research she did into the circumstances that created the residents of Singapore in 1949, so the more she felt that the name of Chit's aunt would not appear on any official list. And that led to the second dilemma; her name.

What Pearl discovered about the Burmese system of naming people almost caused her to abandon the quest before it had begun. With what she knew, what was the chance of tracing Chit's ancestors even if she found the name of the aunt? A major problem was that at least ninety per cent of people (it is claimed) do not have a surname or family name. Members of the same family can have completely different names and, furthermore, the number of words in each name can vary greatly. Because it is the custom to name a child according to the astronomical calculation of the day of the week it is born, so male and female names can be the same, for example "Moe" and "Mya". Designation, apparently very important to its people, adds further to the confusion faced by outsiders. For example, "U" as in U Thant, the third United Nations Secretary-General. In addition, people with one word names face difficulty defining a family name when asked to do so, since the first word such as "U", "Ma" or "Daw" are not their names technically. As if this wasn't enough to throw the inquisitive off the scent, there are honorific salutations before the given name, depending on age, relationship and gender. For example, "Ko" is used as a masculine form of address for a younger person and peer. Yet, it is not unknown for some people to take their father's name, using the British naming system, and Pearl could not help taking satisfaction from deciphering what is probably the Burmese name best known in the West. Aung San Suu Kyi is the daughter of "Aung San".

It was because of these naming difficulties that the decision was taken. Her only chance of tracing the roots of Chit lay in the homeland of Burma where, hopefully, a name might prove less important than local knowledge of the historical circumstances of a young nurse taking care of a critically ill English airman those many years ago. The next task was to find out how to get safely to the second city of a country still sufficiently troubled to be avoided by the mass tourist industry. Tomorrow's lunch break would be devoted to this research. She felt the excitement mounting.

Pearl considered herself neither rich nor poor; rather, somewhere in between. When her dear father retired at the age of 55, he opted to take the permitted 25% of the deemed capital value of his defined benefit pension pot as a tax-free lump sum. This lump sum plus most, but not all, of his savings were used to buy the cottage they shared for the last ten years of his life. His remaining pension, though not large due to his early retirement, and what was left of his savings, was adequate to keep the two of them living quite comfortably. By necessity, due to his gradually increasing poor health, their domestic life was simple and therefore inexpensive. She had taken over the money side of their life together, so, bit by bit, spare cash had been put aside and she had started to study investment strategies. Then, one glorious day that was a highlight in her life, she made her first direct investment on the Stock Exchange. She bought shares in Lloyds Banking Group for the "yield". After her daddy died in 2010 she had to pull her horns in, as she put it.

The Army pension, though willed to her in trust as his dependant, was cut by 50% and her portfolio of shares had taken a knock following the global financial crisis of 2008. Even so, she managed to feed and clothe herself quite well and run the little car. Her income from the library job was a bonus; but still, it would have been nice to have a little more so she could go "bottom fishing" on the Market. Even, perhaps, take a holiday. Pearl reminded herself that she had not set foot in an aeroplane since those giddy days of meeting daddy in some far-flung place in some war-ravished country. Those fabulous times when she was young, he had responsibilities and she had a bright career to look forward to. Mummy was gone, but she and daddy had survived. So, the cost of getting to the Far East was an issue but not one that was going to stop her. Her blood was up and she was raring to go.

The cheapest flight – though, at £1,200 it wasn't cheap – was by taking Emirates Airways to Bangkok via Dubai and then a Bangkok Airways flight doubling back, as Pearl thought of it, to Mandalay. A chill ran down her spine. Eugene had tried, as best he could, to describe the horrors of his tortuous expedition between the, then, Burmese and Siamese cities. Now, when she flew between the same two places in those far off lands, albeit on the outward trip in reverse direction, the journey would take just 1 hour and 47 minutes to cover the 638 air miles. Eugene had gone forward in time by weeks; she would go backwards in time by a mere 30 minutes. How life changes. She wondered: what else had changed?

Pearl had no fear of flying and as her father often said "The bumpier the better darling, let's have some fun while we're here!" Even so, she had turned to her now constant friend, *Mr Wikipedia,* for the answer to two aspects of her adventure that, if detrimental, might have put her off the quest to find the answer to the Chit riddle. First, what was the state of Mandalay airport? Would it for instance be a jumble of old shacks and have a potholed runway? Secondly, what were the chances of flying into a tropical storm? The couple of experiences Eugene had related about his time out there were not exactly designed for comfort.

Any anxiety about storms was put to rest quickly. Much as she was attached to Eugene's roaring log fire, her choice to travel in January proved to be sensible because, according to the climate chart it was the coolest month of the year. Barely a drop of rain would fall and January boasted more hours of sunshine than any other month. As regards the airport, what a surprise from *Mr Wikipedia*. As airports go, Mandalay International Airport is new, having been officially opened in September 2000. Because of this, it was no surprise to learn it is the largest and most modern in Burma. Furthermore, its runway at 4,267 metres, is the longest in use in Southeast Asia. Pearl closed her eyes, leaned back in the library office chair and let her mind wander.

This was not a city teetering on the brink of modernity. There were no broad tree-lined avenues separating swish glass and steel fronted shops displaying outrageously priced fashion garments. No global brand hotels intermingled with smart apartment blocks and definitely no modern-day cars, bumper to bumper, waiting impatiently for the traffic lights to change from red. This was heavy undergrowth jungle bounded by the massive teak trees that Eugene had described. The evening air was rampant with tropical smells. Unseen birds squawked their warning calls and light-brown coloured monkeys leapt from bough to bough in screeching alarm. There were splays of bamboo, palms, hibiscus and casuarinas waiting patiently for the impending tropical storm to strike. But when the strike came it was a gentle tap on the shoulder from a customer returning a book.

★

Pearl had no intention of wasting seven hours on the first leg and six-and-a-half hours on the second, by watching some film she either had no interest in or which she could view in the comfort of her own lounge in Mrs Tiggy-Winkle cottage at some later stage. Nor would she aimlessly chat to some bore whom happened to be sitting next to her on these long-haul flights. In her heart she knew that there was a more than even chance that her mission would be futile. Consequently, she would do what she had always done. She would study and learn. She would extract the maximum possible from the mission undertaken. That is what her daddy would have wanted her to do. What was this place called Mandalay? Where had it come from? Where was it going? How had it spawned the likes of Chit?

The A380-800 had barely crossed the English Channel when Pearl opened her folder and started to read. Mandalay is the second largest city in Burma and is located pretty much in the centre of what is, coincidentally, the second largest country in South-East Asia. Being 445 miles north of the port city of Rangoon, it is sited on the east bank of the Irrawaddy River and has a population of one and a quarter million people. The city is Upper Burma's main commercial, educational (Mandalay College was founded in 1925), cultural and health centre.

Modern Mandalay was founded by King Mindon in 1857 to be a royal capital at the foot of Mandalay Hill, from which it takes its name. This new royal capital was to last only 26 years before the conquering British sent the royal household into exile. The Royal Palace was looted and some of the treasures are still on display in the Victoria and Albert Museum in London. The palace compound was renamed Fort Dufferin and used to billet troops. British rule, not unlike the pattern established in South Africa, witnessed the arrival of immigrants from India.

In April 1942 the Imperial Japanese Army Air Service carried out an extensive assault on the city of Mandalay which was defenceless due to earlier Japanese bombing and the withdrawal of the RAF's fleet of aircraft to the relative safety of India. Three-fifths of the houses were destroyed and some

2,000 civilians killed. The Japanese occupation lasted from May 1942 to March 1945. The Palace Citadel found another use, this time as a supply depot, before finally being burned to the ground by Allied bombing. Only the Royal Mint and the watch tower survived. To Pearl's sympathetic relief, she read that a replica of the Royal Palace was built in the 1990's. She started her list of must see sites.

Apart from what Pearl had read years ago about the Great Fire of London in 1666, she had thought little, if at all, about the impact of fire on the evolution of a city, any city. But now, sipping a glass of Chardonnay during a spot of turbulence over Bulgaria, she realised that drastic change can rise from ashes. Mandalay's single-storey buildings were devastated by fire in May 1981 and again in March 1984. It had been estimated that some 9,000 houses and public buildings were razed to the ground. These fires brought about a huge change in the city's physical character and, as it turned out, ethnic constituent. Huge swathes of land were purchased by immigrant Chinese. Estimates put the number of Yunnanese migrants entering Mandalay in the 1990's at 250,000 to 300,000. The economic paper Pearl was reading put the ethnic Chinese as perhaps 30% to 40% of the current headcount in the city. Would Pearl's visit coincide with a Chinese festival? She hoped so.

It was on the second leg of her long-haul journey whilst over central India that Pearl completed her must-see list. Perhaps it was the effect of a further assault on the excellent Chardonnay, served by the charming and beautiful Malaysian stewardess, that made her question whether this mission to find Chit was merely an excuse for a keen tourist to visit a magical land of pagodas and monasteries. The Royal Palace had slipped to second place behind Mandalay Hill after she recalled Eugene's description of his visit there with Paul, and now realising it was home to many of the city's religious sites. To climb the 790 feet was an absolute must. And so the list, prepared with the care that years with the FT had inculcated, and in her trademark blue ink, emerged as follows:-

1. *Mandalay Hill*
2. *The Mandalay Palace*
3. *Shwenandaw Monastery (The Golden Palace)*
4. *Buddha's Replica Tooth Relic Pagoda*
5. *Mahamuni Buddha Temple*
6. *Kyauktawgyi Pagoda (carved out of a huge single block of marble)*
7. *Atumashi Monastery*

Flying over the Dawna Range of mountains of Eastern Burma, the A320 did bounce a little, but that aside, the most poignant aspect of the third leg of Pearl's adventure was the lie it gave to her preconception that the Far East was teaming with people, jostling cheek-by-jowl for a square foot of space. Hardly. Masses and masses of greenery; huge trees, dense jungle, swamps, cloud-shrouded mountain peaks of over 2,000 ft. and above all, devoid of human habitation. That a young lad, newly emerged from a war-torn weary England, could have been tasked with working in and then required to cross this terrain stretched imagination to breaking point. Yet it happened. If not before, then certainly now, staring out of the aircraft's window, Pearl's admiration for Eugene and his Chit and his mates was profound. As for those toiling to build the death railway… No words were possible. Pearl's cheek was damp; she searched for a paper tissue.

It occurred to Pearl that one problem the planners had failed to solve when conceiving Mandalay International

Airport, was where to locate it. She could tell from the taxi ride that it was nowhere near the city. And this, her first experience in a tropical land, would set a pattern to be repeated constantly; it would be the one aspect to stay with her. The juxtaposition of old and new. The one trying to jostle out the other – and failing. A modern highway of 28 miles, covered in a Nissan Sunny pick-up truck that had to be over twenty-five years old. Why? For the modern tourist arriving at a modern airport fed by a modern highway, surely one expected to find a modern car at the end of the taxi queue? Pearl learnt quickly. Things in different places have arrived in different ways, for different reasons and by different hands. The moral was; accept, adapt, enjoy. She vowed to do so.

Pearl found herself smiling at the prospect of accepting, never mind adapting to and enjoying, the chaotic traffic her driver was attempting to negotiate, even whilst still on the outskirts of the city. Where were all these thousands of bicycles, motorbikes and trishaws heading? Did it actually aid their progress to keep switching from lane to lane? And, as far as she could tell, every other set of traffic lights, and she had never seen so many, was not working, so that it was not just the one-way flow of vehicles her driver was contending with, but cross traffic too. She thought of Brighton seafront and her daddy driving his posh car. The smile turned into a laugh; whether her mission was a success or not, boy, was she going to have an exciting time!

Then, the hustle, bustle, noise and smells all stopped. It was exactly as she had read in the brochure. *An oasis by the landmark Red Canal of local folklore, just minutes from the famed Mandalay Palace and other attractions. The Hotel by the Red Canal is a convenient sanctuary, with its lush tropical greenery and calming water features. Each of the 25 suites is named after and decked in the*

fineries and cultural adornments of one of the four major ethnic groups.
Of these, Pearl had chosen "Chin". It seemed the natural thing
to do.

But she wasn't concentrating on what the charming
reception lady who, adorned in traditional costume, was saying.
The Western guest had use of the free internet connection, the
spa and the fitness facilities. In its place, the voice of the taxi
driver from half an hour earlier broke through as they had
waited in yet another traffic queue. Pointing to an old man
sitting at a table inside an old wooden hut and using a small
hammer with apparent delicate precision,

'See missy, he make gold leaf, you come back later to buy
for temple.'

It was not something one would spot on the front at
Brighton. Was the goldsmith as old as Eugene? He looked to
be, or had the climate taken its toll? This was just one of many
musings Pearl would tuck away over the next two weeks. Any
doubts she may have harboured about the usefulness of this
trip evaporated like the high cloud over the mountain top
as the sun rose over old Burma and the new Myanmar. The
porter carried her two bags and she gave him a generous tip.
The heart of this adventuring English lady was full to bursting.

As she squeezed the fresh lime over the neatly sliced papaya
in this faraway tropical garden and listened to the tinkling of
the water feature, she could still picture daddy hunched over
his fresh grapefruit at breakfast twenty years earlier, saying in
his stern commanding voice, "Pearl darling, business before
pleasure, business before pleasure.' These were surely the first
two steps: education: location.

Her first trishaw ride would be a death-defying, lane-
switching, bell-ringing sally to Yadanabon University, in the
Amarapura District on the outskirts of the city (in partial

defiance of daddy's rule of business first) to hear more of the city's heartbeat than would be possible from the shorter journey to Mandalay University and she was also hoping to couple her business with a trip on Taungthaman Lake.

Kyaw was a second-year student reading English and French and her tutor was delighted to release her for five full days to translate and assist with all the English lady's enquiries, except those of a political nature. To help search for descendants of a citizen who healed an English airman during the war would be an honour. There would be no fee for Kyaw's assistance but she would need her expenses paid. There was much smiling and a slight bowing of the head; the deal was done. Pearl mentally ticked off her education box.

The sun was setting at the end of her first day. Orange and white lights strung discreetly in the overhead branches were starting to appear above the bamboo seat where Pearl had sat that morning. The tropical fruit had been replaced by a bowl of mixed nuts, and a gin and tonic was being sipped thoughtfully as she turned the pages of notes. And there they were, the words in italics, *Mandalay General Hospital – 30th Street – local girl – taken to her home in the next village.*

Pearl was no longer surprised at the abject contrast. The bicycles, trishaws, ancient pick-up trucks, morass of humanity, clatter and odours outside while here inside, as modern as the FT office in London. At the hospital they had been led down a wide corridor leading off from the main reception desks to enter a room with banks of computer screens and all the furniture and equipment so familiar to Pearl from those deadline-pressured days of the past. While she sat in a vacant chair to await events, Kyaw was in a glass panelled corner office talking with, and occasionally gesticulating to, a middle-aged man sitting behind the sole desk. The interview (for that was what it appeared to be) lasted much longer than Pearl had expected and as time passed, so it appeared reasonable to her that this first enquiry would prove more helpful than she could have dared to hope. But when her interpreter emerged and they sat together on a bench in the hospital gardens, the expectation built up in Pearl's mind proved illusory.

Kyaw had been told that the hospital records did not go back to the late 1940's and, even if they had, they would be unlikely to help with any person search. This was because Chit was a very common name for a Burmese girl. The office manager had said in a mocking tone, "My dear girl, it means love as you well know, so it would be popular, wouldn't it?" Kyaw told Pearl that whilst she objected to the manager's attitude, she had to admit that he was correct and this was supported by some research she had done the previous evening at university, once she learned of the name. Looking at her notes, the fact was that the numerological meaning of Chit included someone who expresses high ideals and has an inspirational approach to life. If this person is able to fully realise the potential of her motivation, she will be a very self-sacrificing person who is able to give freely without being concerned about any return or reward. Pearl harboured a degree of scepticism about such pronouncements. But, as Kyaw read out the final few words, a chill ran down her spine.

So, the search at location number one had failed. What about further afield? If the local student was to be of real help, aside from bridging the language barrier, this next assignment would be critical. *Local girl- taken to her home in the next village.* Accepting that Central Burma had grown more slowly than its neighbours over the past seventy years, Mandalay city had expanded out of all proportion, not least due to the immigrants from China. A city of little more than 150,000 residents in

1949 could not now house 1,250,000 without a considerable land push. Such an outwards sprawl would have inevitably led to many *next villages* now being within the greater conurbation.

What chance of identifying Chit's home village? Did it even exist now as a separate entity? Kyaw was tasked with gathering intelligence. Pearl asked her to talk to the locals, the older the better; to pick the brains of the university bigwigs; to visit all the book shops and stalls to find the history buffs; to go back to the hospital and talk to nursing staff rather than the administrators. There was a single objective, to identify the village that a young sixteen year old peasant girl may have come from in order to start a career in nursing at the Mandalay General Hospital. The year would have been 1946 when it was safe, for the first time, for a young girl to come out of hiding and head for the town and a better life.

Pearl had expected her young assistant to fail. Perhaps, being overwhelmed by the scale and complexity of enquiries, even return to her studies. Not so. Using words that were to stay with Pearl for years to come, Kyaw returned to **The Hotel by the Red Canal** in joyful triumph, "Your task was too simple for me". It had taken her two days. Days during which Pearl knew she should be on the tourist trail but instead were spent alone, walking and sitting quietly in the hotel grounds. Her body was acclimatising to the heat and humidity: her mind acclimatising to the inner peace of this Zen-like place. For the very first time she understood the inhuman wrench for Eugene to leave this land of a thousand pagodas and monasteries: where to send a son to become a monk is the most prestigious act a parent can take. How could he ever have been happy in a cold, damp, western land, devoid of divine roots and deprived of his Chit. When she should have been blissfully happy in this wonderland, she was sad and how she wished she could, just one more time, tell her daddy how she now felt about life. How she had grown in mind and spirit and all due to a chance encounter in a small-town library on the far side of the world.

What Kyaw had discovered was that after the Japanese surrender, a programme was launched by the General Hospital to recruit many young girls to train as nurses.

'Yesterday, I was talking to a cleaner who was working in one of the corridors leading to the main Neurology ward and asking about the post-war years, when she invited me to her home to meet her grandfather. He was a very old man but there was nothing wrong with his memory and I really do believe that one thing he recalled will provide the best chance of finding any descendants of this Chit person.

'There is a town sufficiently distant from the city to retain its own identity from which many girls came to be trained for hospital work. What makes that place more likely than others to have been the home village of your friend's healer back in 1948 or thereabouts, is the relative ease of getting to Mandalay City. Madaya is located on National Highway 31 so that, unlike many other villages from which new recruits may have come, transport would not have been an unsurmountable problem. Possibly your hotel could yield an important clue, in that journeys by water were normal and cheap. I researched this back at uni. and found that the Madaya River is connected to the Mandalay Canal, next to which your hotel is located.

It would be a much used means of moving from village to town in those days, especially since the canal goes on to join the Irrawaddy River. My guess is that we should plump for Madaya Town as our best hope of finding the answer to your quest. If we fail, then I'm afraid the task is pretty much hopeless.'

Pearl gave a huge and audible sigh of relief. She invited her young assistant to join her for dinner; maybe the duck again?

If there were records of citizen movements going back to the late 1940's or early 1950's, then Kyaw was sure they would be kept at the Town Hall or be traceable from information held there. It took Pearl and Kyaw, with the help and guidance of the archivist, two whole days of sifting through the annual records of citizen births, deaths and movement records to uncover a story. The story of what happened to Chit. A girl of that name (and given how common the name was – there was miraculously only one on record) did leave the village of Madaya in 1946. The date recorded was two days after her sixteen birthday. She appeared to have then disappeared completely until the 10th April 1950. On that date there was a record of an arrival. It said simply, *Girl named Chit arrived by boat from Mandalay with baby boy named Aung (bui-doi) and now housed with family.* Pearl found herself shaking and, not for the first time on this adventure, a cold shiver ran down her spine.

Holding tight to the chair in the archivist's office, hot tears fell onto the old parchment which held a secret she hadn't expected to find. Kyaw was jumping up and down, waving both arms in the air and yelling in a high-pitched voice. It was as if the tomb of Tutankhamun had been uncovered. The archivist didn't approve of such behaviour but her face was bathed in smiles; it was not every day her records created this sort of reaction. Pearl glanced at her student helper; instinctively they hugged each other. The generation and cultural gap between them had vanished. They were as one. Against all the odds, one winner.

The Town Hall records were excellent. The rest was easy. As time passed and the horrors of the war were slowly swallowed up by the rebuilding of everyday life, so, presumably, the disgrace of a family with a mixed-race war baby dissipated. On the 29th August 1974, Aung married his school-time sweetheart Hlaing and three years later they registered the birth of a first child. It was a girl whom they named Naing.

The archivist had known Naing personally because they had been born the same year and went to the local school. Naing proved to be a restless girl who longed to travel and she gained a place at the University of Dental Medicine in Mandalay.

'Did the Town Hall official know what happened to Naing after she left University?'

'Oh yes, we are still in touch. She went to the UK and is now a partner in a dental practice on the South Coast.'

'Do you know exactly where in England?'

'Certainly I do – it's called *Shoreline Dentistry* and it's in Hove, somewhere near Brighton, I think.'

*

Pearl had even thought of a little joke. It would go something like, Eugene I went all the way to Burma only to discover that on our very doorstep there is something we can really get our teeth stuck into. In her head she had rehearsed a few variations of the wording for the joke and still wasn't quite sure how to break her wonderful news, when the taxi pulled up outside his house.

She rang the bell as usual but he didn't come to the door. It often did take a while, depending on the time of day and whether it was one of his good or bad days. After five minutes or so, and feeling decidedly deflated knowing he must he fast asleep and her enthusiasm would have to wait for another day, a neighbour walked up the short drive,

'It's Pearl isn't it? We have heard so much about you from Mr Whitby. I'm afraid it's bad news. He died on Thursday last week. Really odd. Ok, he was old but still there didn't seem to be anything especially wrong on the Wednesday, no different to when I popped round every day. And yet, oh you're crying, I'm really so terribly sorry to break the news so directly. But I could sense there was something different about him. The instant he told me you had gone on a trip abroad he seemed to slump – mentally, sort of emotionally I mean – I said to the wife, it's almost as if he is in grief or like a puppy taken from its mother, you know, kind of pining.'

★

It was a bitterly cold February morning and the contrast to the heat of Burma and to the elation Pearl had felt walking to his door, couldn't have been starker. Instead of sitting in front of that roaring log fire, sipping his tea, nibbling on one of his ginger biscuits, here she was looking down at the body of an old man she had come to love and respect. His hands were crossed neatly on his chest and he wore his best suit and tie. There was no welcoming smile; no joy at learning that just down the road was his granddaughter. There was nothing but quietness and stillness. The funeral director spoke,

'I was waiting for someone to view the body. By the time we were sent for, your friend had been dead over twelve hours. Rigor mortis had set in and so we had a job extracting it from his hand, but here, you'd better have this, seeing as we're told there are no living relatives.'

Pearl was trying, through her tears, to concentrate on a few lines of writing on a single piece of paper she had taken from an airmail letter. The date stamp had faded badly except for the last two numbers 49. The place was still legible *Kuala Lumpur.* It was written in some form of pidgin English. She failed to make any sense of the first paragraph. It was a mixture of, she assumed, Burmese symbols and the occasional English letter. But the last line of the second and final paragraph was very clear as if she had had a little help writing it. It read;

Mi darling U, baby is cuming, yu be back to me. Chit xxxxxxxxx.

Back in Mrs Tiggy-Winkle's cottage, Pearl held the crumpled airmail letter in her right hand and slowly turned over her notes with her left hand. It took a long time. The central heating must have gone off. She shivered. Finally, she came to the only possible sequence of events; nothing else would fit. The airmail letter had arrived at the Big House. The old man had intercepted it and having read that one decipherable last line, decided to keep the content secret. He was not having his last born return to the Far East – boys make mistakes, the lass should have taken precautions. Eugene's future was within the family.

Only when Hedley Whitby died in 1957 would his private papers come to light. To whose light? Could have been Harold, as the only one left at home but more likely Iris, since if Harold was as lazy as Eugene had always said, surely the tidying up would have fallen to the old lady. Why then didn't she tell her Eugene what was his given right to know? Well, obviously so as not to run any risk of the news affecting his happy marriage. No children after five years but obviously he was capable, so let sleeping dogs lie. No point in upsetting Dot.

If Pearl was following the trail accurately, then how had dear Eugene found the fateful letter? Surely, it must have been amongst Dot's possessions when she died. So, that was it then. The old lady had at some point passed the letter to

Dorothy. Why? Iris was a good Christian woman. She would have believed in the sanctity of life. Eugene must be told he had fathered a child so that if he so chose, that human being could be helped. It would be only right, an act of redemption. But the mother did not tell her son directly. Did she fear for the marriage? And then that wife keeps the secret. Will her husband leave her if she breaks the news? Even with an emerging successful business, even with a virile healthy English wife. She must have feared so.

It was a devastating denouement. Ever since his Dot died, Eugene had known he had made his Burmese girl pregnant. Yet, no word of this to Pearl, no airmail letter amongst the papers handed over. Was he afraid? Did he want to slip away before being told of a Burmese legacy?

★

Dust to dust etc, etc. Pearl threw a handful of soil onto the coffin below. She no longer cared about her make-up or about anything to do with this world, her tears flowed uncontrollably. She stood back from the open grave and tried to commit the scene to memory. There was a sprawling copper beech still showing mournful remnants of its autumnal plumage, a yew tree, two anaemic silver-trunked birches and not much else. No teaks to command attention. No sultry breeze – God, was it only a week ago?

There were a few people to see him laid to rest. She recognised the neighbour, there was an old man who she thought might be Billy and then she saw a second old man. He was short in stature but stood bolt upright. He had a smart suit just showing beneath a half-open camel overcoat. And his features; they were at the same time both familiar and yet not.

He had the longish nose of Eugene but much steelier eyes and the give-away – his right foot in an expensive brogue was turned on its side, not flat to the ground. That was exactly how Eugene would stand.

As the little troupe of mourners turned to walk away she saw the old man hand an envelope to a younger and taller man, who seemed to appear from nowhere, and point a finger at her. This equally well-dressed man walked directly to Pearl and handed her the envelope, using a horizontal hand gesture that clearly implied do not open now. This second man walked back to the old one and together they left the cemetery, went through a wooden gate and, for the first time, Pearl saw a car parked in the driveway beyond. The passenger door was opened by the younger man with something of an exaggerated gesture and perhaps Pearl imagined it but he seemed to half turn in her direction as if to indicate his allegiance to the old man now entering the car. He then walked round to the driver's door. The limousine moved slowly away and disappeared from view.

It could well have been a dream were it not for the envelope sitting on the coffee table. Pearl took a deep breath and picked it up. In neat handwriting it was addressed simply to "Pearl". Inside was a single piece of paper:-

Dear Miss Pearl,
Congratulations on your research. You found a rich man who was lonely and who has always had a soft spot for a pretty lady. No doubt you will be rewarded by inheritance. Well done, very professional. However, you missed one vital clue. A more careful examination of his bank statements would have revealed regular monthly payments to a bank in Jersey. You may have wondered what he was paying for. Let me enlighten you, dear lady. Your darling Eugene murdered

two of his brothers. Rob and Jack. Well, you see, he had to. His business depended on it. The family reputation depended on it. One final thing you ought to know whilst enjoying the spoils of your friendship with my brother Eugene. Did he tell you that as well as finding Paul amongst the engineers repairing the bridges over the Irrawaddy River, there was also Garry? No, I thought not. Garry did not return to civil engineering. He saw a future in the motor trade. He was right, especially for specialists. He became an expert in steering mechanisms. I hope you have similar success with the next sucker you uncover. It will not be me.

Yours sincerely,

Harold.

ACKNOWLEDGEMENTS

Ampltd.co.uk

Asiatours.co.uk

Baby-name-list.com

Babynames.merschat.com

bbc.co.uk/schools

Betterhealth.vic.gov.au

Diabetes.org.uk

Eric Wilson

Fortunecity.co.uk

Globalvoicesonline.org

Gwydir.demon.co.uk

Historic-newspapers.co.uk

History.com

IBM Archives

Madehow.com

News.bbc.co.uk